PRAISE FOR THE NOVELS OF SORAYA LANE

I Knew You Were Trouble

"Readers will fall head-over-heels in love with Nate and Faith. Lane's latest is filled with a huge dose of Southern Texas charm."
—*RT Book Reviews*

"First-rate writing and memorable characters prove that sometimes things are worth the trouble as demonstrated by Ms. Lane."
—*Jenerated Reviews*

"A fun, endearing, yet heartbreaking read that kept me eagerly turning pages just waiting to see how everything works out for Faith and Nate."
—*Romance Junkies*

"For those who love a Texan man and some good flirtation, I recommend *I Knew You Were Trouble*."
—*Harlequin Junkie*

Cowboy Take Me Away

"A sexy, charming Southern read."
—*RT Book Reviews*

"Soraya Lane keeps the story going and exciting to the very end."
—*Reader to Reader Review*

"If you like steamy cowboy romances you'll love this book."
—*Bitten By Love Reviews*

"Captivating on so many levels . . . heartbreakingly memorable."
—*Romance Junkies*

The Devil Wears Spurs

"Hot, handsome cowboys and sharp, amusing banter make Lane's latest a fun, sexy read . . . With down-to-earth characters in a Western setting, Lane tells a story that will keep readers engaged until the very last page."
—*Romantic Times*

"It's no gamble to bet on cowboy Ryder King. Soraya Lane's *The Devil Wears Spurs* is hot as a Texas summer. It's a wild ride you don't want to miss."
—*New York Times* and *USA Today* bestselling author Jennifer Ryan

"Watch out, the Devil has met his match! Sit back with Soraya Lane's *The Devil Wears Spurs* and enjoy the sparks that fly between champion bull rider Ryder and Chloe, a barmaid with a few aces up her sleeve. You won't want their story to end!"
—Laura Moore, bestselling author of *Once Tasted*

"Sassy, sexy, and so much fun, *The Devil Wears Spurs* is a cowboy fantasy come to life. With this rowdy, romantic ride from the ranches of Texas to the casinos of Las Vegas, Soraya Lane proves herself a bright new voice in western romance."
—Melissa Cutler, author of *The Trouble with Cowboys*

Once Upon a Cowboy Christmas

Soraya Lane

St. Martin's Paperbacks

This is a work of fiction. All of the characters, organizations, and events portrayed in this novel are either products of the author's imagination or are used fictitiously.

First published in the United States by St. Martin's Paperbacks, an imprint of St. Martin's Publishing Group.

ONCE UPON A COWBOY CHRISTMAS

Copyright © 2019 by Soraya Lane.

All rights reserved.

For information, address St. Martin's Publishing Group, 120 Broadway, New York, NY 10271.

www.stmartins.com

ISBN: 978-1-250-22428-6

Our books may be purchased in bulk for promotional, educational, or business use. Please contact your local bookseller or the Macmillan Corporate and Premium Sales Department at 1-800-221-7945, ext. 5442, or by email at MacmillanSpecialMarkets@macmillan.com.

Printed in the United States of America

St. Martin's Paperbacks edition / November 2019

10 9 8 7 6 5 4 3 2 1

Chapter 1

CODY Ford tugged at his tie, loosening it and undoing his top button as he stared out the small window. The airport was slowly coming in to focus, the ground becoming more visible as the plane lowered, and he quickly finished his drink before the flight attendant took his glass.

"Can I get you anything else before we land, sir?" she asked.

Cody shook his head. "No, I'm fine. Thanks." Another whiskey would have gone down nicely, but the last thing he wanted was to arrive home under the influence.

The three-hour flight from New York had passed quickly, and he closed up his laptop and filed his papers, placing them all in his briefcase before leaning back into the wide leather seat. He'd given everyone else in his office the week off, but he still had enough emails landing in his inbox to keep him busy all day. His international clients never seemed to sleep, let alone take a day off work.

Soon the plane touched down and he waited for the

attendant to appear again before standing and waiting for her to open the door. Nothing beat flying private and having a jet ready and on call 24/7, and it was a luxury he still never took for granted.

"I hope you enjoyed your flight, Mr. Ford."

"I did. Merry Christmas." He nodded and smiled, reaching into his pocket for a tip. "A little something to say thank you," he said, putting the bills in her palm before turning and walking down the steps, a bag in each hand as he stepped out onto the tarmac and crossed over to the main airport building. Within minutes he was walking out the doors, scanning for the car he'd booked.

"Looking for your limo?" A deep voice drawled from behind.

Cody spun around and found his brother standing behind him, one eyebrow cocked as he stood, looking anything other than a chauffeur in his snug jeans, plaid shirt, and wide-brimmed hat.

"Yeah, actually, I was." Cody laughed and dropped his bags, opening his arms and giving Tanner a big, back-slapping hug.

"I cancelled your driver. Thought I'd get you myself."

"You're all done at school?" Cody asked as he picked up his briefcase and Tanner collected his overnight bag. "I didn't think I'd be seeing you until the weekend."

"School's out," Tanner said. "And thank God, because it's kicking my butt. I'd rather ride bulls any day than study."

Cody laughed and followed Tanner to his car, spotting the black Range Rover almost instantly. It stood out against the oversize pickup trucks it was parked beside. He jumped in the passenger side and watched Tanner as he walked around the car and got in, noticing how tired his brother looked. His face—usually tanned dark brown from all the hours he spent outside—looked pale, and there were shadows under his eyes. He'd already told him he thought the MBA would be too much in addition to managing their ranches, but his little brother hadn't wanted to hear it.

"So how's the MBA going, anyway? Is it tough going back after such a long break?"

Up until recently, Tanner had held the title as the top pro-bull rider in the state, but he'd given it all away after a bad accident and decided to take over the running of the family ranch and the Ford family property interests in Texas. Which meant he'd also decided to go back to school to get the letters after his name, deciding he wanted to be taken seriously as a businessman. Cody still wasn't sure his brother was the studying type though.

"Let's just say it's taken some adjustment," Tanner said with a grin as he started the engine. "It's tough going from being the best at what you do to bottom of the class, but I'm getting there. I haven't taken up bull riding again yet, so that's something."

Cody grunted. "You know, we all would've supported you regardless. You didn't have to go back to school just to prove your worth."

He saw the way Tanner's jaw went tight, eyes fixed straight ahead on the road. "Maybe I didn't want everyone wondering why the black sheep of the family was given the reins over his fancy, Harvard-educated brother. Ever think of that?"

Damn. As was often the case when it came to his brother, he couldn't think of a comeback. "You always were a straight shooter; glad to see nothing's changed. But seriously, you're the right man for the job. So whatever this going-back-to-college thing was about, don't blame us for it." He paused. "You have my full support, if that's what you want to hear. I fully respect the old man's decision to put you at the helm."

"Thanks," Tanner mumbled, glancing at him. "It's nice to hear."

They drove along in silence for a while as Cody stared out the window, feeling the familiar pull back to Texas. When he'd first left home for Harvard, he'd been desperate to start his own life and leave his home state behind. Then as an adult, he'd readily moved to New York, his career planned out ahead of him and the big city being the only place he could ever see himself working and living. But he'd always had this notion of not belonging anywhere, that home was still Texas. And yet when he was home, he always got itchy feet, ready to get back to work and away from River Ranch. Maybe he was scared of the ranch life getting under his skin again. Or maybe he was just an asshole workaholic who needed to be in his glass office overlooking New York City in order to feel like himself. He had a string of ex-girlfriends who'd attest to that. Or maybe, just maybe, he was too scared of coming back to everything he'd left behind because the memories still hurt.

"You heading home on the twenty-seventh again?" Tanner asked.

"Yeah, if not sooner. I need to get back to work. Why?"

"No reason. I just thought you might have stayed for longer this year." Tanner glanced at him, taking his eyes off the road for a split second. "You know, to spend more time with Dad."

Cody breathed deep. "He's getting worse?"

Tanner shrugged. "I wouldn't say worse, but he's, well, he just doesn't look like Dad anymore. He's smaller, seems less imposing I guess. You'll see when we get home."

Cody nodded. "Old bastard's always telling me over the phone that he's fine, and it's you all making a fuss over him. It's easy to believe him when his voice doesn't seem any different."

"Yeah, that sounds like Dad. Making out like we're the problem when he's the one with cancer."

Soon they were driving past the start of River Ranch, the post and rail fences immaculate as always, stretching as far as the eye could see. The entrance to their property was marked by two enormous oak trees, standing guard on either side of the driveway, and Tanner turned in and drove slowly, the gravel crunching beneath the tires. It was almost a mile long, and just before they reached the main house, they passed his sister Mia's old home. She'd built her own modern house tucked away from view, as contemporary as the main house was traditional, with her own swimming pool and stables. Until she'd met Sam, Cody couldn't ever have imagined her leaving the place, but then she'd gotten married and moved to her husband's ranch.

"You think Mia will ever move back here, or are they happy living at Sam's place? I heard they were thinking of building a new house to accommodate that growing brood of theirs."

"I think they're happy there. Sam loves it and Mia's happy, but I've heard them talk about building," Tanner replied. "We've been living in her old house, thought it was stupid to buy something of my own when that's sitting there unused. I'm starting to see why she liked the place so much."

Cody laughed. "You just need a pair of tight jodhpurs

and you'd fit right in over at her stable block, too. You making good use of her show-jumping course?"

"Whatever," Tanner scowled, but Cody didn't miss his grin. They'd always teased Mia about living in her riding breeches even before she'd become a professional show jumper, because no one else in their family would be seen dead in them.

"You remember when Mom tried to make us all go to pony club?" Cody asked. "She had those perfect little outfits all lined up for us, and you walked out in your wranglers and boots with a look on your face like thunder."

Tanner's laugh was deep. "Oh, I remember. I don't think she ever bothered with trying that again."

Cody smiled at the memory, but he was pleased they didn't keep talking about the past. It wasn't like him to bring it up; it was usually one of his siblings laughing and bringing up things from their childhood, and him trying *not* to walk down memory lane.

As the car rolled to a stop, they both unbuckled their seat belts and jumped out. Cody looked up at the sky, surprised to find a perfect blue canopy overhead with barely a cloud to see. New York had been bitterly cold, but it wasn't as bad as he'd expected here. He was starting to doubt he'd even see snow.

"Go inside and find Dad. I've just got to check on a few things first," Tanner called out, throwing Cody the keys before waving and disappearing. "He spends most of his time in the library these days, so try there first."

Cody walked to the door, checking his boots were clean out of habit before going inside. It made him laugh—the dirtiest his boots got now was if he was too busy staring at his phone and accidentally walked through a puddle on the sidewalk—but the habit was still there.

"Anyone home?" he called out, standing in the entranceway, the big staircase to one side of him and a long, timber-floored hallway stretching out in front. "Dad?"

No one answered, so he kept walking. The house was quiet and it didn't feel right to him. He'd grown up with three siblings, and the house had always been loud and full of life, their things sprawled from one end of the place to the other. Now it was more like a museum, every footstep loud, his voice echoing back to him as he called out. He wondered how his dad had been able to stand it, living on his own all this time. Cody's worst fear for years had been finding out his dad was seeing someone romantically, having the awkward first meeting and then progressing to having a stepmom. Now, as he walked through the enormous empty house, he was starting to realize how selfish he'd been.

He frowned to himself as he made for the kitchen, wishing he'd eaten on the plane. His stomach was starting to rumble loudly. He made for the fridge and opened it, scanning the contents for something to eat. Not finding anything, he reached for the orange juice, opening the top and guzzling half of it.

"Can I help you?"

Cody spluttered and almost dropped the bottle, spinning around to find a woman standing, hands on hips, watching him from the other side of the kitchen. A woman with curves in all the right places, who he definitely hadn't been expecting to find in the house.

He slowly wiped his mouth with the back of his hand and screwed the top back on the carton.

"Sorry, you are?" he asked, clearing his throat of the juice still lodged there.

"Your father's caregiver," she said, her eyes wide as she backed up a few steps, as if she'd found a thief in the kitchen. "I was just, ah, about to make him lunch if you're hungry?"

Cody smiled and stepped forward, holding out his hand. "Sorry, I should have known. I'm Cody Ford." Why the hell hadn't Tanner warned him there was a gorgeous woman in the house? He'd probably done it on purpose just to catch him off guard. He knew his dad had a nurse, but no one had ever said she looked like, well, *this*.

"Alexandra," she said, looking like she'd rather run away than step forward to shake his hand, hiding her gaze beneath her hair. Her palm was warm in his, but her gaze only flickered past his, as if she didn't want to make eye contact "Your father's been looking forward to having you home."

Cody had the distinct feeling that he knew the woman standing before him, the peek of her brown eyes so familiar, but he couldn't put his finger on it. "Sorry, but do I know you from somewhere? I'm sure . . ." His voice trailed off when she gave him a blank expression. He ran his eyes back over her long hair, the warm almond eyes and the full pout. She looked so damn familiar. "Sorry, I must be mistaken. You remind me of someone, that's all." He put the juice back in the fridge and gave the woman his full attention, suddenly less interested in filling his stomach and more about finding out everything there was to know about the nurse.

Alexandra had already moved away from him, disappearing into the pantry behind the kitchen and returning with a carton of eggs. *Alexandra*. Why was that ringing a bell? He waited, more than happy to see her emerge again and get another eyeful of the skin-tight jeans and scoop neck T-shirt she was wearing. He took his jacket off, slinging it over the back of a chair. It might be frigid cold outside, but the central heating through the house made it impossible to know it was winter.

"If you want lunch, I'm making a bacon and egg sandwich for your father."

"I thought you were his nurse?"

She shrugged. "I'm his nurse slash chef slash chauffeur. He employed me to look after him and keep everything running smoothly."

Cody laughed. "I didn't think a nurse would encourage a sick man to eat bacon. But I see you're more girl Friday than nurse, am I right?"

The look she shot him was withering. "*Girl Friday?*"

Cody held up his hands, realizing how sexist that had sounded. "Sorry, bad terminology. If you're making my dad happy and keeping him alive, keep up the good work. That came out all kinds of wrong."

He was seriously losing his touch. Alexandra was looking at him like he had rocks in his head, and he was starting to wonder if he did. He needed to shut his mouth and only open it when he'd thought through his lines better. And why the hell did he still feel like he knew her from somewhere?

"What happened to his housekeeper anyway?" Cody asked, thinking back. Last year she'd still been here, but he'd missed Thanksgiving so it'd been a while since he'd come home.

"She's taking a sabbatical. I'll be off chef duties when she returns," Alexandra said dryly. "So do you want a sandwich or not?"

"Yes," he said quickly. "Please."

"He's in the library if you want to go see him. I'll be there soon."

Cody watched Alexandra for a moment, still struck by the feeling of how familiar she looked, but he walked out of the kitchen before she thought he was weird for lingering too long. Maybe he'd become too used to city girls, with their single-minded determination to find a wealthy husband. It had been a long time since he'd had to use his charm and work hard for a woman's attention, especially one who was looking at him like she wasn't at all impressed. Thank God Tanner hadn't seen him make such a fool of himself. But there was something else about her he couldn't put his finger on, an abruptness with him, like she was pissed off with him for even being in the house. She might be beautiful, but she hadn't exactly been warm, and he couldn't imagine his dad liking someone who wasn't friendly. Was there a reason she didn't like him?

He knocked, then pushed open the door to his dad's library, wondering if she'd been employed for reasons other than her level of care or her resume.

"You look good, Dad," Lexi heard Cody say as she walked back into Walter Ford's library. "Except for the fact you've been running marathons or working out too hard to lose so much weight. Are you trying to look good for your sexy nurse? Because you've seriously dropped some pounds."

If any of Walter's other children had cracked a joke about Walter's weight instead of being shocked by it, she'd have laughed, but just the sight of Cody made her blood boil. And he'd unsettled her with his wide brown gaze, the way he'd seemed to study her so casually and still not realize who she was. Had she changed so much, or was she just easy to forget? A long time had passed since they'd seen each other, but part of her had always hoped he'd see her and wish things had been different.

"He's cut out sugar, caffeine, and alcohol to get that svelte figure," Lexi said, giving Walter a grin. "It's supposed to help slow the growth of his cancer, so I'm trying to keep him on the straight and narrow."

"Not *all* the alcohol though, isn't that right?" Walter said, chuckling as he raised his eyebrows at her. "Just don't tell your sister. A man has to have at least a little whiskey each night."

She listened to Cody's easy laugh as he sat across from his father. When he was younger, she hadn't been able see the resemblance, but now it was clear they were cut from the same cloth. Both men were tall, easily over six feet, and with the same broad shoulders, although Walter's frame seemed to have shrunk during the weeks she'd been with him whereas Cody's was well filled out; and Walter's thick head of hair was white compared to Cody's dark blond. They had the same big, easy smile, and they both sat back as if they owned the world—legs spread, languid as hell, not threatened by anyone or anything. And from what she'd read and heard about Cody, he had the same ruthless drive to succeed as his father always had. Although she was probably seeing a much more laid back Walter than the man he'd once been.

"I'll leave this here with you and let you two catch up," she said, setting both plates down. She crossed over to Walter's fridge, hidden by a wood-paneled door among the mahogany bookshelves, and took out two bottles of water along with two ice-cold glasses. Her patient was very particular about what he liked, which made her job easier. The man liked his drinks cold and his food regularly throughout the day, and he sipped a single glass of whiskey before she left for the night. Add to that his medications and keeping an eye on his blood pressure and oxygen levels, and he was one of the easiest patients she'd ever had. Walter was easy to talk to, friendly, and he seemed to genuinely appreciate her company—not to mention the generous sum he was paying her.

Which had all been perfect until Cody had showed up.

"I thought *you* two would be the ones wanting to catch up," Walter said, winking at his son as he took a bite of his sandwich.

She stiffened, swallowing as she slowly met Cody's gaze across the room. After he had not recognized her straightaway, she'd thought the penny wouldn't drop until later, when she'd finished work for the day and was long gone for the night. She bravely kept staring, not wanting to be the one to look away first. She sure as hell hadn't expected Walter to bring it up.

"Catching up?" Cody asked, clearly confused. "Why would I be catching up with your caregiver?"

Walter looked between them, waving his hand in the air. "I don't care if you two have history. It was years ago, so no need to hide it on my behalf. You think I didn't do my research before hiring the woman who was going to care for me every day?" He laughed. "Son, you look like you've seen a ghost."

Lexi squirmed, wishing the carpet could swallow her whole. Maybe it would have been easier to just tell him in the kitchen.

"So I *do* know you?" Cody asked, and the moment his eyes widened she cleared her throat and found the nerve to reply. "Before, when I asked—"

"It's me, Lexi," she said, interrupting him, not wanting Walter to hear any more about the conversation they'd already had in the kitchen. "I usually go by Alexandra professionally."

Cody's jaw dropped, and if she hadn't been so embarrassed that the scene was unfolding in front of her employer, she'd almost have enjoyed it. Because she'd imagined Cody coming back for such a long time, what she'd say to him, how badly she wanted to show him what he'd missed, and what his face might look like when he saw her. But it hadn't exactly gone to plan, even if there was some satisfaction in seeing his shock right now.

Chapter 2

"LEXI, you're . . ." Cody took a moment, his eyebrows arched high as he leaned forward and stared at her. "Well, you're all grown up, I'll give you that." He laughed and stood up, setting his plate down and shaking his head as he came toward her. "Geez, Lexi, *look* at you."

If they'd been in a bar or anywhere else away from sensitive ears, she'd have told him that they were the exact same age, so yeah, she was all grown up just like *he* was. But she respected Walter—and she needed her job—so she wasn't about to engage or let old wounds open up.

Cody opened his arms and pulled her in for a hug, arms wrapping around her, stifling her, making it impossible for her to breathe. She knew that she must feel like a corpse, hell, she probably looked like one too, so she forced herself to raise her arms, to hug Cody back so his father didn't wonder what the hell was wrong with her. Cody's lips brushed her cheek and she stopped breathing, hating that her body was betraying her, that her natural reaction was to lean into him and hold his big, strong body; to put her lips against his smooth cheek in return and inhale the citrusy scent of his cologne. He was older now, but being in his arms was still the same, her head still only reaching into his shoulder.

When he released her she stepped back, almost tripping over her own feet. Hugging him had definitely not been part of her plan.

"Like I said, I'll, ah, let you two enjoy some time together," she said, backing away toward the door. "Call me if you need anything."

She turned and quickly shut the door behind her, back pressed to it for a moment as she caught her breath. Lexi closed her eyes and tried to breathe slowly, tried to push down the anger catching in her throat and rising through her body at seeing him again. Why did he have to look so good? Why couldn't he be grossly overweight and bald? Why did he have to look like the same All-American, handsome quarterback from high school, albeit one dressed in fancier clothes? And why did he have to *smell* so good and *feel* so damn good?

Lexi pushed away from the door in case he tried to follow her, not wanting to tumble back into the room if it was swung open, and walked back to the kitchen, checking the time on the big round clock hanging high above the counter. She had another couple of hours before the school bus arrived, and with Cody in the house, she had a feeling the time was going to drag. Especially when all she could think of was the way his close-cut suit trousers fit him like a glove, his shirt slim fitting and showing her that despite not working on the ranch anymore, his muscles were very much still there. And as much as she hated him, a part of her had never forgotten what it had felt like to be wrapped in the arms of that particular rancher. Or what it felt like to belong to him and know that every time she saw him, her heart was going to race like she'd just finished running across a field.

"Lexi?" a deep call came down the hall.

She grimaced, crossing the kitchen to get as far to the other side as she could. She did not need to be close to him. She needed to remember what he'd done, what he was still doing to her, and keep her distance. The guy was a category-A jerk.

"Lexi?" the call came again, followed by Cody's dark blond head.

"It's Alexandra," she said, meeting his stare. "No one's called me Lexi since high school."

"Why?" he asked, rubbing his chin and managing to fill the doorway as he braced against it. "Lexi suits you. You'll always be Lexi to me."

Lexi shrugged. "Let's just say I've been trying to forget about high school and the person who used to call me that. It was a long time ago," she said, hating the catch in her voice, the way just looking at him brought back memories she'd long since buried.

He frowned. "Why didn't you say anything? Before, when I first saw you? You must have known I was going to find out. I thought you'd be happy to see me." Cody paused. "It's sure great to see *you* again. Honestly, it's been forever since our paths have crossed. How've you been?"

She tried not to bristle. "I thought you'd recognize me the minute you walked in the door, but I guess you find it easy to forget things."

His jaw tightened and she felt a flutter of victory that for once she'd managed to deliver a decent comeback. She was usually thinking of something good to say in

reply an hour after a conversation, but not today. Something about Cody had her firing on all cylinders, even if
she hated how much he still appealed to her physically.

"You look so different, I mean . . ." His voice trailed
off and she noticed the way his lips tipped up into a
smile, same way they always had. "Your hair used to
be so much darker, and curly, and you always wore it
pulled up in a ponytail. And you used to have the cutest
freckles across your nose." He chuckled. "But now I
look at you, I can see it."

He moved closer, and she wished she wasn't already
pressed against the far counter. She had nowhere else
to go. And going for a slow, descriptive trip down
memory lane hadn't been part of her plan with Cody.
He was right though—she probably did look different, she just hadn't expected him not to see past it. Her
mom hadn't let her wear makeup in high school, but
she'd made up for it the day she'd graduated, learning
how to apply foundation and highlighter, experiment-
ing with smoky eyes, and having her hair streaked with
gold highlights and wearing it out, long and wild. But
then that's when Cody had disappeared from her life,
and although she'd waited, expecting to hear from him,
expecting to see him during holidays or even on week-
ends, he'd never come back.

Cody stopped at the island in the center of the
kitchen, splaying his hands on the marble and leaning forward. "So how've you been anyway? It's been
what"—his brow furrowed—"fourteen years since we
last saw each other?"

*Fifteen, actually. Fifteen years since you left town
without even bothering to say goodbye.*

"Yeah, something like that."

"Well, you look great," he said, before groaning and

leaning forward, elbows on the counter now. "I'm terrible at small talk, aren't I?"

She refused to smile at him, so she nodded instead. There was no way she was going to let him charm her. "Hey, it's nice to see there's one thing you're not good at."

"What's that supposed to mean?"

Lexi studied him, wondering if he even knew how much he'd hurt her, or if he'd just forgotten about what he'd done. "Nothing. I shouldn't have said it."

"No, come on, shoot. You may as well say it. You were always good at talking straight."

She took a deep breath. "You were always good at everything, Cody, that's all. School, football, horseback riding, you name it." Lexi breathed deep and wished his eyes weren't so blue, wished that she didn't feel the familiar pull toward him that she'd thought was long buried. "The only thing you were shitty at was saying goodbye to your girlfriend the day you left town, but I guess you don't even remember that, do you?"

Cody looked like she'd sucker punched him, but as his mouth opened, a squeal followed by fast running little feet interrupted them.

"Cody!" Mia Ford called, chasing after her oldest daughter, Sophia. "You're home."

Cody watched as Lexi turned away, seeing how hurt she was and hating that he was the reason for it. Had he been that careless when he left? It had been a long time ago, the same time his mom had found out she was terminal, and he'd left because it was easier than staying. He bent to catch Sophia, who was holding on to his leg and jumping up and down like she'd been waiting her entire life to see him again.

"Hey, cutie pie," he said, grinning as he scooped Sophia up, pretending she was almost too heavy to lift and slowly rising, groaning like she was killing his arms. "When did you get so big? I can hardly get you up here!"

His niece giggled, and he reached for his sister once Sophia was happily positioned in one arm, her little arms wound tight around his neck.

"It's good to see you, Mia," he said, kissing her cheek and then looking down at the baby asleep in her other arm. "Someone looks just like her big sister, huh?"

Before he could glance back at Lexi, his brother strode back into the room. "Has no one told Cody that he's in Texas yet?" Tanner said, shaking his head in obvious disgust. "Dude, how many times do I have to tell you? You look like a complete asshole wearing a shirt and tie. It must be like being in a straitjacket all day. How the hell do you do it?"

Cody glowered at him. "Says the idiot wearing a dirty shirt and scuffed boots? I think I'm just fine in the clothes I'm in, thanks. And I just got here, in case you've forgotten."

Tanner looked down at his shirt then back up again. "I just finished dealing with a thousand-pound mama cattle-beast who didn't want me within a hundred yards of her calf, so I'm okay with a little dirt to show for it." Tanner laughed as he came closer. "Oh look, you got a little ink on you. You have to wrestle a fountain pen?"

Cody carefully set Sophia down and then leapt at his brother, as Tanner roared with laughter and tried to get him in a choke hold. Cody swung and missed, grunting as he tried to escape Tanner's grip, expertly ducking and reaching for his arm to pin it behind his back.

"Boys!" Mia's call pierced the air. "Enough! This is not a frat house!"

Cody dropped Tanner's arm, stepping back and throwing his sister what he hoped was an apologetic look. Tanner grinned at him and Cody glared, yanking off his tie and undoing a couple of his shirt buttons. He was so used to dressing in a suit and tie every day, he hadn't thought about how out of place he might look on the ranch—and it wasn't like Tanner had said anything in the car before. Besides, his wardrobe consisted of Armani and Hugo Boss black suits and white shirts, and an assortment of neutral ties for when he needed them. He didn't even think about what he put on each day, he just reached into his wardrobe and put on a clean version of the day before. Wear. Rinse. Repeat. In New York, it served him well.

"I came straight from the office," he muttered. "I don't think anyone there would appreciate me going casual Friday."

Tanner shrugged and gestured at himself. "Just came from the office too. No one seemed to mind."

"When did you become such an asshole, Tanner? Was it when you stopped taking your frustration out on bulls and joined the real world?" What had happened to his brother in the time from arriving home until now? "Or are you trying to show off in front of the ladies?"

Mia looked unimpressed. "You two idiots are supposed to be role models to your niece, remember? And we have company, so knock it off."

Cody looked down at Sophia, who was all wide eyed, but she flashed him a smile almost immediately. "Sorry honey, Uncle Tanner was being an idiot, so I had to knock . . ."

"Whoa! Enough!" Mia yelped.

Tanner had walked over to the fridge, pulled out a beer, and held it up. Cody nodded and stepped closer, taking it from his brother and unscrewing the top. They stared at each other a while longer, before Tanner raised a brow and grinned, and Cody clinked his bottle to his brother's. Then he took a long, slow slug of it before letting his eyes settle on Lexi again. She was smiling at Sophia and fussing over the baby, but he saw her stiffen, knew that she'd felt his gaze on her. Why the hell had he behaved like that in front of her? It was like seeing her had sent him straight back to his senior year of high school. He and Tanner hadn't goofed around like that in a long time.

"Lexi, would you like a beer?" he asked.

She looked up, her expression impossible to read until she eventually shook her head. "I'm still on the clock, so I'd better not."

Mia was the one to encourage her, slinging an arm around her. "It's almost time for you to finish and besides, it's Christmas. You're the best thing that's ever happened to Dad, letting him be home instead of in the hospital, so no one's going to begrudge you the odd festive drink."

He saw the change in Lexi, the way she was with his sister, and he remembered what it had been like to be the recipient of her smile. She'd been pretty when they'd been in school, all coltish legs and long hair, her brown eyes as warm as hot chocolate on a cold winter's night. But now she was more beautiful than pretty, her brown hair lighter and streaked with shades of gold, her figure ever more filled out. If he'd met her in a bar or she'd walked into his office, he would have stopped whatever he was doing just to find out who she was. Yet somehow he'd walked into his own home and not recognized her.

"You're sure?" Lexi asked.

"Positive," Mia said, as Cody walked straight to the fridge and pulled out another beer, opening it and passing it to Lexi. Her fingers curled around the bottle, her eyes fixed on the drink, not once looking up at him.

"In case you're wondering, he's even more of an asshole now than he was when he left here," Tanner teased.

Cody swilled his beer and ignored his brother. He bet Tanner was enjoying seeing him squirm with his ex in the room. But instead of reacting, he smiled at Lexi, wishing they could start over and he could walk into the kitchen and think before opening his mouth.

"Yeah," Lexi said softly. "I can see that."

And just like that, the entire room erupted into laughter, except for Cody. He should never have come home. If it hadn't been for his father, he'd have walked straight back out the door and driven to the airport, firing up the jet to go home to New York. The last thing he needed was a walk down memory lane.

"What time does the bus arrive?" Mia asked.

Lexi set down her beer, trying hard not to keep glancing at Cody. Her willpower was only valid every other time, and she stole another look at him. "About four. He'll be so excited it's his last day of school tomorrow."

"What bus?" asked Cody.

She turned, trying to be polite for the sake of the other Ford siblings and deciding to face him head-on. They'd been nothing but lovely to her since she started, and she didn't want to tar them all with the same brush as Cody just because they were related. Besides, if she was going to glance at him, she may as well look at him without hiding it. "My son rides the school bus," she said.

"Your son?" he asked, eyes widening. "You have a *son*?"

She nodded. "I sure do. His name's Harry."

"And he's, ah . . ." Cody frowned and his voice seemed to lower an octave. "How old is he exactly?"

Lexi laughed. She couldn't help it. But his sister answered before she could so much as get a word out.

"Quit the deer-in-headlights impersonation, Cody, he's not yours," Mia said with a look bordering on an eye roll. "Seriously, what is with you today?"

He gave Mia what Lexi imagined was an apologetic look. "I'm sorry, it's just, I thought . . ."

"You thought that your high-school girlfriend had hidden a secret love child from you for the past decade and a half, and your family was in on it?" Mia asked. "Why is it that men can be so pathetic? Trust me, I'd have hunted you down and told you if that was the case."

Lexi swapped smiles with Mia. "For the record, he's six," she told Cody. "So you're completely out of the woods there."

She could tell he wanted to know more, could see the curiosity written plainly all over his face, but she wasn't going to indulge him. If Cody wanted to know how she'd ended up being a single mom to the most delicious boy on the planet, then he'd have to man up and ask her outright.

"Speaking of my son, I'd better go check on your father and then wait for the school bus to arrive," she said, relieved to leave the kitchen and the Ford family for the rest of the day. "I might see you when I stop by after dinner to give Walter his meds."

Everyone called out goodbye, but as she walked away, it felt like Cody's eyes were burning a hole into the back of her head. She kept putting one foot in front of the other until she was at the door, wishing they were alone and she had the courage to march back and demand to know how he'd treated her the way he had. But they weren't alone and she doubted she would ever have the nerve to properly confront him anyway.

She looked in on Walter, not disturbing him when she saw he was resting, and walking quietly down the hallway instead. She reached for her coat and scarf, buttoned up, and walked out the door. She needed to see Harrison, to snuggle him and soak up everything about him, to listen to him give her the blow-by-blow account of his day at school. Because then she'd remember why Cody leaving had been the best thing that had ever happened to her, because without Cody, she'd have never had her son.

She took her phone out of her pocket as she made her way over to the converted barn she was living in to get her car. The driveway was almost a mile long, so she always drove to the gate. The only message she'd missed was from her mom, and just reading it sent waves of anxiety through her.

A letter just came and I have four weeks to move. I don't understand.

She couldn't read the rest. Her eyes just kept going back and forth over the first line, her breath shuddering from her as everything came crashing down around her.

Four weeks to move her mom from her assisted-care facility. Four weeks to find someone to care for a woman with Alzheimer's. *Four weeks.*

She blinked away tears and fumbled in her pocket for her keys, trying not to let them spill. Harry always knew when she was sad, could tell from the second he looked at her if she'd been crying, and the last thing she wanted was for her sweet little boy to know what was going on.

Lexi got in the driver's seat and fell forward, her head against the steering wheel, trying to breathe, trying not to let the weight of everything suffocate her. It'd been hard enough when she'd had a little boy to look after on her own, even when her mom had been helping out, but now it was *all* on her. In the cruel twist of fate that had taken her mother's mind from her, leaving her swinging from normal, smart-thinking mom to messed-up, forgetful mom, Lexi had ended up being responsible for everyone. Her mother thought she was still capable sometimes, but was confused periodically about why she was even in assisted living, and she certainly didn't seem to remember or understand that her daughter was having to pay most of her monthly bills to keep her there. The financial strain was suffocating—it woke her up many nights in a hot sweat, sheets tangled frantically around her as she gulped for air and saw the digits in her dwindling bank account in her mind's eye. Her every decision was fraught with fear, that spending too much at the supermarket could start a downward spiral that she wouldn't be able to claw her way out from.

It's going to be fine, she told herself as she started the car. *You have to believe that it's all going to be fine.*

She lifted her head and breathed, focusing on each inhale, holding the air in her lungs for four counts before slowly letting it go, then repeating the pattern. Without her job caring for Walter, and the perk of having her accommodation paid for, she could lose everything. And then she'd have a mother with Alzheimer's to care for on her own, no place to live, and a little boy who needed so much of her. All she wanted was to keep him safe and happy, to know her mom was being cared for, and to somehow find the joy she'd once had in her life. Only it seemed like a very, very long time ago that she'd even known the meaning of joy, unless it was to do with her son's smile and the way she felt whenever he was in the room.

And now Cody was home. Cody Ford. Cody who'd broken her heart. Cody who she knew, deep down, that she'd never, ever stopped loving.

Cody who'd left Texas—*and her*—behind like he was running from the Devil himself.

Chapter 3

CODY left his siblings in the kitchen and walked down the hall and upstairs, stopping as he always did when he was home to look at the photographs lining the walls. Their mom had been all about capturing every single image on camera, and he still remembered the sound of her humming a tune as she sorted through images and put them in frames, adding them to the never-ending collection on the walls. Upstairs, there was virtually no wall space left, and even though he knew all the photos from memory, he always stopped, without fail, to study them.

There were chubby baby photos and toddlers playing naked, family shots of them out on the ranch or away on vacation, their entire family smiling at the rodeo and at a local fair. There was every sort of family photo and pictures of every child, but the collection ended abruptly during Cody's senior year of high school.

He moved on, not wanting to think about their mom. A lot of things had ended when she'd died, and for him, that included wanting to stay at home. The house had never felt the same without her in it, and although he knew that was cruel to his younger siblings who'd had no choice but to stay, at a time when they'd probably needed their big brother around, it had been easier to start his own life and stay far, far away from the pain.

Cody walked into his bedroom, which was more or less the same as he'd left it. The high-school trophies had been cleared away, probably for the sake of whomever was dusting the house each week, and the posters had come down from the walls long ago, but it still felt familiar. The same feel, the same look, the same smell. He closed the door behind him and stood beside the bed, unbuttoning his shirt and then taking off the rest of his clothes, until he was standing in his briefs. He hung his trousers up and put his shoes away, before staring into his closet and feeling the pull down memory lane, the clothes alone enough to bring him crashing headfirst back into the life he'd left behind.

He pulled out a pair of well-worn jeans and put them on, followed by a white T-shirt and a plaid shirt, another old favorite that he'd never parted with. As he was doing the buttons he crossed to the big window that faced the driveway, but instead of staring at the landscape he saw the tail end of Lexi as she got into a car. He moved to the next window to get a better look, wondering what she was doing when the car never moved. And then he saw her lean forward, her arms on the steering wheel as he her head came down, and she just sat there, immobile, as he watched on.

She was crying. Either that or she was so exhausted she couldn't move; but she hadn't looked exhausted in the kitchen before. Something had upset her.

"Hey, you want to come finish moving the bulls with me?"

Cody jumped back from the window and found Tanner standing in his doorway.

"Ah, yeah, sure," he said. "Just give me a sec to find some socks."

"What're you looking at out there?" Tanner asked.

Cody didn't answer, he just crossed the room and opened a drawer, pulling out a thick wooly pair so his toes wouldn't freeze in his boots.

"That's Lexi's car," Tanner said. "What's she doing in there like that?"

Cody looked out the window again, wishing his brother hadn't seen. "She looks upset. She's been like that a while." He sighed. "You don't think it was seeing me again do you?"

Tanner laughed. "Don't flatter yourself. She's got a lot more to worry about than a shitty ex-boyfriend coming back to town."

Cody scowled back at him. "What the hell's that supposed to mean?"

Tanner shrugged and gestured for him to follow, and Cody did, leaving the rest of his city clothes on the bed and padding down the hall after his brother. "We've got to get a move on before it's dark. Last thing we need is a herd of young bulls acting up because we've left it too late."

"Why are you doing all the work? Don't we have our foreman and ranch hands to keep the place running smoothly?" He stopped short of saying that they paid people so none of them *had* to do the grunt work.

"Yeah, we do, but they've all worked their asses off for us for years, so I told most of them to take some time off this Christmas, go see their families," Tanner said, pulling on his boots at the back door. Cody hunted around for his and tipped them upside down to check for mice and any other critters that might have nestled in there since last year. "I knew you were going to be home, so I figured there was nothing we couldn't handle, right?"

"Right." Except Cody hadn't expected to spend his time at home working like a dog on the ranch. "Going back to Lexi, what did you mean she has more going on than me coming back?"

Tanner grunted. "She's real quiet about her personal life, unless it's to do with her son, Harry. He's a real little dude, loves being on the ranch, and you can tell he means the world to her."

Cody waited, wanting to hear the rest. "But?"

"But Dad did a little digging, when she applied for the job. Just routine stuff, contacted old references and talked to some former employers." Tanner leaned on a post and looked back at him. "Turns out her mom's got Alzheimer's—she must have been pretty young to get it—and Lexi's working her ass off to pay for her care. Not to mention she's raising her boy all on her own."

"Some asshole left her holding the baby?"

Tanner scowled. "Some asshole doesn't pay his child support I'd say, but she never talks about it. Trust me, I'd have done something about it if she'd told me enough to figure it out, but she's a pretty closed book on that subject."

"So Dad gave her the job because he felt sorry for her? Is that it?"

"Hell no! She was the most qualified nurse for the job, overqualified in fact, but the hours suited her and he wanted her. She brings out something in him, I don't know what, but he seems to light up around her, you can see that she makes him feel better just by being with him. She has a way with him that a lot of other women wouldn't."

Cody had noticed that himself, the way his father had smiled at Lexi. Or maybe he'd imagined it when he was trying to figure out who the hell she was.

"After she started, Dad asked her a few questions, wanted to know how she was getting on, and he told her to give up the lease on her place and move in. He was deteriorating and he wanted her close, and she couldn't afford her rent, so it was a win-win situation for both of them."

Tanner started to walk again, his long stride eating up the dirt, and Cody followed him, inhaling the smell of the ranch, noticing the way even the air felt different in Texas compared to New York. It filled his lungs, made him feel lighter somehow, had a different bite to the taste of city air tinged with car fumes and the scent of a hundred things wafting together at once. Maybe that's what scared him about the ranch—the pace was too slow for him, the memories always flooding back because there weren't enough other things happening to distract him. He wasn't even sure if he wanted to see Lexi, how he felt about being near her again. He didn't want to be reminded of what he'd left or how he'd behaved, but then he should have been used to women making him feel like an asshole when it came to relationships. He hadn't gotten any better at it.

"Why the hell didn't you tell me about her?" Cody asked.

"You knew her a long time ago, it never really crossed my mind. Besides, you don't exactly come home often."

Cody wasn't buying it. More likely his brother wanted

to see the look on his face when he realized that his ex-girlfriend had turned into one of the most stunning, sexy women he'd ever laid eyes on. If Tanner hadn't proposed to Lauren, he'd have thought his little brother wanted to keep Lexi all to himself.

"You gonna help me with these bulls or daydream about your pretty little ex?" Tanner asked.

Cody snapped out of it and followed him into the field, suddenly not thinking of anything else as fifty young, testosterone-fueled bulls stared him down, their wide brown eyes sizing him up, just as he was doing to them.

"I'm going to get on the quad and they should follow me straight through; they know the drill," Tanner called out. "I just need you to keep an eye on any stragglers and get the gate shut behind them."

Cody nodded and watched as his brother gunned the quad to life and set off, most of the bulls happily following him in the knowledge that there would be food in the next part of the field for them. But one stared back at him, unblinking, as if trying to figure out who he was and what he was going to do to him.

He raised a hand and tried to encourage him on, but still the cattle beast didn't move. And all of a sudden, Cody wondered how different his life might have been if his mom hadn't died and he hadn't felt the sudden urge to flee the ranch and never look back.

That night, Cody sat in the library with his dad in front of a big fire, listening to the sounds of his sister in the kitchen. He had his niece curled asleep in his arms, and his father was holding baby Isobel, bouncing her on his knee to keep her from crying. He would have helped Mia clean up, but when Sophia had fallen asleep on him she'd insisted he stay still and not move a muscle—

and he knew better than to disobey his sister. She might be the youngest, but she'd always been able to boss her brothers around. Besides, he was guessing it was a relief to have someone else mind the children for a bit.

His dad turned the television down and shifted in his chair. "So how's work going? You're usually straight into talking shop with me, but you haven't said a word yet."

"Work's good," he replied, realizing how caught up he'd been in his thoughts. "I've hired some new people so I can be out there doing deals instead of being stuck in my office so much."

Walter chuckled. "I've never thought of you as being *stuck* in your office. Strikes me that you love every minute you spend in there."

"Takes one to know one," Cody replied.

They both laughed, but his dad's expression changed then. "You look tired, son. Your mom used to tell me that sometimes, and I hated to hear it, but it's true. Sometimes we need a break. Take it from someone who never took one and wishes he had."

Cody shifted his weight slightly, glancing down at Sophia. She was so blissfully asleep, her lips parted as she breathed quietly in slumber. "I *am* tired," he admitted. "I mean, I'm always tired—sleeping's not exactly my thing—but I've had a lot of deals to close, money to raise, a never-ending number of investors wanting face-to-face meetings. It's been one hell of a big year but I can't exactly complain."

"I hope you're staying a few days then," his father said. "We like to think we're invincible, but we can't burn the candle at both ends forever without paying for it."

Cody watched his father, saw the stiff way he moved, noticed the slight grimace that bracketed his mouth whenever he had to strain too much. Even holding the baby was probably pushing it for him, having to jiggle her all the time to stop her from fussing, but he wasn't game enough to tell his father, the man who'd run their family dynasty for so many years without so much as a chink in his armor, that he wasn't capable of holding an infant.

"I find it hard to shut off. There's always more to do, my head's always spinning," Cody admitted. "It's goddamn exhausting being me sometimes."

"Son, I know. Trust me, I know."

"You're damn hard to live up to, Dad." He chuckled. "It's tough having an old man who's trodden the path before and done it so well."

"I don't think *Fortune* magazine would agree with that," his dad said with a deep laugh that turned to a cough.

Cody waited for him to catch his breath. "You saw that? I was hoping it had stayed under the radar."

"When your son's named on *Fortune* magazine's 40 Under 40 list, you don't miss it. Besides, I have more time for reading these days, so there's no chance of me missing anything."

Cody couldn't help the smile that spread slowly across his lips. "Pretty insane, huh?"

"I'd like to think the apple doesn't fall too far from the tree. But I sure as hell wouldn't be worrying about not living up to your old man."

They both laughed at the same time as a knock echoed out against the open door behind them.

"Sorry to interrupt," came a soft voice.

Cody turned and saw Lexi standing there, her hair pulled back into a ponytail and an oversize cashmere cardigan wrapped around her body. He gulped. Seeing her like that took him straight back to high school—a look on her face that was more innocent than the guarded expression earlier, and her hair so similar to how she'd once worn it every day back then. If he'd walked in on her looking like that earlier in the day, she'd have stolen his breath away with how familiar she looked, and there wasn't a chance he wouldn't have recognized her. And then he saw a little boy peeking from around his mother's legs, and he grinned when those eyes connected with his.

"You're not interrupting at all," Walter said, at the same moment as Mia came back in and took the baby from him, as if on cue. "You should know by now that seeing you is my favorite part of the day."

"Come on," Mia said, cooing at her little daughter. "Time to get you to sleep. Cody, when you're ready can you carry Sophia up to bed?"

He nodded but his focus was on the woman in the room who *wasn't* his sister. He watched the way she moved, the way she smiled at his father as she sat down beside him, taking his hand and putting his finger into a machine. The way she pointed to the chair in the corner for her son to sit in, and the way he obediently did as he was told.

"What are you doing?" Cody asked, giving the boy a wink as he turned his attention back to Lexi.

"Checking his oxygen levels," she said, barely glancing up. "Then I'll take his temperature and administer his pills, as well as give him a little injection."

His father didn't look at him, but he felt the silence stretch out.

"What kind of injection?" Cody asked, wondering if he wasn't going to like the answer.

He saw the way Lexi glanced at his father, as if asking his permission to share. They seemed to have an unspoken language, a closeness that almost made him jealous. This must have been what Tanner was trying to explain, the way they seemed to have an understanding, the way his father lit up when she was in the room. He could see why they all thought she was good for him.

"Morphine," she said eventually, her voice low. "To help with the pain."

"Morphine?" Cody repeated. "I didn't know your pain was that bad, Dad. Why didn't you say?"

"It's just to help me sleep," the old man muttered. "Don't go getting all worried about it or telling your siblings."

But he could see that look again, that something passed between him and Lexi, and he knew there was more to it. Was his dad worse than he realized?

"Dad?"

Walter sighed. "What good would it do me, telling you all how bad my pain is? As far as I'm concerned, I'm lucky to be alive and that's the end of it. Moaning never got anyone anywhere, did it?"

Cody blew out a breath. "I just wish I'd known." He would have come home more, he would have called more. He sure as hell wouldn't have missed Thanksgiving. Or maybe he would have, maybe it would have made him even more scared to come home. "I'm sorry."

His father held out his arm, and Cody watched as Lexi gently held him, carefully injecting him and smiling down at him the entire time. There was a softness there, a warmth that took him back in time. She'd been a sweet girl even in school, maybe too sweet for him. He'd been so focused on what he wanted, determined to do what he wanted to do, and maybe she'd been so quiet and kind, he'd been able to ignore how she felt about it all. And since then, he'd somehow steered clear of the good girl and gone for all the wrong types of women. Why the hell hadn't he been man enough to say goodbye to her, or had he been so into himself it hadn't even crossed his mind?

Watching her now, it was like looking in a window and seeing a flashback of what he'd done wrong in the past, memories slowly trickling back to him.

Cody rose, lifting Sophia in his arms and walking past the boy.

"Hey, little dude," he whispered, "want me to come back for you once I put this one to bed? We can go make hot chocolates while your mom works."

The boy nodded, but he glanced over at his mother first before answering. She gave a quick nod.

"Yeah," he whispered back.

Cody grinned and walked from the room, heading straight up the stairs. His sister's husband was away traveling for work and wasn't due back until Christmas Eve, which was why Mia was staying in the house with the kids, and he was happy for the children as a distraction. Having them in the house made it easier to stay busy, and stopped him from trying to find an excuse to fly out and go back to work.

"Shhh," he whispered as he lowered Sophia, reaching for the soft toy bunny she liked to snuggle and tucking them both beneath the covers. He watched her for a moment, her dark hair splayed across the pillow, cupid lips parted in slumber, before dropping a kiss to her forehead and tiptoeing out.

"She loves her uncle Cody," Mia said, her voice low as they stood outside the bedroom.

"She's got me wrapped around her little finger already, that's for sure."

"You're a natural with her. Seeing you like that, it reminds me of how you were with me when we were little." Mia leaned into him, her head to his shoulder. "Tanner was always trying to toughen me up, but you were always so kind to me. I don't remember you punching me or pushing me out of a tree even once."

He chuckled. "At least I was nice to *you*."

She pulled back and he met her gaze. "As opposed to?"

Cody cleared his throat, shoving his hands into his pockets. "Lexi. I was an ass to her and until now I've never really thought about how I left her. I was so happy to be moving on, and I didn't think about her being left behind."

Mia frowned. "She's never said anything."

"She doesn't need to. It was written all over her face when I saw her today for the first time. I hurt her and I didn't even know. Or maybe I did know and I was just too juvenile to understand it."

Mia stifled a yawn. "It's never too late to grow a conscience, Cody. If you have something to apologize for, spit it out before it's too late. That's my advice."

"Thanks." He looked at her properly. "You look dog-tired."

She yawned again. "I am. You try having an unsettled baby half the night, and a little girl who wakes at six a.m. and thinks it's party time. Not having Sam to help is killing me."

"Send her to me then," he said. "I don't care. I'm usually up before six anyway."

She laughed. "You'd seriously take her at that time of the morning? Man, you're gonna make a great dad one day."

Cody held up his hands. "Not me. I've got no plans to have kids; work is more than enough of a baby for me."

"*What?*"

He backed away from his sister, not about to get drawn into a conversation with her about children or his lack of desire to ever settle down. "Forget I said anything, other than the part about helping out. You need me, just holler. Right now, I have hot chocolate to make."

He ran back down the stairs and ducked his head into the library. The kid was waiting, watching out for him.

"Come with me," he said, before glancing in Lexi's direction to make sure she was still okay with it. "We'll just be in the kitchen."

The boy looked nervous, so Cody stuck out his hand. "I'm Cody," he said. "And you're the famous Harry, right?"

Harry giggled. "I'm not famous."

"You sure? Because I'm sure your mom told me you were famous."

He was clearly trying hard not to laugh, but it wasn't working. "I'm not famous. Honestly!"

"I must have gotten that wrong. It's just she had the biggest smile on her face when she told me about you, I thought you must have been a movie star or something."

Harry walked closer to him now, and Cody was relieved he'd managed to break the ice between them. He might have been a fool in front of Lexi earlier, but at least he wasn't tongue-tied now.

"So you like hot chocolate?" he asked.

"Yup."

"What about cookies?"

Harry grinned. "I love them."

Cody disappeared and brought out some cookies

from the pantry, sliding them across the counter. Then he helped boost Harry up onto one of the stools.

"So what happened at school today?"

Harry shrugged as he ate his first cookie. "Not much."

"You like taking the bus home?" he asked. "I used to love the bus ride. It was even better than recess, getting to sit and talk with all my friends."

"I don't like school. I just want to stay here, on the ranch."

Cody poured milk into a pot and stirred in some cocoa. This was how he remembered hot chocolates when he was a kid, he just hadn't had to make them himself before. He hoped he was doing it right.

"I remember that, too. But school's important. It'll help you get even smarter."

Harry was staring at him, and Cody smiled, not worried about the kid studying him.

"My mom says the same thing."

"That's because she's so smart," Cody replied, still stirring and waiting for the cocoa to dissolve. He remembered exactly how smart she was, too, always refusing to fool around with him until she'd studied first, and making him hit the books all the time. "You know, you have the same eyes as her."

"How do you know my mom?"

Cody sighed and turned the gas off, finding two big mugs and pouring the drink into them. "We were really good friends, a very long time ago."

"Why doesn't she like you then?"

Cody laughed. He couldn't help it. "She said that?"

"No, but she gave you the same look that she gives my dad, and the dentist, and I know she doesn't like either of them."

He had no idea what to say to that. "Here you go," he

said, sliding the steaming mug over to Harry. "Just be careful, it's hot."

Cody stood and Harry sat, both blowing on their hot chocolate and taking small sips. It wasn't quite the same as he remembered, but it wasn't bad.

"So tell me about your mom. What do you guys do for fun?"

Harry giggled. "We eat so much pizza that she tells me we're gonna pop! And we watch movies."

Cody wasn't going to mention Harry's dad—it seemed safer not to—but he guessed the guy was completely out of the picture. "You have a favorite restaurant or anything?"

The kid shook his head. "Mom keeps saying that she loves going out for dinner and she wishes someone else would cook for her, but we mostly eat at home." He smiled. "Did you used to go out for dinner with her? Were you, like, boyfriend and girlfriend?"

Cody put down his mug and held up his hands. "I'm not telling you that, you'll have to ask your mom, but yeah, we went out for dinner a lot. Your mom used to love getting all dressed up and going out. We thought we were so grown up, but we were only eighteen."

"Ask your mom what?" Lexi asked as she walked into the room.

Cody cringed. "We were just talking about the past, about how we used to know each other." She must have supersonic hearing, or else it was just a mom thing.

She'd walked in so confidently, but he didn't miss the way her cheeks turned a deeper shade of pink as she put an arm around her son and dropped a kiss to the top of his head. She clearly didn't want to talk about the past in front of Harry.

"How's that hot chocolate?" she asked, and Cody

watched the tender way she brushed the hair from Harry's forehead, so gentle and warm with him.

"Awesome," Harry said after draining the last of it.

"You want one?" Cody asked. "Honestly, it wouldn't take me a second to—"

"Thanks, but I need to get this one into bed," she said quickly. "I appreciate you taking him though. Harry, what do you have to say?"

"Thank you," Harry said quietly, jumping off the stool and holding his mom's hand.

"No problem, buddy. Anytime."

He stood and watched as Lexi led her son from the room, a million things racing through his head as he thought of what to say. Talking to Harry, reminiscing about the past just now, it was making him remember what a good time he'd had with Lexi. It had been a long while since he'd thought about it, but not everything about his home state had been so bad.

"Lexi, wait up," he said, knowing he needed to say something before she left. Suddenly all he could think about was how crestfallen she'd looked earlier in the day, when he'd watched her out the window in her car, and he hoped he hadn't been the cause of it, even though Tanner had insisted he couldn't be. She was almost at the front door, her back to him, but she slowly turned at his call.

"I really need to get Harry into bed," she said, as if the last thing she wanted to do was waste time talking to him.

"I know, I just . . ." He looked at her, at the guarded expression she wore around him that was so different from the look she gave his father. Or the look she gave her son. He sucked back a breath. "I just want to say sorry."

"Sorry?" she repeated.

"Seeing you again, it's reminded me of everything that happened between us." He glanced at Harry standing beside his mom, knowing he had to be careful with his choice of words. "I just want to say that I'm sorry for the way I left. It wasn't right."

She laughed as she planted her hands over Harry's ears. "After all this time, you're saying *sorry*? Wow."

Cody shifted uncomfortably, hands back in his pockets. "I didn't realize there was anything funny about it, but yeah. After all this time, I'm saying sorry."

"I appreciate the thought," she said, taking her hands off Harry's ears and pulling on her coat, her eyes like a storm about to lash out with lightning, "and I'd like to say that it's about time. But it's not. You're more than a decade late, Cody. Some things you just can't make up for, no matter what you say."

He went to open his mouth, but before he could say anything else, she'd already yanked open the door and disappeared out into the bitter-cold darkness.

Cody stared at the door for a second before walking slowly into the kitchen and going to the liquor cabinet, deciding to pour himself a drink. What had he expected? Her to say she accepted his apology followed by some reminiscing about the past? He groaned and drained a short glass of whiskey. Stupid. That's what he was. God-damn stupid.

Trouble was, he'd forgotten about Lexi without a second thought all those years ago, but there was something about the woman she'd become that made him think she'd be a whole lot harder to forget the second time around.

He poured another drink and stared at the dark amber

liquid before knocking it back, looking up at the ceiling as he savored the gentle burn in his throat. He knew why he was so scared of Lexi—she reminded him of the type of woman his mother had been, and the second he'd known she was terminal, he'd wanted to run. And he had. Away from home, away from the pain, away from anything that made him *feel*. Nothing had changed, either. He was still the scared son of a bitch who'd bolted all those years ago, and being at home terrified him in case he ever had to deal with those thoughts and feelings again.

He pushed the bottle of whiskey away, not wanting to drown his sorrows in liquor. Work was usually his way to stay focused, and if he had any downtime he'd head straight to his local boxing joint and pull on his gloves, working out with his trainer. In the morning he'd run instead, and he sure as hell wasn't going to be able to do that with a hangover.

Cody put his glass and the mugs in the dishwasher and turned out the lights, walking past his father's library and noticing the light was still drifting out from beneath the door. He paused outside, listening but not hearing anything, so he knocked softly and waited for a reply.

Nothing.

Cody nudged the door open and saw him lying on the big leather sofa, the ottoman pressed up close to it for his legs, and a soft blanket tucked around him. His mouth was open slightly in slumber, and he walked quietly over to him, pulling the blanket up a little higher and flicking the lamp off.

He steeled his jaw as he walked from the room, closing the door behind him as he trudged upstairs. Tears pricked his eyes but he refused to let them fall. But there was something about seeing his once-imposing, big, strong father asleep in his den because he didn't have the strength to make it upstairs—in a morphine-induced slumber at that.

Chapter 4

LEXI stared out the window, wondering if it was going to snow. Trouble was, every time she looked out at the weather, her gaze drifted to the big house across the driveway, and she couldn't stop thinking about the man inside. When she started working for the Ford family, she'd had a funny tingle about being there, her memories of Cody always drifting somewhere in her mind. She'd refused to look at the photos of him in Walter's office, never letting her thoughts wander, staying focused on what she was there to do. And for months it'd worked out just fine. But the energy in the house had shifted having him there, and she had no idea how she was going to get through the next week with him in residence.

She gulped. And there he was, standing outside the house, stretching in the cold, looking like he was about to go for a run. Lexi watched the way he arched his body, limbering up, and something inside of her warmed as she admired him. Yet another reason why she'd been so hung up on him—he had muscles in *all* the right places. She took another sip of coffee, as Cody started to jog away from the house, enjoying being able to look at him without him knowing.

"Mommy, is it snowing?" Harry asked.

She turned, coffee mug in hand, and smiled at her son. He was sitting at the table, eating Fruit Loops, his attention mostly caught by the television playing a cartoon. That was another reason she couldn't stop thinking about Cody—seeing him with Harry had twisted her up in knots. He'd been so sweet with him, which of course had won her son over instantly. Not giving in to her attraction to him wasn't going to be as easy as she'd thought.

"Not yet, honey. Maybe later today."

"Do I have to go to school?"

"Yes," she said, expecting the question. "It's your last day, and then you'll be home for two weeks."

He grinned and she moved closer to wipe the milk from his chin. For some reason her kid always had a messy face, no matter what he was eating.

"Cool."

She glanced back at the house again, before tipping out the last of her coffee and stacking the few dirty dishes they had in the sink, ruffling Harry's hair on the way past.

"Let's go, little man. We can't be late for the bus."

She brushed his teeth and hair, told him to put on his shoes and quickly finished getting herself ready. Lexi looked in the mirror and smiled, before the smile turned to a frown and she scrambled to find her lipstick, adding some extra highlighter to her cheeks and dabbing perfume to her wrists and neck.

"Mmm, you smell nice, Mommy."

Lexi dropped a kiss to his head. "Thanks, bud."

Maybe it was stupid making an extra effort, but the least she could do was make Cody see what he'd missed.

Although compared to the girls he probably dated, she bet she was little more than a country bumpkin. She shuddered thinking about the never-ending stream of women who tripped in and out of his apartment on a weekly basis.

She bundled Harry in the car and jumped in the driver's seat, starting the engine and rubbing her hands together. It was only a short drive, but without the heater blasting she was convinced they could actually freeze to death.

She reached for her son's hand as they drove, squeezing it and flashing him a smile, slowing as they got to the end of the driveway. They sat like that, waiting for the bus, as they did every morning. Just the two of them; she and her boy, warming each other's hands as they quietly waited.

Within minutes the bus appeared, chugging along down the road, and she leaned over and gave him a kiss.

"Have a great day," she said.

"You too, Mom."

He got out of the car as she looked on, slamming the door and running toward the bus. She smiled at his little hand raised in a wave to the bus driver, and the way he turned, as he always did before he stepped in, to give her a quick little wave too. And then he was gone, the bus on its way again as she took a big breath and turned the car around, driving back up the mile-long driveway to the Ford residence.

Only today was different. Because today she was going to have to face Cody headfirst again, and she had no idea how she was going to do it.

Cody finished his run and bent over to catch his breath, gulping down mouthfuls of ice-cold, pure country air.

He'd pushed himself hard, sprinting through field after field, slowing only periodically before sprinting again, running like the devil was on his back. And now his lungs were screaming out in pain, his legs aching, but he enjoyed every inch of the burn. This was what he'd needed, to push his body and tire himself out. The gym was one thing, and he went early every morning at home, but there was something about running outside that made him feel better. More alive somehow.

He looked up at the noise of tires crunching gravel, standing upright as a car pulled slowly in by the converted barn. His father had kitted it out when they were younger, hoping to keep his sons close by giving them their own space to live on the ranch, but even the lure of his own place hadn't been enough to tempt Cody into staying. He watched as Lexi emerged from the car, her dark hair hiding her face as she bent in to retrieve something. Cody took a few steps forward, his eyes never leaving her.

He quickly took off his T-shirt, wiping his face and then tucking it into his waistband. The air might be frigid, but he was still flushed and the cool breeze felt good.

"Hey," he said.

Lexi spun around, hand to her heart. "Shit, Cody! You scared the life out of me."

He grimaced. "Sorry, I thought you'd seen me before."

She shook her head, staring back at him wide eyed. "You'll catch your death out here if you walk around half-naked like that."

Cody took a step back as she glanced at his bare chest, her eyes fluttering slowly down before going sharply back up again.

"I'll be fine," he said, before asking, "You okay?"

"Yeah, I'm fine. I need to get to work though."

Not fine was written all over her face, but he doubted she'd admit it. Cody gestured toward the house. "I'll walk you." He waited for her to move and then fell into step beside her just as the cold finally chilled his skin. He contemplated pulling his T-shirt back on but decided he was better bare than wearing a dripping wet top. "You just dropped your son at the school bus?"

She nodded. "Sure did. He wasn't impressed about going today; I think he thought it would snow and school would get cancelled."

"I remember the feeling like it was yesterday," Cody said, grinning. "I used to pray that school would be cancelled all winter, and every day I'd be disappointed."

They walked in silence then, until they reached the door and he stepped forward to open it for her, waiting for her to walk in.

"Lexi?"

She turned, and he thought he saw a smile, just a faint one, but a smile nonetheless. Or maybe it was wishful thinking.

"I meant what I said last night, about being sorry. I get that it's too late, but I want you to know that I'm genuinely sorry for anything I did to hurt you."

Her gaze fixed on his. "Did you even have any idea how much you'd hurt me back then?"

Cody inhaled, deciding in that split second that he needed to answer honestly even if it wasn't the answer she wanted to hear. "No. I didn't."

She nodded. "And that's why your apology doesn't mean anything to me," she said, walking away. "But I appreciate your sincerity."

Cody stifled a groan and jogged a few steps to catch

up with her. "Since I'm only home for a few days, is there any way we can get past this and . . ."

"What? Go on a date or something?" she asked.

Cody laughed. "Well yeah, you beat me to the question but—"

"Seriously?"

He grinned, his shoulders relaxing at how easy it had been to break the ice with her. "Seriously."

Lexi moved closer, so close he wondered if her breasts were actually going to rub against his bare chest. His nipples hardened in anticipation.

"Not if you were the last man on Earth," she whispered in his ear.

Cody stared after her as she spun and marched down the hallway, her shoes clicking against the timber floor. He opened his mouth and shut it again, not even sure what to say or whether to just burst out laughing. Lexi sure as hell wasn't the sweet little girl he'd left behind in Texas, or else she just hated him so bad that she was showing him a completely different side of herself.

He crossed the hall and ran up the stairs, not bothering to call after her, taking two at a time and making his way to his bedroom. He stripped down and walked naked into the bathroom, turning on the faucet and waiting until the water ran hot before stepping under the steady stream. Cody shut his eyes and leaned forward, hands up with his forehead pressed into them, the showerhead dumping water down his neck and over his back.

He might not have wanted Lexi back then, but he sure as hell wanted her now.

When he wanted a business deal, he didn't take no for an answer, no matter how high the stakes, and it wasn't any different when it came to women. He just needed to figure out how to get what he wanted.

He slipped his hand down, hard as a rock with Lexi on his mind. If he couldn't have her, then this was the next best thing.

Cody liked a challenge, and it'd been a long time since any woman had been a challenge for him.

"Are you sure you don't want any breakfast?" Lexi asked Walter as she plumped up the cushions on his sofa, trying to disguise the fact that he'd slept there. Again. The man was as stubborn as a mule, refusing to let her set up a proper bed in his library turned home office, so she helped him to maintain the façade he seemed determined to continue with. Although she doubted his family was so easily fooled.

"Today's not my best day," he said. For a man who'd always ruled with an iron fist, he was as polite and kind to her as could be. Even on his worst days, when she knew the pain was no doubt unbearable and he couldn't stomach any food, he never failed to be nice to her.

"Morning, Dad." Cody's head appeared through the door, hair still wet, but thankfully with clothes on this time. She guessed he'd just showered.

"Today isn't a good day, Cody," she said gently, nodding toward his father.

Cody's smile faltered and he came closer, but his dad waved at him, clearly trying to dismiss her words. He never liked to let on when he was struggling, and certainly not to his children.

"Anything I can do?" he asked.

"Stop fussing," his father said.

"Fussing?" Cody laughed. "I have no idea how to fuss, so count me out of doing that."

Walter laughed, and Lexi blew out a breath she hadn't even realized she'd been holding. She might not like

Cody, but he wasn't doing his father any harm—quite the opposite almost. And it reminded her of how nice he'd always been to her, and to everyone else at school. He might have been one of the wealthiest kids around, but he'd never acted like it, always sticking up for anyone getting bullied or pushed around. And the way he'd been with Harry the night before had shown her that he wasn't any different now, which was why she was having a hard time remembering why she hated him so much.

"I think we should do something today, get you out of this room and out on the ranch. What do you think?"

Lexi's eyebrows shot up at his suggestion. "It's cold outside, Cody, I don't know if that's a good id—"

"Yes!" Walter boomed. "That's exactly what I need. I need to get back on a goddamn horse or a tractor or something. Get me the hell out of this room, Cody. Thank God you're home, son."

Lexi gave Cody a sharp look, but he didn't seem to get the message. Either that or he was *trying* not to get it. So much for thinking nice thoughts about him.

"I'm not so sure," she said, looking between the two men. "How about we see how the morning goes and then decide? I don't want to push things too far."

"How about you come with us?" Cody asked. "Then we won't have anything to worry about, right, Dad?"

Walter nodded enthusiastically and Lexi gulped down some air as she slowly raised her eyes and stared at Cody. His smile was sweet as pie, but the wink he gave her made it clear that she'd just been played. Clearly this was punishment for laughing at his offer of a date. He'd figured out a way for them to spend time together, and he obviously wasn't going to take no for an answer.

She straightened her shoulders and refused to let

him rattle her. If Walter wanted to go, then she had no choice but to comply, but she wasn't going to make it easy for Cody.

"I'll get everything prepared, then," she said, smiling at Walter and going to assist him. "Cody, why don't you be in charge of snacks? Heck, lunch even? You can rustle up something good for us to eat, can't you?"

She glanced at him and saw one of his brows arch high, but all he did was smile in return. He had a perfect poker face.

One point Cody, one point Lexi, she thought smugly. If he thought he was the only one who could play at this game then he was sorely mistaken. She should have been telling her patient not to overexert himself, to stay put and rest, but she knew that just wasn't Walter's nature and frankly, she'd rather spend whatever last months she had left doing what she loved if it were her, so she got it. A picnic with the old man or an outing on the ranch would have actually been quite nice; *without Cody, that was.*

Half an hour later, she left Walter and found Cody in the kitchen. It seemed to be the place she always ran into him, although this time she had come looking.

"It suits you," she said. "Quite the domestic. I wouldn't have picked it."

He grinned but didn't look up, and she leaned against the doorframe as he finished making sandwiches. She thought he'd have balked, but it looked to her like he'd gotten straight to work.

"What are you making?"

He looked up, licking his finger, his eyes bright. "Peanut butter and jelly sandwiches."

She laughed. "You can make them? Wow, I'm impressed."

"I googled it, actually. You know, just to make sure I did them right."

"Hold up, you *googled* how to make PB and J sandwiches? The title kind of gives you everything you need to know, in case you hadn't realized."

He shrugged. "I wanted to be sure. In case you didn't know, I'm a full-blown type-A personality. I have to do things perfectly."

Lexi groaned. "Right, of course. A type A with a personal chef, who doesn't even make his own breakfast probably. No wonder you needed instructions for how to make sandwiches."

"Ouch. I'll have you know that my chef only cooks me dinner. I get a granola cup on the way to work and my assistant organizes lunch."

Lexi fought the childish urge to roll her eyes. "Of course you do. You do realize you'd be the laughing stock of Texas if you admitted to any of the ranchers here that you stop for a *granola cup* on the way to work though, right?" She laughed. "And don't tell me you take almond milk now instead of *actual* milk?"

"First of all, no, I don't drink goddamn almond milk, and second, ranchers eating eggs and bacon would be better eating something healthier. It's not rocket science."

"Hmm, sounds like someone has a bit of an attitude about things around here. But that's right, you couldn't leave our beautiful part of the country fast enough, could you? Was it the first flight after school let out, or did you wait until the next day at least?"

Cody turned to the fridge and took out a carton of juice, setting in on the counter before planting his hands wide and staring at her. She tried not to squirm, not expecting his full attention to be leveled at her.

"As much as I enjoy these little sparring sessions, it'd be much easier just to get along."

She laughed, before covering her mouth with her hand. "Sorry, were you trying to be funny?"

"No. I'm trying to be a grown-up. Have you heard of it? Less bickering, more understanding, forgetting about the past, that kind of thing."

"Ahhh, right, sorry I must have missed that. Most of us don't have to *try* to be an adult after we've hit thirty."

"We ready to go?" Walter's deep voice still boomed with authority, even if his body didn't seem to match the tone any longer.

"We are," she said, turning to Walter and holding out her arm. "I'm looking forward to this, it'll be so nice to see the ranch properly again."

She shot a look over her shoulder at Cody.

"Catch up when you can, *Cody*," she said sweetly, leaving him to carry everything.

Lexi smiled to herself, knowing she was being petty but unable to help herself. She deserved to get some of her own back, and she was going to ride him hard all day. If he didn't like it, well then he could back the hell off and leave her alone. This year had kicked her butt big-time, and she knew she had a chip on her shoulder because of it, but she was sick of being the nice girl, the one who always did as she was told and ended up getting trampled all over.

She'd put a wall around her heart since Cody had vanished, and the only time she'd let it down was for Harrison's dad. Without Harry, the entire relationship would have been an epic mistake, but she'd never regretted having her son for a second, even if it had shown her that her wall had been built for a reason, and it was never, ever coming down again.

Or maybe, as that little voice in her head kept telling her, there was something about her that made men run in the opposite direction. Either way, she wasn't going to find out for a third time.

"So do you remember how to ride a horse?" Cody asked.

Lexi nodded even though she was mildly terrified of the beast saddled up in front of her. *Why did they look so much bigger than they used to?* "It's been a while, but it's one of those things you never forget, right?"

Walter grunted beside her. "I'm starting to think a vehicle would have been a better idea."

"Horseback will do you good, Dad. The fresh air in your lungs, it's exactly what you need."

Tanner poked his head out of the barn then, and Lexi wished she could have captured the look on his face— shock merged with horror that instantly seemed to turn to panic. "When you said to saddle up the horses I didn't think you meant for the old man," he muttered. "You sure about this? Dad, when did you even last ride a horse?"

"I'll have you know I spent my childhood on horseback. You gonna help an old man or not?"

Tanner moved fast, and with Cody holding the horse steady, she watched as Tanner helped to boost his dad up into the saddle. She also watched something pass between the boys, some unspoken words, before Tanner stepped back, his hand drifting hesitantly from his father's leg.

"You want me to saddle up and ride with you?" Tanner asked. "If you could use another pair of hands—"

"No, I got this," Cody said. "You can't take the ranch out of the rancher, right?"

"Ah, in your case, I think you can."

She smiled at Cody's scowl, finding it amusing the way Tanner seemed to be able to rile him so easily. The younger Ford brother was a whole lot more easygoing than the older one, that was for sure. But part of her wondered about Cody, whether he had actually left the ranch behind or if he just liked pretending that he had. For all the subtle changes, she thought that maybe he was just a rancher in fancier clothing, one who slipped straight back into rancher mode the second he let his guard down. She dragged her eyes from him, not wanting to start down the slippery slope of wondering what he was like now.

"Lexi, you need help mounting?" Cody asked.

She stared back at him standing there, hands by his side, eyes so clear as he fixed them on her, and slowly shook her head, not wanting any part of him that close to her.

"I'm fine. Thanks."

He gestured to the smaller of the two horses remaining, and she bravely took a step forward. *He taught you how to ride. Remember all those days under the sun on horseback?* She pushed the thoughts away and gave the chestnut mare a pat on the neck as Cody untied her. Lexi gathered up the reins. She had this.

"She'll go easy on you," Tanner called out, standing in front of the barn now. "She's the sweetest horse on the property, so don't worry if you're feeling rusty."

Trust Tanner to be the one to reassure her, not Cody.

She lifted her left leg high and pushed it into the stirrup, her thigh muscle screaming out as she bounced and struggled to get high enough to swing her other leg over onto the saddle. She tried again. When the hell had this gotten so hard? She remembered being so flexible and easily bouncing three times before landing in the saddle, but this was tough.

"Here, let me help," Cody said, his palms closing over her hips before she had a chance to yelp out *no.* "First time back in the saddle can be rough."

If she could even get in the damn saddle, that was!

"One, two, *three!*" he counted, boosting her on the final number, his hands pushing under her butt as he guided her up. She landed with an embarrassing *thump* and cringed as the horse shifted beneath her.

"Sorry, girl," she muttered, before looking down and seeing that Cody's hand was still resting on her leg.

Heat flooded her and she hated it, her body betraying her as the man she'd never forgotten stood with his warm palm on her jean-clad thigh. So much for swearing off men—her body clearly hadn't received the memo!

"You need any reminders?" he asked.

"Pretty sure you taught me everything I needed to know when I was seventeen," she muttered, regretting the words the second they left her mouth. Because they both knew that horseback riding wasn't the only thing Cody had taught her that first summer they were together.

"Good, well, I'm glad it was so memorable."

If his father hadn't been watching, she'd have kicked him, but instead she rode out the heat wave passing through her body, wishing the ground would just open up and swallow him as she brazenly stared back at him.

"Come on then, let's get moving before the weather closes in," Cody said, slinging his bag over his shoulder and mounting his horse so easily it made Lexi cringe. She had no idea when he'd last been in the saddle, but

clearly his limbs were still capable of moving correctly,
unlike hers. How had he made it look so damn easy?
Was it something to do with being born on the ranch?
Maybe it was just in his blood.

"Where's the food?" she asked as Cody nudged his
horse in the side and started to walk.

"Tanner's bringing it, he's going to meet us at that
nice place by the river, with the big tree hanging over
the water. You remember the spot?" His voice didn't
even hint that he was teasing her, it was an inside joke,
but it still made her bristle.

"Of course he is." She would have laughed at the fact
he'd made his brother their servant, except for the fact
that he'd name-dropped the place they were riding to for
a reason.

On a hot summer's day, with the sun on their backs
and the wind on their skin, beneath the enormous over-
hanging tree by the river, she'd given her virginity to
Cody, and he was taking her back to the one place on
the ranch she sure as hell didn't want to go with him.
Not today, not ever. Because remembering how good
that summer had been, how happy they'd been, it hurt.
And she was dealing with enough hurt to last a lifetime
already.

Chapter 5

CODY would never admit it, but his legs were starting to ache. It had taken every inch of his strength to push up into the saddle, his thigh muscles screaming out as he'd forced his foot high in the stirrup, and he'd only been pleased that Lexi hadn't been able to see the look on his face as he'd landed in the saddle. Or maybe he was lucky Tanner hadn't seen it, because his brother never would have let him live it down.

There was something about being back in the saddle again though, something peaceful about watching the world from the back of a horse. Time passed at a different pace on the ranch, and as much as he loved being at work and living in a high-pressure world, he liked the dip in pace here too. As a kid he'd felt trapped by the sameness of it all, but now he could appreciate it for what it was.

"You ever miss this, just being able to hop on a horse and ride? How does it compare to city life?"

Lexi's question made him stumble from his thoughts. "I don't miss it when I'm not here," he said. "That probably doesn't make sense, but when I'm in the city, I don't look back. It's only when I come to visit that I remember what I left."

If she were a canine, he was certain her back would have physically bristled, and he regretted his choice of words given their history.

"You can't stay away too long," his father chimed in. "You do that, you forget what's in your blood."

He started to cough then and Cody wondered if the air was too cold, whether it had been selfish of him to bring his father out just so he could spend time with Lexi.

"Do we need to head back?" he asked her, keeping his voice low so his father didn't hear.

She shook her head. "He coughs when he talks too much sometimes, but I think he's enjoying it."

Cody nodded and they kept riding, the three of them fanning out three-abreast now with Lexi in the middle. He watched her, seeing the way her body had relaxed, moving gently with the horse. Her long hair was pulled back into a ponytail, and he had the sudden urge to ride closer and slide the tie out so he could see it tumble down her back like it had been the day before.

"So why did you actually want to go riding today? You suddenly had a yearning to be back in the saddle and play rancher?"

Cody chuckled. "I think you know why I suggested this."

She kept her gaze fixed ahead but he saw the faint smirk of a smile pass her lips. That was the girl he remembered, always keeping him on his toes. "Maybe I want to hear you say it."

"Is it so bad that I want to spend time with you?" he asked. "I mean, I'm feeling like an absolute idiot for how things played out in the past, and I thought we could reconnect. I'm not going to lie, it's nice seeing you again."

She laughed. "More like you thought I'd forgive you and you'd have a plaything for the next few days. Am I right?"

Cody looked over at his father, pleased to see the old man gazing in the other direction, clearly lost in his thoughts. "Your words, Lexi, not mine."

"So there's no one special back in New York? No Mrs. Ford? Or are you more of a 'play while the cat's away' kind of guy."

Cody was the one bristling now. "I'm a lot of things, Lexi, but a cheater is not one of them."

She looked amused, and it annoyed him even more than her comment. "You don't strike me as a one-woman kind of guy."

At that he shrugged. "Never said I was. But I don't cheat," he kept his voice low. "There's a big difference between setting out clear parameters and being unfaithful. Besides, I'm not really interested in relationships, to be honest. I'm too busy."

"Ahh, of course. So if it's only a one-night thing, you can't cheat, right?"

He was about to nod when he realized she was being sarcastic.

"I know all about guys like that. You see, I used to date you, then my son's father. I really seem to be able to pick 'em."

Walter cleared his throat and Cody looked over. "You okay, Dad?"

"I was just wondering if you two think I'm deaf as well as dying?" he said dryly.

A quick glance at Lexi showed burning red cheeks, and Cody cleared his own throat, embarrassed at being caught like that. His dad had never been a fool, so he didn't know why he'd thought he wouldn't be listening.

"We have history, that's all," Cody muttered. "Sorry."

"Don't apologize. It's amusing as hell to an old man listening in. But I think you're digging yourself a pretty big hole there, son."

Lexi's laughter should have driven him mad, but he couldn't help smiling back at his father. He was right, trying to justify his lifestyle to an ex-girlfriend who was already pissed with him might not have been his cleverest move.

"How about we call a truce?" Cody asked. "For everyone's sake. While I'm home, we get along and don't mention the past. Deal?"

Her shoulders pushed up, but she finally released them into a shrug. "Fine. Deal. But only because I have way too much respect for your father to bicker about the past."

"Heard that too," Walter muttered smugly.

Cody rode closer to her, using his outside leg to nudge his horse over, and held out his hand. He watched as Lexi stared at it, before fumbling with her reins and putting them in one hand so she could reach him. They shook, and he stared into eyes the color of almonds.

"So do you spend Christmas Day with your own family or—"

"She's spending it with us," his father boomed, sounding more like his old self for a moment. "Aren't you, Alexandra? I want you by my side having the best Christmas lunch that money can buy."

Cody watched as she shifted, maybe unsettled by the offer. "Dad, she might have plans already."

Lexi shook her head. "Actually I don't. My mother's

in an assisted-care facility right now, and it's just me and Harrison, so other than going to visit Mom, we're just hanging out the two of us."

"With us," Walter insisted.

Cody hated seeing the sadness pass over Lexi's face. Anger he could deal with, but not sadness. Sadness was why he'd left Texas in the first place. "Lexi? You know you're welcome, right? Don't decide not to come just because I'm here." For some reason he couldn't stop thinking about how Harry had said they didn't go out for dinner much, even though he knew she'd like to. Was it because she was worried about money, because she was supporting her mom? He made a mental note to ask another time, when his father wouldn't be listening in— or anyone else for that matter.

She glanced at him, more vulnerable, more like the girl he remembered all of a sudden. "Thanks, Cody."

They rode farther, covering the long stretch of land between the barn and the river, and he suddenly felt like a jerk for taking her back to where it had all begun between them. He'd never been short of attention from women. Hell, since moving to New York he hadn't had to work for it at all, it just seemed to fall into his lap as often as he invited it. But those women were all after him, they wanted something from him, whether it be money or status or a leg up into the world of finance and investment. Lexi wanted nothing from him, she never had, and he suddenly had no goddamn idea what to even do with that.

"So tell me about your son," he said, realizing that was the only thing he could bring up that didn't involve their past or antagonize her in any way. "He seems like a good little guy."

"What do you want to know?"

"What's he like? Does he have his dad in the picture? Would he like to play ball on Christmas Day?" he laughed. "Does he like horses?"

"Ahh, well, yes to playing ball and horses, but it's a no to having his dad around. His father is great at making promises and not so great at keeping them, so I try to keep expectations pretty low."

"When you say pretty low . . . ?" Cody asked.

"As in, 'you're lucky to hear from him on your birthday' and 'don't expect a present' kind of expectation," she said sarcastically. "Oh, or if he wants to hit me up for money, then he'll be father of the year for a few days, until he disappears again. But now that I have none, suffice to say he's now completely absent from our lives."

Cody sighed. He had an instant mental picture of the guy, and he hated that a nice girl like Lexi had to deal with it. "Anything I can do?"

She made a weird noise in her throat. "Like what?"

"I don't know, but if you think of something, well, I like kids. If he needs a guy to kick a ball around with, I'm happy to do it while I'm here." He would have outright offered to help her financially if she needed it, but he knew she was far too proud to ever say yes.

"City slicker like you remembers how to kick a ball around?" Her brows shot up and she started to laugh.

"Yeah, I do actually. Just like I can still ride a horse, in case you hadn't noticed."

"You're serious?" she asked. "About doing stuff with him?"

Cody nodded. "I might have been an ass to you in the past, but I'm not a bad guy. If you need help while I'm here, just ask for it. I really enjoyed hanging out with him the other night, there's something about him." He laughed. "Actually, he kind of reminds me of you, so maybe that's why I like him so much."

Lexi smiled over at him, an actual smile that wasn't a smirk or a half scowl.

"Now that you two have made up, can someone tell me when your brother is joining us?" Walter muttered. "If I sit any longer in this goddamn saddle I'm gonna fall out of it!"

Cody laughed, harder than he'd laughed in a long time, and he winked at Lexi. "You might have a sore ass, Dad, but I bet this ride has done you the world of good."

Walter grinned. "Any day above ground is a good one, son, but this one's been pretty memorable so far."

Cody nodded. "Good to hear."

"But you two are like listening to one of those bad lunchtime soap operas. Are you done with all the talking?"

Cody shot his dad a look. "Old man, any more moaning and I'll make you trot the rest of the way."

Walter gave him a mock salute. "Noted. Now call your brother, would you?"

Cody reached into his pocket for his phone, then patted his other pocket. *Dammit!* "Ah, that might be easier said than done."

Lexi produced a phone before Cody's father could even curse him. "Got one here. I'd be a terrible nurse if I wasn't prepared for emergencies." He watched as she sent a message before his dad called out again.

"You got any more pain meds in there for me?" Walter asked, and despite all the jovialness of before, he could suddenly hear the crack in his dad's voice.

"We okay here?" Cody asked. "If you need something, if we need to stop . . . ?"

Lexi waved her hand at him, down low, as if she were trying to get him to be quiet. "We're fine here," she said quietly. "Nothing a little painkillers won't help."

They reined the horses in and stood in a semicircle, Cody ready to grab his father's reins if he needed to. Hell, he was prepared to leap off if need be and break his father's fall, but right now he didn't look like he was in danger of keeling over.

The rumble of a vehicle approaching alerted him to Tanner arriving, and he stood in his stirrups, waving out to him. Tanner was driving slowly so he didn't spook the horses, and Cody watched as his brother stopped and leapt out of the car, breaking into a run.

"Everything alright here?" he called out. "Why have you stopped?"

"Did you text him?" Cody asked.

Lexi nodded. "Yeah. Just to make sure he was on his way. I didn't say anything to make him worry though."

"We're fine," Cody called back, dismounting as Tanner approached. 'He just needs some pain meds and—"

"You never should have taken him out in the first place, you should know better!" Tanner fumed. "This is bullshit, exposing him to the cold like that and—"

"Bullshit is my two grown sons telling their father what he can and can't do," Walter grumbled. "I can make my own damn mind up, and I said yes to this ride."

Cody and Tanner both fell silent. Cody might spend his days brokering deals and telling people what to do, but when his father spoke, he listened, and when his father told him to do something, he did that too.

"You want to switch to riding in the car with Tanner?" Lexi asked, her hand resting on Walter's arm as she leaned toward him from her horse.

His father softened before his eyes then, but to Cody's surprise, he shook his head.

"No. To hell with it! If this is my last Christmas, I'd rather fall off this damn horse than spend it riding in a car."

Cody swallowed and looked at his brother. He watched as Tanner did the same, looking like he was swallowing a rock as his Adam's apple bobbed up and down. They weren't exactly words either of them wanted to hear, but the old man was right.

"Let's get a move on then," Cody said, mounting up again.

Tanner stood back and Cody gave him a wave, eventually hearing the rumble of the farm vehicle's engine starting behind them. They had about fifteen minutes left to ride if they just walked, and as he shifted his horse to ride beside his father, he couldn't help but wonder if it was the last time they were ever going to be on their family ranch together again.

Don't take him yet, he thought silently, looking skyward. *It was hard enough losing you, Mom, I don't need to lose Dad too.* But it was inevitable and he knew it. When his mom had passed, he'd been in college still, trying to find his way in the world and wishing he didn't have to go home and see his mother take her last breath. When school had finished, he'd run far away to avoid being with her through it all, terrified of seeing her long, beautiful hair falling out in clumps, and even more scared of seeing her bald head that she proudly covered in bright-colored scarves. Or of how tiny she became, how thin, until there was nothing physically left of the woman he'd spent his childhood with. The woman who'd cuddled him and listened to him, the woman who'd never been too busy to drop everything whenever he'd needed her. He might not need his dad in the same way, but deep down he knew he was still that boy terrified of seeing the end. And of saying goodbye.

Lexi shut her eyes and felt the movement of the horse beneath her, the gentle sway of her body somehow easing the tension in her head. Maybe it was a combination of the movement, the cool wind against her cheeks, and the fresh air, but whatever it was, it was the first time she hadn't felt like she was sinking in weeks. Maybe months.

But how long was that feeling going to last? Until Harrison outgrew all his clothes and she had to find the money for them? Or when she got a message from her mom? Or when the mail arrived and told her there were only two weeks left to find a new facility or that her payments were too far in arrears? A wave of heat flooded her, thoughts muddling in her head, and she pushed her thoughts away, trying to refocus on the horse again, on how she felt being away from everything.

She wasn't about to give Cody credit, but maybe it hadn't been such a bad idea of his to get away from the house for the day. The cold air wasn't great for anyone who wasn't well, but Walter was long past the point of getting better, and she could see he was enjoying it, even if he was slightly uncomfortable. Although she might change her mind about how sensible it was if he ended up with pneumonia.

"When I kick the bucket, I want you to put me there."

Lexi's eyes flew open and she pulled on the reins to stop her horse when she saw that Walter had halted. He was staring straight ahead, a big smile stretching across his face and making him look younger than she'd ever seen him look.

"Seriously? I thought you wanted to be put in the family burial plot?" Cody asked.

"Not anymore. I love this goddamn river, and I want to be cremated and left there in peace. Just sprinkle me around and leave me be."

"Okay, so you're telling me this so I can tell the others?" Cody asked. "Because everyone thought you wanted—"

"I want this, and that's final."

Walter rode off and left them to catch up with him.

"It's not unusual, you know," Lexi quietly told Cody. "People often change their minds or become very firm about their plans as they cope with being terminal. It's something we talk about a lot in respite care."

Cody grunted, and Lexi's heart fell as she saw tears shining in his eyes. They'd been so busy sparring, she hadn't taken the time to think how he might be feeling, but suddenly her heart went out to him.

"Oh, Cody, I'm so sorry. All this bickering between us and I didn't even stop to think what this must be like for you." How could she have been so heartless? He might have been a jerk in the past, but right now he was just a son watching his dad deteriorate before his eyes. *A son who'd already seen his mom die only a decade earlier.* It was no different than her coming to terms with her mother's illness.

He cleared his throat loudly and she watched him swallow a few times, his jaw steeled as he moved his horse on and followed his father. She nudged her mare gently in the side and rode beside him, reaching out as she got closer.

"This isn't the end for him," she said in a low voice. "He's not well, but he's got a lot longer to go. So don't go thinking this is the last time you're going to see him, because it's not. I promise."

Cody's gaze met hers and she couldn't read what was reflected in his eyes. "Have you heard how often I come home?"

"Well, make it more often then," she said. "At least you have the chance to spend time with him before he goes. You've been given something so many people would love to have, and that's time."

"What's that supposed to mean? That I was given it before and didn't use it?"

She blew out a breath. "No, of course not! I just . . ." Her voice disappeared and she sat a little straighter before finding the words to continue. "My mom has Alzheimer's, Cody. One month she was my mom, and the next . . . everything seemed to change. There was no warning, no time to prepare myself, and the next thing. I'm putting her in care and I lost my best friend and my son lost his grandma. Up until then, she'd been like a second mom to him. He spent all his time with her, and then it was just the two of us."

"I'm sorry," Cody said, as if somehow it was his fault. "I'm so sorry, Lexi."

And this time when he said "sorry," she didn't call him out. Instead she took hold of his hand and squeezed it, and for a few beats she didn't let go, hoping he knew that whatever their past might have been, right now she would have done anything to help him through his pain.

Walter reached the river before they did, and she saw Tanner waiting up ahead, hovering. It was strange to see him like that, because she'd known him for years and he was usually so relaxed he could have fallen over backward.

"If you still want to spend some time together, maybe we could have dinner tonight?" she suggested. "But it's not a date. This is just two old friends catching up, for old times' sake." She wondered if she'd regret it, but seeing him suffering as he watched his dad, it made her realize that she needed to let go of the past, at least a little.

Cody was silent for a moment. "Hold up, now you're *volunteering* to spend time alone with me?"

She shrugged. "I could easily change my mind, but I'm starting to think I was a little hard on you. You were an easy target when I was feeling low, but there's no reason we can't get along. Especially given the circumstances."

"I deserved it."

She wasn't going to say she agreed, but she also didn't have to say anything in reply.

"Cody, you couldn't have splurged on a better lunch?" Tanner yelled out.

"Made it myself!" he called back. "Don't be so particular, there's nothing wrong with peanut butter and jelly sandwiches!"

Walter made a roaring noise as he glared back at his son. "Peanut butter and *jelly*? I rode all that way for a goddamn kid's lunch?"

Cody looked guilty and put his hands up in the air, and Lexi couldn't help but laugh. Here was a man who probably dominated a boardroom every day of the week, who did multimillion-dollar deals without blinking, and yet he was just a regular guy who couldn't make a decent lunch to save himself.

"Want me to take you back home in the car and make

you a proper lunch, Walter?" she asked, as sweet as pie as she grinned at Cody.

"Hell yes! It's bloody freezing out here anyway."

Lexi dismounted, her feet making a loud *thump* as she landed. She stroked the mare's neck and took the reins over her head, offering them up to Cody.

"See you back at the house."

He took the reins. "This isn't exactly how I planned our day."

"Is that right? How exactly did you plan it?"

Cody shrugged. "I thought Dad would be tired from the ride, and after lunch he'd fall asleep against a tree and I'd be able to remind you why we were so good together back in the day."

"Really. *That's* how you thought this day was going to go?"

"Really."

"Man, you always did have a vivid imagination." She tried not to laugh. Or say *in your dreams* to him.

"I guess I'm riding a horse back, huh?" Tanner called over.

As she passed him he smiled and patted her shoulder, and she watched as he took his father's horse and easily swung up into the saddle.

"Looks like it," Cody muttered.

She walked behind Walter, biting her tongue as the old man insisted on opening the door for her. Southern men did things the old-fashioned way, and she wasn't going to complain. Maybe that's where she'd gone wrong with her ex-husband—going for the guy who *didn't* think to open her door for her.

She started the engine and watched the retreating figures of the three horses and the two Ford brothers, both as broad and tall as each other, so relaxed in the saddle, looking no different than any ranch hand riding around the land. But they were different—they were heirs to a multimillion-dollar fortune, and Cody was easily the most eligible bachelor in Texas right now.

And for some crazy reason, she'd ended up asking him out for dinner.

Chapter 6

"YOU know, you don't have to go out with my son just to be nice to me."

Lexi stopped what she was doing and turned to look at Walter. The morning out had been a lot for him, and she'd insisted he rest afterward, but instead of sleeping, he was sitting up and tracking her as she moved about the room. She'd known the man long enough to think that he was enjoying himself.

"Cody and I have history. It's complicated between us," she said.

"He's a loner and he's terrible at relaxing or coming home, that's what he is," Walter muttered. "Did he treat you badly in the past? Is that why there's so much fire between the two of you?"

She inhaled and let her hands rest on the desk in front of her, carefully considering her words. Walter treated her well, in a familiar way like he treated his daughter, but it didn't mean she wanted to open up to him when it came to his own flesh and blood.

"We were young, but yeah, he did treat me badly."

He broke my heart. "I should have forgotten all about it by now, but to be honest, I've never forgiven him. Seeing him suddenly brought the past roaring back to life for me."

"Huh," Walter grunted. "Well, take it from an old man, it's not worth dwelling on those things. I spent years angry at the world for taking my wife so young, and I wished later that I'd just got on with life. I had a lot of living left to do, and I should have enjoyed it instead of being bitter."

She listened to him, not sure what to say in reply. In the end, she went with honesty. "I can't get past the anger stage over my mom," she admitted. "Sometimes it's all I think about, and I think it makes me react badly to other things that I'd usually be level-headed about."

"There anything I can help you with?" Walter asked. "You've been so good to me, Lexi."

She wished he understood that he'd been the good one, just by giving her a well-paying job and putting a roof over her head.

"Enough talk, it's time for you to rest," she said, switching back to nurse mode. "I'm going to leave you for a bit. Call if you need anything, otherwise I'll check in on you every hour."

Walter was silent, but she heard him moving. She opened the door, but before she could walk out, he spoke again.

"There's an old saying that leopards don't change their spots, Alexandra," he said softly. "But when I first met my wife, I was too young and stupid to see how incredible she was, and we broke up after a few months of dating. But when we crossed paths again five years later, I knew that I needed to grow up and be the man she needed. I proved myself to her, that she was more important to me than anything else, and my marriage, well, it was the best twenty-five years of my life."

Lexi leaned into the door for a second, eyes shut, wishing he hadn't said that. She didn't want to pin her hopes on Cody or let herself go back in time and feel that way all over again.

"Thanks, Walter," she murmured, before shutting the door behind her and standing in the hallway to catch her breath.

Cody was a wolf in sheep's clothing on the ranch. Even if he wanted to change his spots, he couldn't, because he had a life in New York now, a life that would never, *could* never include her, and there was no point in ever letting herself get lost in that fantasy. And it wasn't just her now, she had to think of Harrison, and he was already seeing enough of sad mommy as it was these days.

She'd have dinner with Cody, clear the air, and then they could both move on. Nothing more, nothing less.

Cody rode alongside his brother, the mare Lexi had been riding walking between them as Tanner rode with one hand and led her by the other. The weather was crisp and clear, still with no sign of snow, and even though the day hadn't gone to plan, Cody was still happy he'd taken his dad out. He gave his horse more rein so she could stretch her neck out, stroking one hand down her neck as she did exactly that, her nose almost touching the ground she stretched so long and low.

"So how did it go today, with Lexi?"

Cody grunted. "Ah, good as can be expected I guess."

"She still hate you?"

"Hey, *hate*'s a strong word." Cody sighed. "But yeah, I guess so. Although she did agree to have dinner with me, which was weird."

"Huh, well, *that's* something." Tanner grinned at him. "You need me to babysit Harry for you or will he be tagging along?"

"Aw hell," Cody groaned. "I never thought about the boy. She'll probably organize family or a babysitter or something, right?" How could he not have thought about Harry?

Tanner gave him a strange look. "She hasn't told you anything? Her mom is in care now, there's no dad in the picture with her boy, and I don't think she has any other family."

"Ah, yeah, she did kinda tell me all that."

"Yet you still thought she was going to just snap her fingers and have someone look after her kid tonight?" Tanner laughed. "Man, you don't live in the real world, do you? I think you've been living the bachelor-in-his-immaculate-apartment lifestyle waaay too long now."

"Says the guy who lived in fantasy land riding bulls when his body was broken and refused to give up?" Cody shot back. "Don't go lecturing me on lifestyle, *brother.*"

"Okay, fair enough. But the point is I *did* grow the hell up and figure out what I should be doing."

"And I grew up in college and did the same. Just because you don't understand living in the city doesn't mean I'm doing anything wrong. I'm just not used to kids, or dating women with kids for that matter." *Dating* was probably pushing it, but Tanner didn't seem to notice.

They were silent awhile, before Tanner finally broke

the silence. "Sorry. It's stupid to be fighting. I'm just glad you came home."

"Yeah, me too." Cody watched his brother, the easy way he sat astride the horse, so sure of his place on the ranch. He wished he felt like that, that he'd had the connection to the land and an affinity with animals like Tanner had. As a kid he'd loved the ranch, but as the years had passed he'd started to feel like a prisoner counting down the days to see more of the world, to get away from the pain at home.

Tanner suddenly started to trot and Cody gathered up his reins and nudged his horse in the sides, taking a second to find the rhythm before rising up and down to the beat of the trot.

"You know, some asshole's bought the Bright Life Retirement center to develop for some high-rise apartment complex or something," Tanner said. "Lexi was telling Mia about it the other day. Means her mom's going to be kicked out and she can't find anywhere else for her to go. I've been trying to think how we could help her, but I haven't brought it up with Dad yet."

"Fuck," Cody swore as he kept up with Tanner's fast pace.

"What?"

Cody groaned. "That asshole is *me*."

"You? What the hell would you do that for?"

"Why the hell *wouldn't* I do it? That piece of land's been underutilized for years as an assisted-living facility, and it's going to be a homerun getting the land re-zoned for development. We'll make a fortune from it. And besides, I'd thought you'd all be happy that I was looking at investments closer to home."

Tanner slowed and Cody did the same, his breath

making white puffs in front of him as the air become colder.

"Hold up. *You're* kicking all those old people out to develop the land for condos or something?"

"It's just business, Tan. And I'm giving them a decent amount of time to find somewhere new, I'm not just kicking them out onto the street. This is a huge deal for me, and I'm starting to realize why Dad liked developing land so much. Property gives me more of a buzz than the share market or buying businesses."

Tanner nodded and broke into a trot again, but Cody knew he was holding something back.

"What? You don't approve?" he called out as he trotted fast to catch up.

His brother shrugged. "I never said that. I just didn't expect it to be you, that's all."

"You'd do the same in my shoes. It's a great deal, it makes sense on paper. There's no emotion in business, Tanner."

"Yeah, I get that. You don't need to talk to me like I'm a kid."

"Well, you're acting like a kid right now," Cody said, surprised that his brother wasn't being more supportive. "What part of *great deal* and *lots of money* didn't you hear?"

"Cody, I'm just a part of this community still, that's all," Tanner said, his words cutting deep. But then Cody guessed that had been the purpose, reminding him that he'd turned his back on Texas and never looked back. "Business might be business, but you don't hurt your own, Cody. There's a lot of folk we know who'll be affected by this, and I don't care how much it's worth, it's not good business."

"You're acting like I'm the bad guy here. It's just a business deal. Dad would have done the same thing if he'd been given the opportunity, and if I hadn't done it, someone else would have. It's inevitable." Cody couldn't believe the way his brother was behaving. "There's no point having a fancy MBA if you don't have the back-bone."

Tanner shot him a look and suddenly launched into a canter, leaving Cody to play catch-up again, only a whole lot faster this time. What the hell was it with this place? He dug his heels in and sat forward in the saddle, urging his horse faster as he raced to catch up with Tanner, but he knew he'd never get past him. Tanner had spent his life being competitive on the back of an animal, and if he was angry, there was no way he was going to be beaten back to the barn.

When they finally got back, Tanner at least a full thirty seconds before him, Cody's lungs were burning and he could feel his horse heaving beneath him. She'd seemed to love the race though, her ears pricked and her pace fast as they'd rocketed across the field. He'd thought Tanner might have been handicapped by having to lead another horse beside him, but it hadn't seemed to slow him at all.

"Keep walking her until she cools," Tanner ordered as he dismounted and started to walk, a horse on each side of him.

Cody did as he was told, walking a few paces behind. "Were you serious about offering to babysit tonight?" he asked.

"You going to tell Lexi that you're the one kicking her mom out onto the street?"

Cody grit his teeth. "No. Not yet, anyway."

Tanner all but growled back at him. "Goddamn it,

Cody, if she finds out and you're not the one to tell her . . ."

"I'll tell her, just not tonight."

"Fine, I'll babysit for you. Lauren's back tonight and we can make a fun night of it. But don't come crying to me if it all turns to shit when she finds out, okay?"

Cody shrugged. "It'll be fine."

"Wishful thinking, brother. Wishful goddamn thinking."

"Hold up, Tanner's going to babysit Harrison so we can have dinner?" Lexi was certain she'd heard that wrong. "We can't ask him to do that! Harrison can just come along. He'll be quiet as a mouse if I let him have his iPad and—"

"When was the last time you went out without your son?"

She planted her hands on her hips. "Today. Horseback riding with you. Which he'll be furious about by the way, because he's dying to ride a horse."

Cody's smile made her uncomfortable. She liked him too much, *felt* too much when she was around him, and she didn't like it.

"I meant going out socially, as a woman, not as a mom. Out for dinner, getting dressed up, just letting your hair down like old times?"

She laughed. "I'm always a mom, Cody. It's not like I can just switch it off whenever I want to."

"You know what I meant," Cody said. "So will you let Tanner and Lauren babysit or not? There's a great new restaurant my assistant told me to try."

"Your *assistant*? Do you realize how pompous you sound, dropping that in there?"

Cody frowned. "Should I walk out the door and

come back in, so we can start this conversation all over again?"

"Fine. Dinner. Babysitter. No being a mom." She had to admit that a night out on Cody wasn't exactly a chore. She hadn't been able to afford to eat out since she'd taken over her mom's bills, and she'd do anything for a couple of glasses of good wine and great food.

"You're sure?"

Her phone buzzed then and she glanced down, moving fast when she saw it was Walter. He liked his privacy, but when he needed her he sent her a text, and she never left him waiting.

"I have to go, but yes."

"I'll pick you up at eight."

She spun around and walked backward. "Eight? Can't we make it seven? I'll fall asleep on you if you we go out too late."

She saw Cody hide his smile, but he nodded. "Sure. Seven it is."

Her stomach fluttered as she walked quickly down the hall, and she placed a hand there, trying to settle it. This wasn't a date. This was two old friends going out. She knew all about getting her hopes up when it came to Cody Ford, and she wasn't letting it happen again. Ever. But there was nothing wrong about looking forward to dinner with a handsome man, was there?

She found Walter out of bed and at his desk, glancing up at her as if she were his secretary popping her head in instead of his nurse.

"What are you doing?"

"Bah, I can rest when I'm dead," he said. "I was just wanting something to eat, I'm starving. And, ah, something to help with the pain a little."

She planted her hands on her hips. "So you *should* be resting and not working."

He shrugged. "I thought about something I hadn't attended to."

"You know, you have two very capable sons, including one who's chomping at the bit to be working right now. You could always ask one of them for help."

Lexi turned to leave but Walter's voice made her turn back.

"It's nice to see you smile, Lexi. You look happy today."

She laughed, shaking her head at him. It was almost as if he knew that his son was to thank for her newfound smile. She only hoped it didn't falter when she went to visit her mom the next day.

"Dad," Cody said in a low voice, not wanting to wake the sleeping child on his chest. He didn't ever remember his dad being quite so hands on when they were kids, but he was practically attached to his grandkids when they were around. It was nice to see a softer side of him, to see that beneath his intense work ethic was a man who knew what was important in life now. *Maybe he needed to take a leaf from his dad's book.*

He watched as his father reached for the remote and turned the volume down, his gaze settling on him as he waited for him to speak.

"I was talking to Tanner today, about the deal I'm putting together on a piece of land here," he said. "I think I talked to you about it last time I was here?"

His father chuckled. "No, you told me about it when I was in the hospital, when I begged you to talk work to me like I wasn't an old man dying. You remember how everyone else was fussing over me?"

Cody cracked up laughing, shaking his head. His father had hated being cooped up in the hospital and being treated like an old man incapable of working from his bed. In fact, it was also then that he'd insisted Cody sneak his laptop and work files into his room, so he had something to do when everyone was gone. His father never had been the sit-idle-and-watch-television or read-a-book kind of guy.

"It's one of the biggest deals I've put together in Texas. I'm so used to working in New York and LA, but it's going to be huge. I've spent the past month living and breathing it."

"So what's the problem? Cash flow?" He turned slightly in his chair so he was facing Cody now. "You don't have to talk around it, son. You need money from me you just have to ask. It's a solid deal and I'm happy to partner with you."

Cody frowned. "It's not that, I don't need money, I just wanted to sound you out. Tanner thinks I shouldn't be messing with land so close to home, even though someone else would have snapped it up if I hadn't." He laughed as he thought it through. "Hell, *you* might have bought it if I hadn't."

"Trust me, son, the thought crossed my mind." His father's frowned. "You know, this is the first time I've ever seen you doubt yourself."

"So you don't think I should be, I don't know, more careful about upsetting the local folk?" Cody asked. "Business has always been business to me. It's nothing personal, but yeah, I guess he rattled me."

He watched his dad shift position, and he glanced away as he saw the grimace of pain cross his face as he moved. Talking to his dad, it was like nothing had changed, but physically, the signs were terrifying. He wondered if it was as obvious to Mia and Tanner because they saw him so often and the deterioration was probably slow, whereas he went months without seeing his old man and the truth hit hard when he did.

"Your brother has a lot of heart, Cody. Always has, always will," he said. "He followed his heart with his career until he retired, and he's as passionate about this ranch and our other ranching interests as you are about closing deals and acquiring land. It's the reason I let him take over that part of our business, and why you'll step into my shoes when I'm no longer capable. If you want to, that is."

"You know I want to," he said without hesitating.

"The apple hasn't fallen far from the tree when it comes to you, Cody. I know you're the right person to grow our family business."

Cody let it all sink in, his father's words washing over him. It was strange, talking about a time when his dad might not be the family patriarch, but he knew how much it meant to his old man to have everything planned for every possible situation, including his own death. And he was right about how different he was from his brother too. Tanner was more like their mom had been, with a head for business but more inclined to follow her heart when she needed to, whereas Cody had learned from his father, inherited his desire to conquer any obstacle in his path. He thought with his head and his bank balance, and he didn't let anything get in the way of his success.

"So I don't need to start second-guessing myself then?" he asked. "I thought maybe I'd started to lose perspective."

"The day you start second-guessing yourself is the day you fail," Walter said. "It's not healthy and if you do it once, you'll never trust your instincts again. It doesn't mean you shouldn't do things differently next time, or that you won't make mistakes, but don't let anyone else get in your head and influence your decisions."

Cody nodded, rising when Mia came in looking for her daughter. He glanced at his watch, happy to see it was almost seven.

"Where are you heading out to dressed so sharp?" Mia asked, eyebrows raised as she studied him.

"Just dinner, that's all."

"Dinner with who?" she asked.

Cody laughed. "Sorry, Mom, I didn't know I had to tell you everything. Do I have a curfew?"

Mia narrowed her gaze, and Cody laughed at her.

"If you must know, I'm going out with Lexi."

"For *dinner*?"

"Yes, for dinner," he replied. "Is that okay with you? You don't have to sound quite so shocked that a beautiful woman wants to have dinner with me."

"I don't think it's such a good idea."

Cody folded his arms. "Hold up. Last night you told me to apologize and make amends. Which for the record, I did."

"Leave him to go have fun," Walter interrupted, waving his hand. "But if you do something stupid and lose me my nurse, you'll be the one caring for me until my last breath."

Cody blew out a breath and looked from his sister to his father. He had no idea whom to be more afraid of.

"Don't wait up for me," he said, making his getaway and heading out the door.

"Wouldn't dream of it!" Mia called back.

Cody headed to the front door, feeling a weight on his shoulders that certainly hadn't been there the last time he'd taken Lexi out. Or maybe he just couldn't remember back that far.

Chapter 7

AS Cody walked the short distance between the main house and the guesthouse, he looked up, seeing how unusual the sky appeared. It had a lightness about it that reminded him of snow, and he wished he'd checked the forecast. As much as he was starting to enjoy being back, the last thing he wanted was a heavy snowfall to ground him longer than the few more days he had left.

Why was that always where his mind turned to? He was like a flighty animal always needing to see an exit, needing to know he could flee if and when he needed to.

"Wait up!" he heard Tanner's call and turned, tugging his scarf up higher against the chill of the wind as it slowly started to pick up.

Cody opened his arms as they neared, happy to see Lauren tucked against Tanner's side. She stepped out to hug him, and he kissed her cheek as he pulled her close.

"Good to see you, Lauren," he said, before his brother had his arm around her again. They'd been parted for a while and it showed.

"You boys been behaving while I was gone?" she asked.

"Ahhh, I don't know if I'd call it behaving exactly," Cody teased. "It depends on your definition."

"Well, it's good to have you back anyway. Now can we please get moving? It's freezing out here!"

Tanner somehow bundled her even closer as Cody walked beside them.

"Thanks for doing this tonight," he said. "I know babysitting probably wasn't on your list of things to do on your first night back."

"Hey, we're all just waiting to see what a train wreck this turns into," Tanner joked. "It's kind of like watching reality television, but in our own backyard."

Cody balled and flexed his fists a few times, refusing to take the bait and explode at his brother. "There's no train wreck. I'm just taking an old friend out for dinner, that's all." He raised his hand to knock, rapping three times lightly on the door.

"So you're going to tell her about the development you're doing?" Tanner asked. "Because that's where the train wreck part comes in, just in case I wasn't clear."

"What development?" Lauren asked. "What exactly am I missing here?"

"Lover boy here is tearing down that assisted-living facility. You know the one that had the big signs out in front saying HELP SAVE BRIGHT LIGHTS a few weeks back?"

Lauren's eyes grew wide. "Oh shit."

"I'll tell her when I'm good and ready. Quit making such a big deal out of it," Cody grumbled.

"Big deal? I think you're the one making the big deal, *literally*. And no, I won't stop, because you wouldn't let up when it came to my career and telling me when you thought I was in the wrong. I remember you being pretty happy to be part of *that* intervention."

"First of all, that was different, and second, can we stop talking about that now before Lexi—"

The door creaked and swung open. "Before Lexi what?" she asked, eyebrows arched, her little boy wrapped around one of her legs and staring up at Cody with a big grin on his face.

"Ahhh, before Lexi opens the door," he said with a smile, hoping she didn't notice the tension between him and Tanner. "Hey, Harry, how are you?"

The kid grinned up at him. "Is this why you asked me what Mom likes to do when we hang out? I told her that's why you knew she'd like dinner at a restaurant."

"Ahhh, you got me," Cody said, bending a little and chuckling at him. "I just thought it'd be our little secret, bud. Now your mom knows I've been asking about her."

He glanced up at Lexi and saw her sucking in her bottom lip to stop from laughing.

"Ooops," Harry said with a shrug. "But she said you were kind of a jerk when she used to know you, so I thought I'd better tell her. Mommy, do you *really* want to have dinner with him?"

"Harry!" Lexi gasped. "That wasn't to be repeated!"

Tanner was cracking up laughing behind him but Cody managed to keep a straight face, bending down farther until he was the same height as Harry and touching the little guy's shoulder.

"Dude, I *was* a jerk back then, but I'll try really hard not to be tonight, okay? If your mom comes home angry, I'll let you beat me up. Deal?"

Harry fist-bumped him, but Lexi put her hands over his ears and glared at him. "No fighting in this house,

Cody." She took her hands off her son's ears and planted her hands on his shoulders instead, leaning forward and kissing his cheek. "Fighting isn't cool, is it? We don't beat anyone up, right?"

Harry shook his head but he mouthed "yes" to Cody over her shoulder, and Cody gave him a quick thumbs-up before rising.

"I saw that," Lexi said.

Cody shook his head. "Moms see everything, Harry. Don't forget that, okay?"

Harry giggled. "Okay."

But then Harry's attention was turned to Tanner, who was already high-fiving him.

"What's the plan tonight, little man? Pizza? Movie?" Tanner asked. "And you remember the prettiest woman in the world other than your mom, don't you? Lauren was so excited about seeing you tonight."

Harry waved. "Yes! Can we go to your place? I really want to see your dog."

Cody reached for Lexi as she turned to him, seeing in her eyes that she was worried about her son and not even thinking about him. "He'll be fine. He's in good hands. Tanner loves kids and so does Lauren."

"I know, it's just . . ." She turned back to Cody, her shoulders slowly falling as if some of the tension was fading away.

"He's your son. I get it. And you're used to it being just the two of you, am I right?"

She nodded. "It's hard to know how it feels unless you're a parent. I feel like half my life is about feeling guilty now, and the other half is about worrying whether I'm doing the right thing or not."

"I've helped my sister when her husband's been away traveling for work, and she's so tired she can barely move from looking after her kids, so I get it," he said gently. "She told me just the other night that parenting is harder than any show-jumping competition she's ever prepared for."

"You can say that again." Lexi smiled at him, her shoulders dropping down at the same time as she sighed. "Maybe you're not such a jerk after all."

Before he could answer Harry came running back into the room, slamming into his mom as he grabbed her leg again.

"Tanner said I have to ask you first, but can we *please* go to their place? They have pizza and ice cream and a dog and, and—"

"Whoa," Lexi said, bending and throwing her arms around him in a fierce hug. "You can do anything you want to do, so long as you listen to Tanner and Lauren, okay? I'm only going to be a couple of hours."

Cody watched as he hugged his mom back before leaping away and running off again, no doubt in search of Tanner.

"You ready to go?"

She took a big breath and reached for her coat, letting him take it so he could help her into it.

"Yes. Ready," she said. "Bye, Harry! Thanks for looking after him, guys!"

Tanner called back and when she looked like she was about to change her mind, Cody took her hand and opened the door with the other.

"Come on, we're going before you decide to stay home instead."

Lexi gripped his hand tight and followed him, just as a light flurry of snow floated through the air. She laughed and held a hand out, catching a snowflake and turning to him.

"Harry will be so excited if it snows all night. He's dying to make a snowman."

They walked across back to the main house, and Cody gestured toward the garage and pointed to the Range Rover, stepping in front of Lexi to open the door. Once he was in, he started the engine and activated the heated seats, turning the heat up as well and the volume on the radio down.

"I think Tanner was the last person to drive this. Who would have the music that loud?"

Lexi laughed and he turned to look at her before backing out. "It was me."

"What do you mean?" he asked.

"I was the last person to drive it! Your dad asked me to run some errands for him, and he always tells me to take this. I had the music blaring."

Cody reached to turn the stereo back up again. "Better?" he asked.

She cranked it up a little more. "Better."

Lexi was full of surprises. And it surprised him how much he liked it.

Lexi unbuttoned her jacket as the seat warmed up and the interior of the car became more summer in LA than winter in Texas. As she settled back, she angled her body so she had a better view of Cody. When she'd first laid eyes on him again, all she'd been able to see was how much he'd hurt her, but now she was wondering if he was just easy to blame because of everything that had happened. It had been a rollercoaster of a year for her, and despite what a jerk he'd been, maybe it was stupid holding onto a grudge. She was starting to see that maybe he might have changed, at least a little bit, and she was the one left feeling stupid for being so easy to rile. Maybe if things had worked out differently for her she wouldn't have been so angry at him still, but nothing had turned out the way she'd expected.

"You seem more relaxed than when you first arrived," she said, her thoughts suddenly spilling from her mind.

Cody shot her a surprised look. "Really? It's just a ruse. Inside I'm slowly driving myself insane wishing I could dive back into work. It's almost impossible to keep my laptop shut."

"So tell me about your life in New York. Is it everything you ever wanted it to be?"

She couldn't read his expression this time, and he didn't answer straightaway, but when he did he let out a breath and a slow smile spread across his lips. "You know, it is and it isn't. I mean, I love New York and I love the work, but sometimes I feel like I'm running from something still."

"Running?" she asked, surprised by his choice of words.

She sat quietly, the only response she received from him a nod, and she wasn't brave enough to ask more. Or maybe she just didn't want to know.

The rest of the drive passed in silence, until Cody slowed and pulled into a parking spot outside the restaurant. She cleared her throat and tugged her jacket tighter around herself before reaching for her bag. But as the engine stopped, Cody's hand curled around her wrist. She froze, before slowly looking up.

"That was really insensitive, what I said before," he said, his thumb rubbing lightly against her skin, making her heart beat way too fast. "About running."

Settle down, girl. You're not a teenager anymore.

"It's fine," she said, staying still and hoping he'd take

his hand off. She didn't want the contact—it was much easier not to like him when he *wasn't* touching her.

"For the record, it wasn't you I was running from. I should have made that clearer."

She nodded and slowly extracted her arm, needing to put some space between them. She looked out the window, using her palm to clear the fogged-up glass. "Have you been here before?" she asked.

"We can go somewhere else if you'd prefer?"

Lexi just smiled, looking at the lights of the restaurant and feeling all her worries start to slowly melt away. It had been a long, long time since she'd been out somewhere nice. First, it had been because of Harry, then because of finances—and she hadn't exactly been dating during all the in-between parts.

"This is perfect."

He chuckled. "I was actually wondering if we should have gone for burgers or something more low key, but I figure I have a lot to make up for. The least I can do is find somewhere nice to take you."

Lexi turned to reply, but he'd already stepped out, the click of his door telling her she had about five seconds to take a deep breath before he appeared and opened her door for her. Like clockwork, Cody appeared and swung her door open, offering her his hand as she stepped out.

"It's slippery out here," he said. "As opposed to me thinking you can't walk on your own."

"Most men around here are so chivalrous I think they actually *do* think women can't open doors or walk on their own."

Cody laughed but she happily kept hold of his hand. "How does the Texas charm work for you in New

York? I bet the girls lap it up, having a man open doors and bend over backward to be polite."

"You know, not so great actually. I had one woman slap me for daring to open her car door, and another give me a stare so cold I may have actually turned to ice. But when you've been brought up around these parts, they're hard habits to forget."

Cody grinned, holding up his jacket to shield her from the snow as they walked quickly to the restaurant. He nudged the door open and waited for her to walk through, and the warmth inside hit her as quickly as the aroma of delicious food.

"You sure you don't want to go for burgers?" he asked, leaning in and whispering in her ear. "We can make a run for it and be gone before they even know we've arrived."

She shook her head and bravely met his gaze, deciding that tonight was on her terms, that she was in charge and she was damn well going to enjoy herself. "Not a chance. You were right, you *do* have a lot of making up to do."

Cody didn't say a word, he just stared back at her a heartbeat too long until the maître d' came over and took their names before ushering them to a table.

They sat and she fingered her menu, looking up and down, her eyes skimming each word but not really reading anything. When she looked up, she saw Cody studying the wine list.

"What do you like? Red? White? Champagne?" he asked, looking at her over it. "Or maybe a beer like the old days?"

She remembered them drinking *a lot* of beer back then. "What the hell, it's Christmas. Why don't we have champagne?" Lexi wondered who the confident, happy-sounding voice belonged to, because she was never one to suggest champagne, and even earlier that day she was hardly feeling Christmas-y, but Cody was paying and she knew he wouldn't care what the bill came to. If she were going out with a mere mortal, she would have been far more conscious of the price.

Cody waved the waiter over. "A bottle of Veuve Clicquot," he said, before turning his attention back to her.

"You do realize it'll take more than ridiculously over-priced champagne and a fancy meal to impress me?"

He studied her, his eyes moving over her face as she refused to squirm, letting him look as she watched him right back. She was surprised how good he looked, when half the guys from back in their school days looked like middle-aged men by the time they hit thirty. Cody had always been confident and good looking, but he was more filled out now, very much a man, and she could see that unlike the exaggerated confidence of his youth, he seemed to know his place in the world now. He'd spoken in a quiet voice to the waiter, not needing anyone else to overhear that he was ordering pricey champagne, and the way he carried himself and spoke exuded old-world confidence. She guessed that was the case for most people who'd grown up with wealth like he had; they didn't have to worry about anything. She only wished she knew what that was like.

"What will it take?" he finally asked.

"Why do you even care? You have your pick of women, Cody," she said softly. "Do you even care about a jilted ex-girlfriend? Or is it just the fact that you want to be nice so I don't walk out on your father? Is it because your family told you to play nice with me?"

For the first time, she seemed to get a reaction out of him, his jaw steeling as he stared more coolly back at her. "I'm a big boy, Lexi. I don't need to make anyone happy, not my family, not my father, not anyone."

She blinked away tears as they filled her eyes, not knowing why she was suddenly overcome with emotion. She wasn't the crying type, she barely cried *ever*, but suddenly sitting across from Cody and trying to be brave and witty, when she was actually crumbling into pieces inside, it was all too much.

"I'm sorry, I . . ." She reached for the perfect white napkin and dabbed at her eyes.

"Hey, I'm sorry. Shit, what did I say? I didn't mean to upset you!"

She took a big, shaky breath. "I'm sorry. It's me, not you. I've been going through a lot and it just hit me like a ton of bricks all of a sudden."

The waiter arrived with their champagne and popped the top, one hand behind his back as he poured first her glass and then Cody's. She slowly curled her fingers around the stem, inhaling as she looked at the bubbles frantically rising to the top, and only exhaling as she felt brave enough to raise it and clink it to Cody's.

"To new beginnings," he said, waiting for her before raising it to his lips.

"New beginnings," she repeated, taking a long, slow sip. The bubbles tickled her throat, and she took another small one before placing the glass down.

"If this is too much for you, if you'd rather go home?" he asked. "You just say the word and we'll go."

"I never thought I'd ever forgive you, Cody," she confessed. "I've spent my entire life hating you, resenting you for the way you left me hanging, wasting my time when I could have been out having fun instead of pining over you, brokenhearted, while you had the time of your life at college."

He grimaced. "And now?"

"Ugh, I don't know." She took another sip. "Given the things that have turned to crap for me this past year or two, I guess it seems stupid to be holding on to such negativity. It's been easy to blame you, I guess. Even when my marriage turned into a disaster, I kept telling myself that you'd broken me, and wondering what it would have been like if things had worked out differently between us." She swallowed slowly, blinking away tears. "But maybe I'm just hard to love. It would explain a lot."

"Don't you dare say that, it's as far from the truth as possible. God, look at you, you're gorgeous and you're intelligent, what's not to love?" Cody moved so fast she didn't have time to pull back, his hand suddenly covering hers, squeezing her fingers. "For the record, I wasn't actually having the time of my life. I was studying like a complete nerd, not going to frat parties, and I was too scared to come home most of the time. I guess I'd just decided that I was done with Texas, and that Texas was done with me."

"But I wasn't done with you, Cody," she said, her voice barely a whisper. "Far from it."

She clenched her fingers against the glass before backing off, scared it might shatter in her hand. But the way Cody was looking at her, the anger that had shifted off her chest and somehow started bubbling up her throat into emotion, it was all too much.

"I wasn't running from you," he ground out, as if he was the one in pain, not her. "All I could see was where I wanted to be, what I wanted to do, and I didn't realize how much I hurt the people I left behind."

"There was someone else you hurt?" she asked. "You said *people*. As in plural. I always thought it was just me."

Cody lifted his glass and she watched his Adam's apple move as he swallowed, holding his glass up a little too long, as if trying to buy himself time.

"Cody?"

"I shouldn't have said anything," he muttered. "Have you looked at the menu? Maybe we should think about what we're going to order?"

She didn't stop staring at him. "You don't get off the hook that easy with me. What were you running from? If it wasn't me, then who?"

Cody stared at his menu, before slowly raising his eyes. "I was never running from you, Lexi. I was running from my family." He took a big breath and shook his head. "I was running away from my mom so I didn't have to see her die right before my eyes."

Lexi's heart broke even further as she saw the sadness pass over Cody's face. Why the hell hadn't she put two and two together? Now it was her reaching for him, but Cody was quick to back away, deftly avoiding her touch.

"I'm so sorry."

"And that right there is why I've never told anyone that. I can't stand being pitied."

She sighed. "It's not pity, Cody. It's empathy." She paused. "Actually it's me feeling like the jerk for not realizing why you left. I just thought you were trying to break up with me without having to actually tell me."

"As a man, I'm sorry for hurting you. But back then, I don't think I was even mature enough to see what I'd done to you, or that what I'd done could hurt you." Cody said, his voice a pitch lower, gravelly as he looked into her eyes. "I would never intentionally hurt a woman now, but there's something selfish about being eighteen that stops you from giving a shit about the people around you sometimes. Or even being perceptive enough to understand the ramifications of a decision."

"Yeah, you can say that again."

Lexi picked up her menu, staring hard at the words but still not seeing. She wasn't sure what hurt more: the fact she'd thought he was just a jerk trying to get out of breaking up with her all these years, or that he hadn't felt he could talk to her instead of turning his back on everything and running away.

"All this time, I believed you had some sense of being too good for this place. Like it was beneath you," she said. "It was like the second you could spread your wings and move on to something better you took it and got the hell out of Dodge."

"Not something better, just something different," he said, lowering his voice as their waiter neared. "Because it was easier to move on than deal with how I felt."

Cody let Lexi order first, wondering why the hell he'd opened up to her like that. Granted, it had broken the ice and at least made her see that he wasn't a heartless beast, but now she had that look about her like she wanted to fix him.

"I'll have the steak with beans and truffle oil, medium rare," he said, smiling up at the waiter as he passed him the menu. "Actually, do you do fries?" It was a fancy restaurant and he hoped he hadn't offended the waiter, who just smiled.

"Of course, sir. To share?"

"Yes. Thank you."

Lexi leveled her gaze on him and he sat back, collecting his drink and finishing what was left in his glass.

"So we're going to drink the best champagne and

eat the most gourmet-sounding food, but we're going to share fries too?"

"Hey, I remember we used to always order fries, didn't we?"

"Yeah, because we were uncouth eighteen-year-olds."

"Nothing much has changed. Except for the expensive threads and—"

"Cody," she interrupted. "*Everything* has changed. You're a hotshot finance guy and I'm just a regular girl who is way out of your league. I know there's no chance I'd be sitting here having dinner with you if you weren't trying to be nice and make it up to me for old times' sake."

He laughed then. He actually burst out laughing, stopping only when he saw the serious look on her face. She hadn't been kidding. "Lexi, if I'd seen you here or in New York, hell, anywhere in the world for that matter, I would have stopped what I was doing just to meet you."

He saw the change in her face, the way her cheeks flushed, her hand quickly reaching out for her drink as if she needed it for courage

"You're just saying that."

Cody refilled her glass and then his. "No, I'm not. When I saw you in the kitchen that first night, I couldn't stop thinking what a beautiful woman you were. Granted, I didn't think you were necessarily that friendly, but so damn gorgeous I wanted to know more. If I'd seen you in New York I'd have asked you out in a heartbeat."

Lexi didn't say anything that time, and he watched as she carefully lifted her glass and took another tiny sip.

"The worst part was wondering how on earth I didn't recognize you, but it's been a long time," he said. "I look like an older version of the teenage me, but you? You don't look like your old self. You went from pretty to goddamn beautiful. You changed your hair, your style is different, I just . . ."

Lexi was still staring at him, an expectant look on her face that he wished he knew how to deal with. He didn't know why, but for some reason he actually cared about her knowing he wasn't a complete asshole.

"Tell me about your mom," Lexi said.

Their fries arrived just at the right time and Cody was able to think for a minute, trying to process how much he wanted to tell her, how much he could actually open up about what he'd been through. All these years, he'd kept it locked inside, refusing to talk to anyone about his grief or what he'd endured. He'd watched from afar as Tanner had immersed himself into bull riding, traveling away on the circuit a lot; his older sister Angelina had bolted just like he had as soon as she could, and Mia had sought solace in the sport their mom had loved—show jumping. But Mia had also had to be there to see their mom slowly wither and eventually pass away, whereas the rest of them had tried to live their own lives away from the pain.

Tanner always tried to make him feel bad for leaving, but the way he saw it, there was no difference between what he'd done and what his brother had done. Other than the fact that the miles he'd put between the family ranch and where he lived were more permanent than Tanner's rotating schedule. But for some reason, he was always seen as the one who'd run away, and the one who was always too scared of ghosts to ever come back.

"I don't talk about her," he finally said, after eating a few fries. "But I think about her a lot."

"You still miss her?"

He nodded. "Yeah, I do. Every time I come home, I have this feeling, and it makes me want to run the hell back out the door and to the airport again." He took another few fries. "It's stupid, I should be way past it now, but it's just easier to stay away. Not dealing with stuff is a whole lot easier than facing up to it."

Lexi ate too, and he wished he had just taken her somewhere more low key. He was trying to impress her, but she was probably the one person who didn't need impressing. She'd made friends with him at school and dated him without seeming to care who he was and what his family was worth, so he didn't know why he thought she'd care now.

"How about we take a rain check on talking about my feelings, and you tell me all the great things you have going on right now? Catch me up on what I missed."

Their dinner arrived then and Cody sat back as the food was placed in front of him. It smelled great, the steak covered in drizzles of sauce, with tiny potatoes and green beans on the side. He was starving.

Lexi had surprised him by having the same, and he waited for her to lean back as the waiter covered her lap with a napkin, before smiling up at him and saying thank you. It suddenly felt like a long time since he'd eaten.

"My stomach's growling. Those PB and J sandwiches weren't enough to keep me going."

"Cody, they weren't enough to keep anyone going."

He ate a few mouthfuls and watched as she did the same, before asking her the question again. He was curious about how things had worked out for her, and everything was slowly starting to come back to him about her. It had been so long since he'd even thought about his past, but now that he had, it was like he'd unleashed a stream of memories he'd long since buried.

"So tell me about what happened after school? You were always talking about becoming an interior designer or an architect, weren't you?"

"Ahhh, so he *does* remember," she said, holding her hand in front of her mouth as she swallowed. "I had grand plans to become an architect, but I didn't get the scholarships I'd applied for and money was too tight without the assistance."

Cody looked down at his plate. He'd been such an ass that he hadn't even known his girlfriend needed financial help. It was something he could easily have done to assist her, and it would have changed everything for her.

"I'm sorry," he said, looking up from cutting his steak. "I should have known. I could have done something about it and your entire life could have gone to plan. Things could have been different for you."

"Hey, if things had been different, I wouldn't be mom to the sweetest kid on the planet, so it hasn't been all bad."

She was making light of what had happened, but he could see the pain in her eyes. Harry or not, life hadn't worked out as she'd hoped, and now he felt partly responsible.

"So you decided to nurse instead?"

"Nope, I decided to become an interior designer, because I could do a course within driving distance of home without moving." Lexi set her fork down and reached for her glass, taking a sip. "And then I met David and we had a whirlwind romance before I finished my course and we ended up getting married."

"That doesn't sound like you. You were always such a planner, I can't imagine you just . . ."

"Being stupid enough to marry an asshole and getting pregnant by mistake?" she asked, finishing with a laugh. "Yeah, I'm pretty sure everyone who knew me thought the same thing. But I was on the rebound"—she paused and took a deep breath—"*from you.*"

Her words were so soft he almost couldn't hear them, but he did. Just like he saw the glint in her eye that told him how much it had genuinely hurt her, and that she was so goddamn strong she wasn't going to sit back and not let him know it.

"So tell me about your ex-husband?" he asked, deciding not to comment on the part about him.

"There's nothing to tell," she said. "Other than the fact that I've had to work full time since Harry was in diapers, as well as retrain and try to keep a roof over our heads. That's my story in a nutshell, which is probably as different from your glamorous city life, with a different girl every night and no responsibilities."

"There's no girl every night. I'm married to my work, so don't go thinking I'm having some kind of Hugh Hefner lifestyle. I already told you that."

"So you're single?" she asked, and then she looked down as if she was embarrassed and shouldn't have asked. "You were serious when you said you don't have anyone special back in New York?"

"Despite managing to hurt you, it's something I'm pretty careful to avoid," he admitted. "I don't do relationships anymore. I don't have enough to give someone and I like them knowing that from the get-go. Work is always going to be the love of my life."

"Bad relationship in the past?" she asked dryly.

"Yeah, you could say that. It involved the throwing of plates—her, not me—and a lot of yelling about me being too focused on work and not giving a shit about her." He spread his hands wide, needing to explain to her that it wasn't her or any other woman, it was just him. "I'm not the husband type; I suppose that's what I'm trying to say."

Lexi nodded and went back to eating, before looking up at him. "This is weird. It's kind of like a date, but not a date, and all we're doing is acting like we're interested in each other's lives despite the fact that we haven't been in contact for over ten years."

He laughed—there was nothing else to do. "Yeah, even champagne and a steak dinner can't disguise it. You want to go or—"

"No." She put her knife and fork down, placing them on her plate as she lowered her voice. "I want to tell you what a fucking jerk you were, that you broke my heart, and that I hate you."

"Okaaaaay," he groaned and put his fork down too, even though he hadn't quite finished. "I'm not sure where to go from there."

"Now that I've gotten that off my chest, can we just forget about the past? You've grown up, I've grown up, we've both moved on and whatever happened, it happened. I'm officially over it." She laughed. "Although it felt damn good telling you that!"

He raised his brows. "Should we start over by having dessert then? Am I pushing it by thinking it's worth celebrating?"

"No," she said, gathering up her bag and standing, the change in her gaze so obvious that he had no idea what she was about to say or do.

"I'm not sure what you want?" He rose too, surprised when she reached for his shirt and tugged him closer, her voice low. "You want to leave?"

"What I want is to be one of your no-strings-attached

dates," she whispered. "I haven't been laid since my husband left me, and my son is out of the house. No confusion, no wanting more than you can give, just a little walk down memory lane." She stared at him, long and hard. "You want to make it up to me for leaving me, this is your chance."

Cody swallowed, trying not to grin. This was definitely not how he'd thought their night was going to pan out. He was expecting it to take a lot longer for her to thaw out, and he hadn't even considered that it might end in sex.

"You're sure about—"

"Get the bill, Cody, and meet me at the car."

He pulled his wallet out. "Yes, ma'am."

Chapter 8

LEXI's heart was pounding. What the hell was she thinking, telling Cody that she wanted to get out of the restaurant? She hadn't even had that much to drink, but suddenly all she could think about was how long it had been since she'd spent the night with a man. But something about the fact that they'd been together before was emboldening her, almost making her feel like it didn't count, that she could have one naughty night without passing judgment on herself. There was a familiarity there that made her think she could actually do this. No commitment, no pain. *Just pleasure.*

She was standing outside the restaurant, beneath the overhang outside so she wasn't getting wet, and she knew that any second now, Cody would be walking out the door. Anticipating what was coming next. And all of a sudden she was terrified that she wouldn't know what to do anymore.

The door creaked and she shut her eyes, listening, feeling, knowing it was him.

"Hey, you must be freezing."

Cody's arm slid around her, tugging her against him

and quickly forward as he propelled them out into the snow toward the car. He unlocked it as they were walking and opened the door, but instead of leaping in out of the cold, she slowly turned, looking up at him as the snow caught in his lashes.

He waited, immobile, as she clutched the front of his coat, inhaling deeply before lifting on her toes to press her lips to his. She kissed him lightly, feeling his mouth move softly beneath hers, not pushing, not claiming the kiss, just like his body wasn't moving toward her. Lexi chose to deepen the kiss, holding him tighter as she pulled him farther forward and tasted his mouth, remembering exactly how her body had always responded to his.

"As much as I'm enjoying this," Cody murmured in her ear, "I think we need to relocate somewhere out of the cold."

Lexi nodded, slowly lowering herself and letting go of his coat. She got into the car and he jogged around to the other side, turning the engine on as she cranked up the heater. And then after he'd reversed the car, Cody reached for her hand and turned it over, tracing circles lightly across her skin the rest of the way home.

It took every ounce of her self-control not to squirm, the combination of the tip of his fingernail and the edge of his skin skimming hers almost too much to bear, but she knew she'd done the right thing. She wanted Cody, and she needed this release more than she'd realized.

The drive home felt agonizingly long compared to the drive to the restaurant, and by the time they pulled into the River Ranch driveway, her stomach was in knots and she was almost ready to back out. But one glance from Cody and she knew she'd regret not taking her chance with him. She needed this.

"I'll drive real slow," he said, voice low as he glanced at her. "Last thing we need is Tanner hearing we're home."

"Or Harry," she said, suddenly finding it hard not to think about her little boy. They were about to drive straight past the house he was in, and it went against her mom instinct not to check on him or put him first. But this was just once. She'd never let someone else look after him before. Surely she was allowed one night of thinking of herself? She gulped, trying to push the thoughts away.

"Shit," Cody swore softly. "What if they didn't go back to Tanner's place?"

She gulped. "We could go to your room?"

He shook his head. "Imagine if my dad heard us? I'm past sneaking girls in the front door." Cody grinned. "What we should have done was find a motel. Why the hell didn't I think of that?"

Lexi smiled straight back at him. "You should be better at all this. I'm way out of practice, but you're supposed to be the king of smooth."

"Smooth? I'll take the compliment but I'm not sure I deserve it." He finally pulled in beside her front door and they sat for a second before he turned in his seat, his hand finding hers again. "You sure about this? You can back out if you want to."

She swallowed, hoping her voice worked. "I'm sure. You?"

Cody nodded. "But just to make this clear, I'm only here for a few days, this doesn't mean—"

She didn't let him finish. "Relax, this time I know you're going. It's no strings." Lexi hoped it came out as carefree as she meant it. "Now would you hurry up and open my door before I get cold feet?"

Cody sprang into action, and within seconds she was at her front door, unlocking it as Cody pushed it open. It was quiet inside; no lights, no TV blaring, nothing.

"I think we're alone," Cody said from behind her.

Lexi took a step forward, clearing her throat and waiting to see if anyone made a noise. "Just let me check, I'd hate if . . ." Her voice trailed off and she didn't bother finishing her sentence.

She left Cody and took a cursory look around, flicking on a lamp and then walking upstairs to the loft area where she and Harry both slept. She checked his room and then hers, but there was nothing. No one.

Which meant she had no excuse not to follow through with what she'd started.

The stairs made a creaking noise, shifting as someone stepped on a tread, as she waited, knowing that Cody had followed her. Lexi gasped as hands closed over her shoulders before slowly, *softly*, tracing down her body until they settled on her hips.

Cody never said a word, letting his body do the talking as he stepped closer, his chest and stomach skimming her back, the pressure just enough for her to feel him against her. She'd worn her long hair down, and Cody stroked it before scooping it up and putting it over one shoulder, while his mouth found her neck, murmuring across the soft, sensitive skin as he tasted her.

She moaned as he kissed down then up, finding her ear and gently nibbling at her lobe before his hands were on her shoulders, taking off her coat. The second he'd discarded it, his hand were on her again, this time his fingertips lightly dancing across her shoulders.

Lexi wanted to tell him to stop as much as she wanted him to keep going, but as he pushed back against her again, as his lips found her skin again, she knew that she was already in too deep to say no to him. She wanted this, even just for one night. She needed to feel wanted, to feel a man's hands on her, to do something for *her* for once instead of putting everyone else in her life first, even just for a few hours.

She laughed. As if she'd last a few hours; she'd probably be equal parts satisfied and exhausted in half that time.

"What?" he murmured. "You think this is funny?"

"No," Lexi replied, slowly turning to face him. She scooped her arms around his neck and looked up at him.

"Then why were you laughing?"

"It's just been a long time since I've done this. And I sure as hell didn't expect my first time back in the saddle to be with you, excuse the pun."

"Hey," he said, bending forward and placing the slowest, most tantalizing kiss on her lips, his mouth moving so slowly that every nerve ending in her body seemed to shudder with the anticipation of more. "It is like riding a horse. You never forget."

Lexi leaned back as she laughed, loving the feel of Cody's big, strong arms around her. "Except I did forget how to ride, didn't I! I couldn't even get on the damn horse in case you've forgotten already!"

Cody chuckled and moved her forward, hard up against his chest again, her hands trapped between them. "Bad analogy," he muttered. "But trust me, your body doesn't forget."

His hold on her tightened, his arms firm around her back as his mouth found hers again. She sure hoped he was right.

Cody needed every inch of will power to take things slow with Lexi, but he wasn't going to hurry her, not even for a second. He owed it to her to give her a damn good night, and that was precisely what he was going to do.

He moved his mouth against hers, loving the feel of her pillowy, warm mouth, the way her tongue was tentatively exploring, as if she wasn't quite sure. Cody stroked her body, from her butt all the way up her back and down again, loving the way she moaned and leaned harder against him, her breasts crushed to his chest. And then he stroked her shoulders, slowly slipping the straps of her camisole down.

"No," she gasped, pulling back a little, and he stopped, shrugging them straight back up again. He wasn't going to push her if she didn't want it.

"You having second thoughts?" he asked.

She shook her head. "You first."

Cody shrugged, happy to oblige, and he tossed off his coat and then tugged at the bottom of his cashmere sweater, pulling it up and over his head so he was standing bare chested.

"More?" he asked, liking the way she was biting her bottom lip as she watched him, wide eyed.

Lexi nodded and he grinned back, bending to take off his shoes and socks, and then undoing his belt and unbuttoning his jeans. He looked at her, slowly taking off his jeans and kicking them off too, until all his clothes sat in a pile. He was about to take off his briefs too, but a squeak from Lexi stopped him.

Her eyes met his before trailing back down again, and he laughed as she shook her head, clearly seeing just how much he was interested in her.

"Your turn," he murmured. And when she didn't move, he moved to her, reaching for her, one finger curling beneath her chin to lift her face. He kissed her, once, gently, before lowering and touching her shoe, waiting for her to lift her foot so he could take it off.

He heard her exhale before lifting one foot and then the other, until she was standing barefoot on the floorboards. Cody rose slowly, watching her face as he touched her straps again. This time there was no protest, and he slipped them down, exposing her bare skin and bending to press a kiss to her collarbone. Lexi's fingers clenched in his hair, holding him there, and he took it as a sign to keep going, exploring her skin more, and then slowly pushing her camisole down until it was at her waist, the lacy bra she was wearing not leaving much to the imagination.

Cody dropped lower to kiss her stomach, caressing the soft skin with his lips before working his way back up again so he could look into her eyes. Lexi's fingers were still in his hair, and she forced his head back down again, taking charge as she claimed his mouth, and suddenly Cody couldn't go slow. He wanted her and if her grip on his hair was anything to go by, she wanted him right back.

He fumbled with the top button of her jeans, hands slipping on the silk of her top, but she helped him, pushing at her pants. But he wasn't waiting for her to shimmy her way out of her tight trousers. He held her and stepped her backward, pushing her onto the bed.

She laughed as he manhandled her, grabbing hold of the denim at her ankles and tugging hard. She almost slipped straight off the bed, but the second he had her jeans off she scrambled back up. The sight of her in her lace panties and bra was too much for him.

"You still want to go slow?" he ground out as he stripped off his briefs and lowered himself over her, propped on his elbows as his body covered hers, staring down into her eyes. He saw the same longing there that he was certain she could see reflected in his.

"Screw that," she whispered. "I've been waiting a long time for a repeat."

Cody pushed himself up, yanking down her panties and throwing them behind him. He was about to reach for her bra, desperate to feel the heaviness of her breasts in his hands, but she was too fast.

Lexi hooked her legs around his waist, her ankles locked as she reached up for him.

"No time," she whispered. "Just . . ."

Cody didn't need to be asked twice. Lexi rocked up to him as he shifted his weight forward, but he stopped, groaning. "Shit, we need . . ."

"Oh my god, yes!" she gasped. "I don't, I mean I haven't need—"

He leapt up, fumbling for his jeans and getting out his wallet. "I've got one, so we better make it count." Then he laughed. "Actually there's two, it's our lucky night."

Lexi's laughter stalled when he dropped on top of her again, nudging her legs apart at the same time she crossed her legs around him again, urging him forward as she arched up. He put his hands beneath her, guiding her up as he rocked inside of her, groaning as she bucked against him, her fingers clawing at his back until he lowered and covered her body with his. Cody's hands bracketed the space on either side of her head as his mouth found hers again, kissing her as he slid in and out, going faster than he wanted because of her fingers digging into him, forcing him faster and faster as she moaned beneath him.

He stopped kissing her and trailed his mouth lower, plucking at her already slick skin, groaning as she held him tighter and he fought to sit upright, forcing him backward into a sitting position as she sat in his lap and took charge. And as he stroked her long, silky hair, as she tipped her head back in his hands and he kissed her long, slender neck, he remembered what it had felt like to love Lexi.

Just like everything else about home, he'd somehow managed to block it out. But not now. Now he remembered every feeling, why everything had felt so right, why he hadn't been able to get enough of her.

"Cody," she gasped, leaning back, her body arched as she moved urgently over him.

He groaned and held her, his arms tightening around her as he felt her body go taut and then suddenly soften, collapsing against him as her sex-drunk eyes met his. He gave in then too, no longer holding back, as Lexi's lace-covered breasts pressed into his chest, her body rocking gently against his as he climaxed.

He stroked his fingers against Lexi's skin, committing her to memory all over again and knowing she'd very well haunt him for the rest of his life now.

Chapter 9

LEXI sighed and stretched out, feeling the most relaxed she had in months. She'd forgotten just how much she enjoyed sex, how much she needed the release.

"Thank you," she murmured to Cody, reaching for him. She'd collapsed alongside him, both of them out of breath and taking a moment to enjoy the aftermath, but instead of moving closer to her as she'd expected, he rolled away.

"Cody?" she said, sitting up.

He was kneeling now, giving her an eyeful of his body and making her want to explore it all over again. He moved closer and caught the light, and she could see his abs, every single one of them, impressive on his tanned torso. His shoulders were big and broad, balanced by large biceps. He was built like an athlete, only he was a six-foot-something businessman who wore Italian suits and was perfectly at ease making multi-million-dollar deals every day.

"It's time for me to pleasure you," he said.

She laughed, but the serious look on his face told her he wasn't kidding. "You just did that. Very well in fact."

He made a grunting sound in his throat. "No, I was like a teenage boy who'd never had sex before, rushing like that. This time, I'm going to take it slow." His smile was wicked. "Very, *very* slow."

"Oh really."

"Yes," he said, moving forward on his knees. "Really."

Lexi sucked in a breath, anticipation licking over every inch of her body. She couldn't breathe, couldn't think, couldn't do anything except watch Cody as he lowered himself and reached for her.

"I want you to lie back and enjoy," he said as he cupped her cheek in one of his hands, staring into her eyes.

"Okay," she murmured back, lips parting as his mouth came closer, happy to obey him as her body tingled with need all over again.

Cody was done talking. His soft kiss and gentle touch turned rough almost immediately. One second he was cupping her face; the next his fingers were tangled in her hair, his mouth rough on her lips and then her neck, his stubble a barely there roughness that reminded her just how damn masculine he was.

His mouth moved down her neck, his warm lips a contrast to his wet tongue that was trailing sensually across her skin. Lexi moaned as one of his hands brushed her breast. She wasn't scared of his hands—she wanted them everywhere.

"Damn," he muttered against her collarbone. "So much for going slow."

She laughed. "You're the one racing ahead. I'm just lying here doing what I'm told."

He grunted and stopped, lifting his head. "It's not my fault you've got such a goddamn irresistible body."

"Touché," Lexi murmured, cupping the back of his skull to force him forward again, looping her other arm around his neck as she kissed him, surrendering to his mouth. Since when did she have sex not once, but *twice*, in one night? It was like her body had been dormant for so long, it had come to life and wasn't going to simmer down anytime soon.

He plucked at her mouth then deepened his kiss, exploring her body with his hands, so painfully slow that she couldn't help but squirm. Every part of her wanted to tell him to stop, not wanting to lie there so exposed when she was never usually so brazen, but another little part of her was telling her to just enjoy herself. To quit with the self-confidence issues and surrender to the pleasure.

Lexi stayed still, *silent,* the only noise the rasping of their breath.

"Is this what you want?" he asked, his mouth against her skin, his tongue tracing across her and teasing her as he tasted down her stomach, teasing as he went lower.

She tensed, her body quivering at his touch.

"Are you sure this is what you want?" he repeated, voice so deep and husky she hardly recognized it. "I want to give you want you want, Lexi."

"Yes," she whispered back, raising her hips, forcing her body against his. His erection was rock solid against her belly, his desire for her more than obvious. It sent sparks of pleasure through her just knowing that she still had the same effect on Cody in the bedroom as she had as a teenager.

Lexi's body was humming now, Cody's touch driving her so close to the edge, but he pulled back, moving away from her. "What did I tell you about hurrying this time around?" he muttered, pushing her down and repositioning himself.

The roughness of his stubble against her thighs was the only distraction from the softness of his tongue, and the lower he moved, the more sensitive she became, squirming beneath him, nails digging into the sheets beneath her as she tried not to squirm away from him. It felt so good she could hardly stand it.

He trailed down her thighs, skipping over the place she wanted him to touch the most, his fingers stroking so close to her, his mouth moving so close, but not quiet touching.

Cody rose slightly then, stroking one finger from her collarbone to the top of her breasts. The circles he was tracing across her skin became smaller, until he was almost touching her nipple. But his mouth got there before his finger, sucking so gently, licking so softly, that she couldn't help but gasp.

"Mmm," he whispered, before moving on to the other one.

"Stop," she moaned. "Let me pleasure you. You can't just . . ."

Cody laughed and sucked harder until she was forced to wriggle away from him, but he wasn't letting her escape. He covered her mouth with his, his hands back to exploring her body. She kept up with his touches, didn't miss a beat, delighted in the feeling of everything he was doing to her. She'd almost forgotten how good it felt to be between the sheets with him.

"Tonight," he said, against her skin, taking her hands and putting them above her head, fingers locked firmly around her wrists, "is all about you."

She wanted to protest, but she didn't. The idea of Cody pleasuring her, lying back and letting him do anything and everything with her? That wasn't something she had the strength to say no to. She tried to retrieve one hand, wanted to run her fingers through his thick blond hair, to grip it hard, but he wasn't relenting. So in the end, she let her body go slack and finally gave in to him.

Cody's breath was hot against her skin, his kisses even hotter, searing as he made a trail across her skin.

She moaned when he lowered his head, wasting no time, his free hand gently pushing her thighs down so he had better access to her most intimate parts. His tongue barely touched her, but it was enough to make her moan.

Everything else drowned out when he started to pleasure her, his mouth doing the most wicked things to her, making it impossible to think of anything except the building heat inside of her. His tongue was doing circles, his mouth clamped over her, and he no longer needed to hold her wrists captive.

"Cody," she moaned, threading her fingers hard through his hair and holding on tight.

If it hurt him, he never said; he just continued to work his magic, not letting up, her climax building fast. She wrapped her legs tight around his head as he pushed her to the edge, spasms of pleasure taking over every bit of her body.

When she released him, finally letting her fingers ease out of his hair and unclamping her thighs, he kissed her intimately one last time before trailing fingers across her skin, up and down her legs. His mouth soon followed, warm kisses against her burning stomach, every part of her still feeling like it was on fire.

Cody had always been an overachiever, he'd always done better than any other kid at sports and in the classroom, and clearly he'd decided to become as skilled in the bedroom as the boardroom.

He was above her now, his mouth closing down on hers, making her eyes pop open.

"It's not over yet, Lexi," he whispered, his deep drawl more delicious than ever, reminding her of the old Cody, the young Cody who she'd been head over heels, hopelessly in love with.

Cody's smile was even more wicked than his words, but instead of saying anything else, he just slid straight inside her, going slow but not stopping until he couldn't push any further.

Lexi's legs wrapped around him, she gripped hard, her body eagerly meeting his. The man was relentless, and she was just as keen as he was to keep going, to ride her way to the edge again.

"I think I've been waiting for another chance for more than a decade," he muttered in her ear. "I just didn't know it until now."

"Yeah," she let out a sharp breath, a hiss of air, as his thrusts became harder, all gentleness long gone. "Me neither." Only she was lying, because she'd been thinking about this for years. She'd never forgotten how good their bodies were together, how much he'd always managed to send her straight over the edge.

He paused, his body still, muscles slick with sweat, but she just she gripped him tighter, digging her fingernails into his shoulders and forcing him down closer, their bodies pressed tight. His chest slid against hers as he wrapped his arms around her, breasts crushed against him.

Cody knew how much she wanted him; it would be impossible for him not to, given how tight she was holding on to him, matching his every movement. But what was turning her on the most was how obviously he wanted her, how much he was enjoying it too.

Just as she started to feel like her body was getting closer to the edge again, just as she thought that she could hardly bear the intense pleasure inside of her any longer, Cody pulled out, kissing her mouth, eyes open as he looked down at her.

"Don't stop," she begged. "*Please.*"

He laughed. "Not stopping. Just trying to figure out how to make this even better for you."

Her mouth was dry, her eyes roving over every inch of him. He was so well built, his body a well-honed machine, every part of him muscled and exquisite. His skin was golden, the only smattering of hair an arrow that extended from his belly button to his . . . She looked up, caught his naughty smile. It would have been more believable that he worked a physical job than an office one.

"How do you like it?" he asked. "Given that the last time you saw me naked I was eighteen."

"Honestly?" she said, panting still, her heart racing. "You look even better."

"So do you," he whispered, smiling down at her. "I love the fullness of your breasts now," he said, reaching to gently fondle her. "And I love the look in your eyes, that confidence that you didn't have then."

She smiled, wanting to believe him even if there was a whisper of self-doubt in her head telling her that her eighteen-year-old body had been so much better than this one. But Cody didn't seem to be having any trouble enjoying himself, and that was all she was going to let herself think about when it came to her body.

Lexi pushed her hands against his chest, palms hard against him until he was flat on his back, the smile on his face telling her he knew exactly what she had in mind. "It's my turn to take the lead now," she said, climbing on top of him, lowering herself as she stared into his eyes, watching his face until her lids fluttered shut.

Cody's hands moved to her hips, fingers spread wide as he guided her back and forth, up and down, holding her as she arched back, tipping her head back too as she lost herself to the feel of him inside of her.

Lexi moved so she could kiss him, bending lower, still rocking gently back and forth as her mouth whispered across his, and even though he kissed her back, slowly, his hands kept her moving, kept guiding her so she didn't stop riding him.

His lips were hot, wet; his body was slick with sweat; and the feel of him inside of her was exactly how she'd remembered, and then some. Sex had never felt this good, not in her lifetime, anyway. And as she sat up again, eyes shut as she rode her final wave of pleasure, she wished she'd jumped him the day he'd arrived home instead of wasting time telling him what an ass he'd been.

As far as she was concerned now, the past was the goddamn past.

Cody stretched out before realizing he wasn't alone in bed. The night before came flooding back, the memories almost as good as the real thing as he stretched out to touch Lexi. He withdrew his hand, though, when he realized she was still asleep, deciding to press a kiss to her cheek instead of rousing her, no matter how tempted he was make her incredible body hum again.

He stroked a strand of her hair, a mental picture

of her sitting astride him while he fisted handfuls of chocolate-colored silk strands around his wrists flashing through his mind. How had he ever walked away from Lexi so easily? He might have been young, but she was something special; she was beautiful, smart, and fun, and she'd obviously cared a lot about him. In his desperation to run, he'd managed to hurt everyone close to him, which meant that Lexi was just another casualty to add to the list. The only difference was that everyone else had long ago forgiven him.

Except for his mom. Although he liked to think she'd forgiven him in her own way before she passed.

He glanced at the clock, seeing it was only two a.m. but wondering whether he should wake her. They'd fallen asleep unexpectedly, which meant she'd no doubt wake up in a panic over not collecting her son from Tanner's place. But they'd all be long asleep by now, so no matter whether she woke—now or at sunrise—there was nothing she could do about it.

He rose and reached for his briefs, pulling them on before padding softly down the stairs, careful not to make any noise. His throat was dry and he was desperate for water, so he stuck his head under the faucet and took a few long gulps to quench his thirst. When he was finished, he stretched and walked around, looking at the place with fresh eyes. It felt so different with Lexi's stuff compared to what he remembered: it had been very much a boys' place for a long while, filled with old leather sofas and rejected furniture from the big house. But now it had a feminine touch, and it made him smile seeing Harry's things strewn around the place. It was tidy but in a relaxed kind of way, and it reminded him of the way his mom had been.

Cody wasn't tired anymore, or he was but knew he'd

never be able to sleep. He was like this all the time, so tired he wanted to crash into bed every night, but when he finally slept it was never for long enough. His brain never seemed to stop, his body incapable of indulging in a decent rest any longer. There was always something to do, something to think about, someone to email, finances to chew over. And even though he was away from the office, when he woke up, his mind always woke up in work mode.

He made his way back into the small kitchen and opened the fridge, hoping it didn't make too much noise. He spied some orange juice and took it out, closing the fridge and wandering back over to the open-plan living space. He sat at the table and unscrewed the lid, feeling a bit guilty drinking from the container so he didn't have to open and shut cupboard doors looking for a glass.

He took a long, slow sip, but as he was doing it, something caught his eye.

Bright Lights Retirement seemed to seek him out, the words staring back at him from the top of a letter lying on the table. It was sticking out from beneath something else, and he had a feeling he knew what it would be.

Cody set the juice down and wiped his mouth with the back of his hand before reaching for the letter. There was a lamp on near the sofa, which sent enough light out for him to read by, and he scanned the words.

It is with a sense of sadness that we inform you that Bright Lights Retirement has been sold. Due to this sale, you will be given 4 weeks to make alternative arrangements for care, as per your agreement with us.

He scanned farther down the page.

We want to thank you for trusting Bright Lights to provide accommodation and ongoing support for your

*loved one. Our staff will do everything they can to make
this transition as smooth and stress-free for you as possible, so please don't hesitate to reach out if you need
any assistance during this time.*

"What are you reading?"

Cody slowly turned, the letter falling to the table as
he let it go. He swallowed and braved a smile. *Fuck.*
Why the hell hadn't he just come clean earlier? For once,
he should have followed his brother's advice. Tanner had
been right, telling her sooner than later would have been
the smart thing to do, and now he either had to keep lying and pray she didn't find out, or just spit it out.

"I, ah . . ."

She came up behind him, casually wrapping an arm
around his waist and pushing against him. "There's nothing private here. I don't care what you were looking at."

And then she let out a big sigh as she reached for the
juice, unscrewing the top and taking a few long sips
herself. "Man, I tell Harry off all the time for doing
that, but it definitely tastes better straight from the carton, right?"

Cody nodded, running his fingers down her back as
he tried to figure out what the hell to do.

"Your mom," he finally said as Lexi looked up at
him. She was wearing a robe that was tied loosely at the
waist, and he wished he could just nudge it aside and
distract her with sex, but if he didn't tell her now, then
he'd look like even more of an asshole than he already
was. "I saw the letter. So she's, ah, relocating?"

Lexi shrugged. "Yeah, she is. Some fucking asshole,
excuse my language, brought the place and now I have
exactly four weeks to find new specialized care for her."

"Four weeks seems long enough, wouldn't you say?"

Lexi choked on her juice that time around and he

took it from her, waiting for her to stop coughing and screwing the lid back on for her. He had a feeling he might end up wearing the juice in about half a minute if he didn't take it from her.

"Four weeks to find specialist care suitable for an Alzheimer's patient? Are you kidding me?" she laughed. "My mom will have to be moved so far away, I'll be lucky to see her once a week. And that's if I can even get her in somewhere. I mean, what kind of company would give notice right before Christmas? With the holiday factored in, I'll have more like two weeks to find somewhere."

"Right," he said, cringing now that he heard how bad it sounded. Making cutthroat decisions from his office wasn't difficult, but hearing firsthand ramifications of them? It was surprisingly confronting.

"So what happens if you don't find another place?" he asked.

He watched as Lexi looked down, squeezing her eyes shut as she rocked back on her heels for a moment. When she opened her eyes and looked up at him, he saw they were swimming with tears, and he caught her hand. Cody used his other hand to wipe them away, gently brushing the back of his knuckles to her cheeks.

"These big corporations, they just don't care. All they see are dollar signs on the land, when their decisions affect real people like my mom," she said quietly. "I wish I knew who'd bought it, but they're keeping a very low profile. All we know is that the facility has been sold."

"Lexi," Cody said, squeezing her hand and staring down at her. "I'm sorry. I truly am sorry."

She looked back up at him. "What are you sorry for? It's not like it's your fault."

Lexi squeezed his hand back and stepped into him,

wrapping her arms around his waist and holding him tight as her cheek touched his chest. Cody started to stroke her back, thrumming his fingers up and down as he held her. *You're a gutless bastard,* he thought as he kissed the top of her head. *An absolutely gutless, asshole bastard who doesn't deserve this.*

"Since I'm the worst mom in the world and my son has ended up on a sleepover, what do you say we make the most of our alone time?" she said, standing on tiptoes and kissing feather-light touches against his neck. "Distract me a little more."

Cody stiffened and rubbed her shoulders before stepping back a little. "Lexi, I need to tell you something."

She frowned, reaching out for him. "We don't need to talk, we can just—"

"I'm the asshole."

Lexi laughed. "What are you talking about?"

He took a deep breath and held up his hands. "You said before that some *fucking* asshole had—

"Stop," she said, her voice sounding more like a choke. "Stop," she ground out, louder the second time. "What the hell . . ." Her voice trailed off.

But Cody knew what was coming. She was about to explode, the way her fists clenched at her sides, the way her eyes started to widen and her nostrils did the littlest flare as she opened her mouth and started to back up away from him.

"You mean to tell me," she whispered, her voice so low he could barely hear her, "that you took me out for dinner and *slept* with me, knowing that you were responsible for turning my life upside down?" She reached for the letter and waved it at him. "That you were responsible for *this*," she seethed.

He shook his head, putting some more distance between them as he watched her. "In fairness, I had no idea what this meant for you. I made the deal, sure, but I didn't take care of any of the finer details, I guess you could say."

If looks could have killed, Cody knew for sure he'd be dead and buried. "Look me in the eye and tell me, Cody. Did you know my mother was at Bright Lights?" she asked, before screaming at him, her eyes wild. "Did you know, Cody? Answer me, goddamn it!"

Cody nodded. "Yes. Yes I did."

Her body was trembling and he wanted so badly to go to her, to comfort her and explain that it wasn't personal, that it had nothing to do with her, but she looked like the thought of him repulsed her, let alone the touch. So he stood still and waited for whatever was coming.

"Lexi, if you'd let me explain," he started, before she pointed with a straight arm at the door.

"Get out," she choked, as tears started to drip steadily down her cheeks.

"Lexi, please," he tried. "I didn't know when—"

"Get the *fuck* out of my house!" she screamed, sobbing as stared at him.

"I didn't know until a day ago that she was there," he tried to say as she screamed.

"Get out!"

Cody didn't bother getting the rest of his clothes, he didn't give a damn about the fact that it was snowing or that all his stuff was upstairs. He looked back at Lexi, wanting to say something but knowing better, and walked straight out into the ice-cold night to run barefoot back to his house.

Lexi watched him go, unable to stop the steady rain of tears as they battered her cheeks. She waited, willed her legs to keep her upright, until the door shut; and only then did she let them buckle beneath her as slipped into a puddle on the kitchen floor.

This was why she should never have let Cody into her heart again. This was why she was supposed to have fences built around her, around her heart and around her family, to stop anyone like Cody from ever getting close. From ever hurting her like he'd already hurt her before. Why had she thought it was a good idea to get tangled up with him again?

But this was different. This wasn't a teenager making a bad decision, this was a grown man making a business decision that had the power to devastate so many lives. And just like always, the rich man got his way and to hell with all the poor people he had to stomp on to get there.

The worst thing was, she had no one to turn to. All she had was an amazing, happy, fun little boy whom she had to shield from everything. She shuffled back so she could lean against the cool of the kitchen cabinetry, slowing her breathing as she tried to pull herself together.

Why hadn't she kept calm and asked him more questions? Maybe she could have changed his mind if she'd only been more rational. Did his family know? Had they been keeping this from her too? They'd seemed so sympathetic to her plight, but maybe it stemmed from guilt?

Lexi dropped her head to her knees as another wave of tears rocked through her body. They were long overdue—the last time she'd cried was when her mother was diagnosed—and once she'd ridden this wave of emotion, she wouldn't cry again. Not over Cody, not over any man.

She smiled through her tears as she remembered

her mom's words: *The only thing crying does, is give you red eyes, darling. The world's a tough place, and you've got to learn to pull yourself up by your bootstraps and kick some butt.* At the time she'd always rolled her eyes, wishing her mom would stop saying it, but now she was glad for all the little things she remembered, all the pep talks her mom had given her. And she'd been right: crying didn't get anyone anywhere. But every now and again, it felt good to let go instead of trying to keep up a brave face.

She slowly rose and wiped her face, trudging upstairs and finding her phone to set her alarm. Part of her was mortified she'd ended up letting Harry stay over without pre-planning it, but there was nothing she could do about it now, and it was the first time in his entire life they'd spent a night apart, so it wasn't like it was a regular habit. She collapsed onto the bed, wishing the sheets didn't smell like Cody, and that her mind didn't keep drifting off into mental images of what they'd done.

It had been so, *so* good, but it was never, ever happening again.

Chapter 10

LEXI woke up when her alarm started dinging, and she felt in the bed for Harry, who usually migrated into her bed at some stage during the night. When she found empty space instead of a warm, delicious little body, she sat bolt upright as memories of the night before trickled through her mind.

She quickly rose, hastily making her bed and going into the bathroom between the two bedrooms. Usually while she was getting ready in the morning, Harry would stumble into the bathroom, yawning and with his hair sticking on end, but today the house was silent and she hated it.

Within minutes she was out of the shower. She dressed, put on a little makeup, and dried her hair. Then she was downstairs to gulp down some breakfast and stare outside at the still-falling snow. It was sticking, but it would take a while for it to become problematic to navigate, which meant she could easily make it on foot or by car over to Tanner's place to retrieve her son. She knew he'd be awake early, but she wasn't sure about going over to the house in case she woke Tanner or Lauren up.

Lexi poured herself coffee and tried to drink it slowly, before finally deciding she couldn't wait any longer. She grabbed her scarf and coat, buttoned up, and pulled on her boots, then stepped out into the frigid air. She stared up for a second, loving the look of the snow flurries as they fell, closing her eyes as snowflakes brushed her cheeks. It wouldn't have felt like Christmas without a little snow, so the timing was perfect.

A very fast five-minute walk later, Lexi was outside Tanner's place, about to raise her hand to knock when the door swung open and Harry came charging at her like a miniature bull. His arms locked around her legs and she dropped to hug him, pleased to see he was happy to see her. She'd almost expected him to be having so much fun that he wouldn't want to leave.

She looked up and found Tanner leaning in the open doorway, his dog appearing at his side, tail wagging as he eyed her up.

"I'm so sorry you ended up having him for the night," Lexi said, knowing from the heat in her face that her cheeks were turning bright red. She hoped he'd think it was from the cold weather. "I . . ."

"Where were you, Mom?" Harry complained, his face scrunched up as he stared at her. "I fell asleep on the sofa watching *Jurassic World*! Tanner has *all* the best movies!"

"*Jurassic World*?" she repeated. Oh boy. Someone was going to be having nightmares.

"That was okay, right? He told us he loved dinosaurs and then—"

Lexi smiled at Tanner, not about to tell him that her

son might be a touch too young for movies like that after he'd cared for him all night. "Of course it's okay. I just appreciate you looking after him."

"I'll go get my stuff!" Harry announced, running off like a bullet back into the house.

"So I take it you had a good night then?" Tanner asked, eyebrows raised as a grin crossed his face.

Lexi sighed. "I wouldn't exactly say that. It started out great but it didn't end so well, and that's putting it lightly."

Tanner grimaced. "My brother was a jerk again, wasn't he? What the hell is wrong with him?"

She saw movement in the living room and wasn't sure if it was Harry coming back or Lauren about to join them. "Tanner, I need to know if you knew about Cody being the developer tearing down the retirement home where my mom is. He said something and I just, I can't stop thinking about whether I've been the butt of the joke and everyone kept it from me."

The uncomfortable look on Tanner's face told her everything she needed to know. "Yeah, I did know. But it's not like you think."

She felt tears prick her eyes again but she refused to let them fall, quickly blinking them away instead. "So you knew all this time I've been here and never said anything?"

Tanner held up his hands. "No, that's not true. When he told me yesterday, the first thing I told him to do was tell you." He grunted. "No, the first thing I told him to do was quit the deal, but he told me if he didn't do it someone else would. And last night I made him promise to tell you."

"So when I told you and your family about my mom and what I was going through, you didn't know then?"

she asked, searching Tanner's face. "Please don't lie to me."

Tanner stepped forward and put his hand on her upper arm, his grip warm but firm. "I didn't know, Lexi, and I'm sure no one else in this family knew either. I'm not in the habit of lying to people I care about, and I'll never forget what you've done for my old man, okay?"

"Hey," Lauren said, appearing and standing by Tanner, her arms wrapped around herself as the cold blew in at her from outside. "What's going on here? Everything okay?"

"Lexi's just found out that my idiot big brother is the asshole responsible for tearing down Bright Lights to make way for luxury high-rise housing," Tanner said.

"Ah, I see," Lauren said, frowning. "Hey, do you feel like a girls' night? You look like you need some loving." She burst out laughing. "I didn't mean loving by a man, either. Just some girl time, you know?"

If Tanner hadn't been standing there watching the exchange, Lexi probably would have thrown her arms around Lauren in a big hug. Instead she tried not to overdo her reaction.

"That'd actually be great," Lexi replied. "But I don't want to leave Harry again."

Lauren waved her hand in the air. "Then let's make it early evening or even afternoon. You can both come over here and I'll ask Mia too, and the kids can play while we have a few drinks and chat. What do you say?"

"I say I'm in," Lexi said, feeling like a weight had fallen from her shoulders just being invited over. She hadn't realized how lonely she'd been, but the offer from Lauren was making her feel the burden of isolation acutely. Talking and sitting around with a couple of other women was exactly what she needed.

"So do I get to come to girls' night?" Tanner asked with a waggle of his eyebrows.

Lauren just groaned and winked at Lexi. "Absolutely not. In fact, why don't you have a boys' night with your dad and brother?"

Tanner frowned. "I'd rather be with the girls."

Harry came flying between Tanner and Lauren then, and Lexi quickly caught his hand. "Thanks again for looking after him," she called over her shoulder as Harry almost yanked her arm from its socket.

"No problem," Tanner called after her.

"Harry, what do you say?" Lexi scolded.

"Thank you for having me!" he yelled, spinning around as snow fell down on him. He laughed and spun until he crashed to the ground, and Lexi couldn't help it if some of the magic was rubbing off on her. It was Christmas and it was snowing; she had Harry to make her feel like nothing was more important than being with him; and she had a girls' night to look forward to.

Cody might have knocked the wind from her sails, but she was still alive and kicking, and she wasn't going to let him crush the life from her twice. Not if she had anything to do with it.

"So let me get this straight," Tanner said, passing Cody a beer and sitting back in the chair across from him. "You thought it was a good idea to take her to bed *before* telling her? I mean, she already hates you for what you did to her, and you've pretty much done the same thing to her all over again."

Cody groaned as he lifted the beer bottle to his lips, swallowing long and hard. Hearing Tanner say it like that only made it all sound even worse than it was.

"Hey, at least you didn't jump on a plane and leave

her. That's something," Sam, Mia's husband, said from the chair to his side. His horse-whisperer brother-in-law hadn't been back in town long, with his most recent tour finally ending in time for him to make it home for Christmas.

"Still, you lost her trust again," Tanner said. "You're not coming back from this."

"Great, thanks for the relationship advice," Cody grunted. He lifted his beer again and took another long sip. At this rate he'd be drunk before dark.

"So what are you going to do about it?" Sam asked. "You like her, or was it just a fun walk down memory lane?"

Cody could feel his brother staring at him, knew Tanner was probably just as curious about his answer to that question as Sam was. He turned to Sam since he was the one who'd asked.

"You know what, I don't know," Cody said, draining his beer and rising to get another for them all, although he'd drunk his a lot faster than the others had theirs. "I think I'd kind of blocked her out, along with almost everything else from back then, but spending time with her again is kind of bringing it all back."

They sat in silence for a bit, all quietly drinking and staring at the fire roaring in the big library. One of the things Cody liked most about being home in winter was the feeling inside the house. The big open fires were always roaring, combining with central heating to make the house cozy enough to be barefoot and in a T-shirt, the lights on outside illuminating the white of snow falling and settling on the ground. An enormous Christmas tree was propped in the corner, covered with decorations that he imagined Mia hung every year, and there were giant wreaths on all the doors and picture-perfect stockings hanging from the mantle. It was Christmas just as he'd remembered from being a kid, although back then his dad had always cut the tree down, and he imagined that tradition had passed to Tanner now.

Cody stood and crossed the room, reaching out to touch a snow globe. He looked at the little scene, a group of reindeer with a perfect-looking little house, and he tipped it upside down, shaking the snow before putting it back down to watch it drift and settle. But then he stepped back, the sharp reminder of his mom placing it there, laughing as she watched the snow fall, hitting him square on.

Fuck. He hated the memories, had spent so long running from them that he'd never learned how to deal with them. *Run again. Get the hell out of here and back on the plane to New York.*

"You know, it doesn't matter whether I do this to Lexi now or not, because it would only take a few months for another investor to do the same," he said, taking up residence on the leather sofa again as he pushed his thoughts away. He sprawled out, suddenly tired as he reached for his beer again. Leaving wasn't an option, not yet. "The zoning was changed and it's a damn good investment for anyone with the cash to inject into it."

"So don't sell it," Tanner said, shrugging as if the decision were that easy. "You can keep it and stay in the aged-care sector."

"Keep it?" Cody laughed. "I do business, not charity work. That place isn't exactly a cash cow. The only thing going for it is the land it's built on."

"Don't speak to me like I'm a goddamn idiot, Cody." Tanner glowered at him as he spoke. "You're not the only person in this family who understands business."

"Whatever, Tanner. Since when did you get so sensitive, anyway?" Cody shook his head. "Being all loved up has turned you soft."

Tanner's stare turned ice cold. "You leave Lauren the fuck out of this argument."

"Whoa!" Sam held his hands out. "You guys are worse than the mustangs I started breaking in today. Now cut it out, it's Christmas."

Cody leaned back again, taking another pull of beer.

"Look, way I see it is that you've got to figure out what's important to you."

"I don't let business and pleasure cross paths," Cody said. "I've got as little interest in breaking hearts as I have in losing money on deals, but business is business."

Tanner didn't say anything, just sat and watched him. But Sam leaned forward. "So think a bit more creatively. Looks to me like you've got a lot of making up to do, and you're going to have bad press to contend with regardless."

Bad press? "Has there been something about this in the media?" he asked.

"Dude," Sam chuckled, but then his laughter died off suddenly, probably in reaction to the stone-faced look Cody gave him in return. "I take it you guys haven't looked on Facebook lately?"

Cody grunted and reached for his phone, but Sam beat him to it, swiping on his own phone and passing it over.

"Sorry, I thought you already knew about this."

Cody reached for the phone and scanned the post, checking to see how many likes and comments were there already. *Goddamn it.* If things weren't already bad, they were catastrophic now, and the last thing he

needed was a shitstorm two days before Christmas Eve
when all his staff were already jetting off on vacation
or back to their families.

Looks like Texas' most eligible bachelor is the de-
veloper behind Bright Lights Retirement Home being
pulled down. Who's with me to march on the 22nd?
Let's show Cody Ford exactly what we all think of him
storming back into town and ripping our community
apart! Every voice counts, come and join us—and don't
forget to share! Our elderly deserve better than some-
one ripping their homes down to make millions!

"Fuck," Cody swore. "I can't believe she'd do this to
me."

"Oh believe it, brother," Tanner said, giving him a sly
grin. "There ain't nothing quite like a woman scorned."

Sam laughed and Cody watched as he exchanged an
amused look with Tanner.

"What am I missing here?"

Tanner shrugged. "Call us pussy whipped if you
want, but we know better than to mess with the women
in our lives."

"Yeah, you got that right." Sam slapped a hand to his
shoulder. "Your sister would kick my ass if I did anything to hurt her or the people she loved, so just be
careful what you're messing with here, Cody, that's all
I'm saying."

He frowned and started to scroll through the comments, annoyed to see that more than two hundred
people had liked the post already. What the hell had she
done? Paid for advertising to boost the damn thing?

What an asshole. Calls himself a Texan?

So this is how he made the Fortune 500 list, by steal-
ing homes from old people?

Oh man, this was worse than he thought. One thing

he didn't agree with in business was the saying that "Any publicity was good publicity." He preferred to stay as low profile as possible, *Fortune* list withstanding, and the last thing he needed was his company's name being dragged through the mud. His foreign investors liked how squeaky clean he was, no skeletons in the closet, that sort of thing. And this was fast becoming the biggest fucking skeleton he could imagine.

And it got worse. The page had been updated with a picture of him. The same one as that ad that appeared in *Fortune* magazine. He grimaced, before realizing that it would be a copyright infringement.

He grabbed his phone and dialed his assistant. It rang and rang, then went to voicemail. Cody glared at his phone, checking the time. She should still be on the clock for another thirty minutes, and given the generous Christmas bonus he'd paid her, he expected her to pick up the goddamn phone.

"What are you going to do?" Tanner asked, and he saw his father had ambled into the room. Cody was going to tell Tanner off for giving their dad a beer, but he didn't bother. He was a grown man, and if he wanted to have a beer in hand, that was his prerogative.

"I'm going to kill the story, and then I'm going to find Lexi and tell her exactly what I think of her petty little stunt."

Tanner laughed and clinked beer bottles with Sam, but he saw his father was watching him with a more serious stare. He met his gaze and swallowed, knowing in that instance that he was still the same little boy so desperate for his old man's approval. There was no way he was going to let his family's name be dragged through the mud by one woman with a vendetta against him, even if that woman was Lexi.

All was fair in love and war, and as far as he was concerned, this was war.

"You okay there, son?" Walter asked.

Cody inhaled as his phone buzzed and he saw it was Katie, his assistant. "Yeah, Dad, I'm fine. Nothing I can't handle, but I do need to take this."

He smiled at his dad, not letting anything betray the cool, calm demeanor he was trying his best to exude. There was a reason he was a good poker player, and he only hoped his father was buying it.

"Katie, I need you," he said quietly as he answered the call. It was loud in the background and he grimaced, imagining everyone who was left in the office having drinks and celebrating the festive season. If Katie was already a few drinks in, he was screwed.

"Cody, it's after five. What's so urgent?"

He felt his back bristle. Since when was he a nine-to-five kind of guy? She knew that better than anyone. "I'm in the middle of a social media shitstorm and I need you to fix it."

There was a long pause and then it went silent on the other end, like she'd moved from whatever party she was part of to somewhere quieter.

"Cody, are you sure this isn't something that can wait until—"

"Facebook, now," he ordered. "I need this sorted, and I need it sorted now. I want my photo taken down and I want the post deleted."

"Cody, it's not as easy as that. Unless there's something that breaches the—"

"I don't care how you do it, just get it done. I'm sending you the links now."

He heard Katie's sigh on the other end and wished he hadn't snapped at her. It wasn't her fault and she worked hard for him all year, always in the office before him and never failing to anticipate what he needed. Cody took a deep breath.

"You still flying out to see your folks in the morning?" he asked.

"Yes," she replied, her voice sounding brighter at the mention of her family.

"Upgrade your ticket to first class, use the company card," he said. "And take your parents out for a nice meal somewhere too, tell them Merry Christmas from me."

He could almost hear Katie smiling down the line. "Thanks, Cody. You're a real sweetheart sometimes."

"Hey, I've got to make up for the uptight asshole part somehow, don't I?"

She asked him a few more questions before saying goodbye. He ended the call, taking a minute to calm down as he stared out into the dark. Maybe he should just go. Would anyone really care if he wasn't there? If he was gone, the storm might pass over a whole lot faster.

A hand closed over his shoulder and he turned to find his father standing behind him. He was holding a glass tumbler filled with amber liquid, and Cody took it as it was passed to him.

"Son, you look like you need something strong."

Cody lifted it to his lips, inhaling the familiar aroma of his old man's favorite whiskey. He swallowed it down in one long gulp, savoring the hot burn as it traced a tumbling path down his throat all the way to his stomach.

"Thanks," he said, patting his father on the shoulder. "You want to sit?"

"I want to know who the hell organized a boys' night and didn't invite me?" he growled. "No more business tonight, Cody. Your old man here wants to sit and drink without anyone taking my blood pressure or telling me what I should be doing."

"Fair enough," Cody said. "Who wants some of the good stuff?"

All three men facing him let out a roar of approval, and Cody went to get the whiskey and more glasses.

"Hey, we didn't organize this. The girls kicked us out to have their own get-together," he told his father as he passed him.

Sam laughed. "Yeah, we had nowhere else to go."

Cody stood and watched as they laughed and joked, wishing he didn't feel so uptight and that a certain woman wasn't circling his mind, driving him crazy. Being with her had felt so damn right: the weight of her in his arms; the softness of her lips; the fact that he actually, for once in his goddamn life, felt like he could just be himself.

He poured the drinks and passed them out, including a large one for himself. It was Christmas, he was with his family, and that was what he should be focusing on. Not chasing tail and stressing over business deals that were as good as done.

Chapter 11

LEXI watched as Harry played with Sophia, pretending she was listening to whatever Mia and Lauren were chatting about. They were all sitting at the kitchen counter, but Lexi's mind was a million miles away. She resisted the urge to check her iPhone, guilt creeping through at what she'd done. Cody deserved what was coming to him. If he was going to do something like this, then his name was going to be leaked at some point, but she still felt bad about the fallout on his family. And how they might react.

If Walter Ford got wind of what she'd done and decided to side with his son, which she knew was more likely than not, then it wouldn't just be her mom who became homeless. Lexi gulped and started to reach for her phone, wondering if she should just delete her post and go beg Cody to reconsider instead.

"Hey, Earth to Lexi?" Mia said, tapping her hand from the other side of the counter where she was leaning. "Bubbles or wine?"

Lexi sighed and forced herself to smile. This was why she felt bad. The Ford family had, on the whole, been so kind and welcoming to her. But maybe they'd all agree with what Cody was doing. The family was wealthy beyond her wildest dreams, and she knew they didn't end up that way from being pushovers.

"What are you girls having?" she asked.

Lauren held up her tall champagne glass, the bubbles rising in rapid succession to the top. "I don't get out a lot, so I'm making the most of it. I've been all work and no play for way too long."

"I'll have the same, thanks," she said, reaching for an olive from the platter in front of her.

"So Lauren told me a little before you arrived, about a big fight you and Cody had," Mia said. "I was really hoping you guys would have a great night together."

The last thing Lexi was going to do was tell Cody's sister and sister-in-law exactly what she thought of him, so she decided to water it down a little. She'd probably said too much this morning to Tanner as it was.

"We just have a lot of history, so I guess it was never going to be easy between us," Lexi said, gratefully taking the champagne and clinking glasses with the other two. She took a sip and the bubbles tickled her throat, relaxing her almost instantly.

"Cody's biggest downfall has also been his biggest success," Mia said. "He has prioritized work all his life, and he doesn't seem to see how badly the people around him need him sometimes."

Lexi just nodded, trying to find the right words, but she was saved from having to say anything at all when a bang signaled the front door had opened and a woman called out.

"Where's my welcoming party?"

Mia's daughter squealed and ran through the kitchen and Mia burst out laughing at the commotion.

"That'll be my sister," she muttered. "Always one to make an entrance, and someone loves her Aunty Angie."

"She's the only one allowed to call me that," Angelina Ford said as she stepped into the room with Sophia on her hip and a Louis Vuitton bag in her hand. Lexi smiled as she stared at her, wondering if the woman's handbag was more expensive than every item of clothing and jewelry Lexi was wearing. She guessed yes. "What's with the party tonight?"

"We decided to have a girls' night," Mia said as she hugged her sister and then peppered Sophia with kisses while she hung on tight to her aunt.

Angelina gave Lauren a one-armed hug too, and then turned to Lexi and held out her hand. "You look familiar, but I can't quite place you."

"Lexi," she said, taking in the warm smile that counterbalanced the tailored trousers, silk shirt, and high heels. "I'm your father's nurse and I think we met a long time ago when I dated your brother."

Angelina's smile turned into a full-wattage grin. "Oh wow, you look different but I definitely remember you. It hadn't clicked when the others told me Dad had a caregiver."

"No one told Cody either," Mia said with a sigh.

"And suddenly I can see why we're having a girls' night," Angelina said with a wink. "Well, come on then, pour me a drink and let's get this night started!"

Lexi felt a pang then, a deep longing to be part of the Ford family. They were all so different, a mix of full-blood ranchers and successful city dwellers, but there was something about each and every one of them that made Lexi want to be close to them. Not to mention how much she'd always longed to be part of a big family, instead of having only her mom to count on when things were tough. *Or just herself.*

"So tell me," Angelina said, sitting beside Lexi as Sophia ran back to play with Harry. She kicked her shoes off and took a sip of her champagne. "Is Cody all twisted in knots over you being here? You were the one who got away, right?"

Lexi snorted, making both her and Angelina laugh. "More like he was the one who got away," she said. "I wasn't the one running."

"Oh please," Angelina waved her hand dismissively, "Cody wasn't running from you. I bet he would have tucked you into his suitcase if he could."

She studied the elegant features of the woman sitting across from her, wondering just how much she knew. Mia was younger than Cody, but Angelina was the oldest, and Lexi wondered if she knew a whole lot more about everything.

"You know, Cody and I are a lot the same. We didn't feel the same deep connection to the ranch as Mia and Tanner did. They were born to ride and live on the land, but we had that fire in our bellies to spread our wings. And things were rough at home." Angelina sighed. "I told Cody to walk away from everything he knew and make a new life for himself. He was suffocating here, seeing Mom getting sicker and sicker and feeling so helpless, and he needed to run while he could. The longer he stayed, the harder it would have been."

Lexi's hand started to shake as she took a little sip of her drink. It had been Angelina who told Cody to move? Had he been simply following his big sister's advice?

"So you told him to leave me?" she finally asked, and the room suddenly fell silent.

"I didn't even know you, not properly," Angelina said. "I never told him to leave you, I just told him to do the right thing and look at the bigger picture. He'd never have been happy staying here, but I guess I expected you two to figure things out if it was meant to be."

Wow. It was such a long time ago, but she still felt the blow of Angelina's words. It didn't change anything, though. Cody could have talked to her and they could have made long-distance work. *Or not.* What kind of eighteen-year-olds can do long distance and survive? But anything would have been better than the way he'd left.

"Lexi, are you okay? You look a little pale," Mia said, coming around to stand beside her. She looked up in time to see the angry look she was flashing her older sister.

"I'm fine," Lexi said, forcing a smile.

"This girl hasn't exactly had the best day," Mia continued. "Idiot brother has taken on a deal waaay too close to home, and Lexi's feeling the brunt of it on top of everything else. So let's go easy on her, okay?"

"What kind of deal?" Angelina asked.

"Oh, you'll find out soon enough," Mia said, topping up their glasses. "Now how about we toast the gorgeous Lexi, who not only has the capacity to drive our brother crazy, but can also make taming our father look so easy! She has the old man eating out of her hand, and it's sure taken a big load off my mind."

Lexi held her glass up, giving Angelina a wary side-glance. Cody's sister had only been honest, but she couldn't stop thinking about what she'd said. But one thing she said was right: she and Cody were cut from a different cloth than her sweet sister Mia and burly brother Tanner. Only when they were kids she hadn't been able to see it so clearly.

"I upset you, didn't I?" Angelina's words were more softly spoken this time, after moving her chair closer to Lexi's. "You've been a great help with Dad, and I never meant to hurt you back when—"

Lexi held up her hand. "It was a decade ago, it's water under the bridge," she said bravely, trying to convince herself as much as Angelina. "You just took me by surprise, that's all. I shouldn't have let it rattle me. How about we just let the past stay in the past, okay?"

"Look, Cody's a good man," Angelina said. "He's been incredibly successful and he's a great brother to me, but he's married to his work. Whatever happened between you guys back then, just be grateful you didn't stay together, because he would have made a lousy husband."

Lexi nodded. This wasn't exactly a conversation she wanted to be having, not with his sister. Mia, maybe, because they were closer, and Cody's younger sister was so much more like her, but not with Angelina. Even as a teenager, she'd been mildly terrified of the beautiful, confident oldest Ford sibling; the belle of every school dance and top of her class, not to mention the captain of the softball team. She seemed to be good at anything and everything without looking as if she even tried.

"You know how Cody seems to have zero tact sometimes?" Mia asked, leaning over and sliding her sister's drink down the counter and away from Lexi. "Well, my darling sister is exactly the same. If not worse."

"You say that like it's not a compliment," Angelina said dryly, moving down the counter after her champagne.

"It's not," Mia snapped. "Come on, Lexi, tell us about your mom. It must be really hard on you right now. What about Harry's dad, is he at least around for Christmas?"

Lexi braved a smile, feeling more relaxed now it was just Mia talking to her. Lauren was great too, but thankfully she'd engaged Angelina and they were laughing about something as Mia waited for Lexi to answer.

"It's pretty rough. I don't know what I'm going to do about my mom to be honest." She sipped her drink and found Mia studying her, the sweetest look on her face. "And as for my deadbeat ex, no, he won't show his face. The only Christmas he did that was to sneak in and write his name on all the gifts under the tree, so Harry thought they were all from him."

Mia made a sour-looking face. "How did that go down?"

Lexi grinned. "Great, actually, because he was too stupid to realize that Harry couldn't read yet! There was no way I'd have let him get away with it otherwise, not after I'd worked my ass off to buy all those presents on my own."

"You're doing a great job, mama," Mia said.

Lexi held up her glass. "Takes one to know one."

"I'm serious though," Mia said after they'd both clinked glasses and sipped. "He's a great kid. You *are* doing a really good job with him."

"Aw, thanks," she said, feeling a warm fuzz pass through her body as the champagne started to relax her.

There was a knock at the door and Lexi turned. "You expecting someone else?"

Mia touched her shoulder as she passed. "I ordered

dinner. I thought we could all do without cooking tonight, so there's pizza for the kids and Thai for us."

"I bet you got something for the boys," Angelina called out as Mia walked down the hall. "No way you'd let them fend for themselves!"

"Of course I did! We're angry with Cody, not the entire male population."

Lexi burst out laughing, loving Cody's fiery little sister even more. And when she met Lauren's eye, she started laughing too, with Angelina watching them both as if they were crazy. Lexi hardly even knew why she was laughing, but maybe if she wasn't she'd have burst into tears. Because as much as she hated the deal he was doing, and what he'd done to her in the past, they were a special family, and once upon a time she'd have given anything to be a part of it.

The next day, Lexi drove over to Lauren's place, her hands sweaty despite the cold. She was freaking out with nerves, but she was trying her best to pretend they weren't real. Her worst fear was that the family was going to terminate her employment now that she'd gone public with her feud against Cody's company, but she wasn't going to let fear rule her decisions.

Lauren must have seen her coming because she'd opened the door before Lexi even turned off the engine. She leaned over and kissed the top of Harry's head, smiling down at him.

"I'm sorry I have to leave you again, but I promise it'll be the last time this vacation, okay?"

He shrugged. "I love coming here. Can you go out all morning?"

Lexi laughed. There she was suffering serious mom guilt, and he was worried she might come back too soon.

"Yeah, sure. I'll make sure I'm gone at least half the day."

She got out and followed Harry as he ran up to the door, going straight past Lauren and running inside.

"Sorry, but I think he's as excited about seeing your dog as he is you," Lexi apologized.

"No worries. Hey, do you mind if he comes with me to see the horses later? The weather seems to have cleared a little and Tanner wanted me to meet him. Apparently he's got a really sweet old pony in the yards too, a horse they rode as kids, so I thought Harry might like to see her."

"He might never want to come back to me!" Lexi teased. "But yes, of course, just have fun. I really appreciate you helping me out. Again."

Lauren reached for her hand and squeezed it. "You sure you want to do this? I mean, is it worth picking a fight like this with Cody?"

She nodded. "Yeah, it is. Because this is the one stunt that might actually help."

Lauren let go of her. "I haven't breathed a word to anyone else. Good luck."

Lexi had had just a little too much to drink last night and spilled everything to Lauren, and she liked that she was able to trust her with her secret. She wouldn't have blamed her for telling Tanner—he was her husband after all—but it was nice knowing she could tell her something and it wouldn't go any further. Mia had gone back to her own ranch now that Sam was home, so at least she didn't have to explain everything to her.

"Give 'em death," Lauren called out after her as she stepped carefully over the slowly defrosting snow. "Those Ford boys need to be told they're not God's gift sometimes. Trust me, I know!"

Lexi was laughing to herself as she got in her car, glancing in the back at the placard she'd made that morning. Cody was going to hate his name being dragged through the mud, and if the local television station came along he'd hate that even more. Her phone beeped and she glanced down at the screen, half expecting it to be her mother. But it was another woman, Rosie Brown, a new friend of hers who had her mother in the retirement home, too.

The Facebook post has been deleted!

Lexi glared at the screen as heat prickled her skin and her pulse started to thump. Her thumb was quivering as she replied.

Can we try to repost? She realized as she replied that there was no point; they were supposed to be marching in less than an hour. How long had the post been down? Anger thudded through her as she imagined how conceited Cody would be at wielding his power like that to get it removed. He probably had Zuckerberg on speed dial.

Do you have confirmation on numbers? I think there might only be a handful of us. Five at most.

Lexi smiled to herself as she quietly hatched a plan.

Then let's get the old people to march with us! Anyone who can walk can join, maybe some of the staff will come too?

. She started her engine and drove slowly down the drive, smiling to herself at her plan. If this didn't stop Cody from going ahead with the development, then she didn't know what would.

"What's Lauren doing with Lexi's kid?"

Cody waved back at the young boy as he approached,

a huge grin on his face as he bounded along beside Cody's sister-in-law.

"No idea. Lauren probably offered to help while Lexi was working or something."

"Huh," Cody grunted. As much as he'd grumbled about Lexi the night before, furiously refreshing Facebook every fifteen minutes or so to see if the post and his photo had been deleted, he still wanted to see her. Part of him actually admired her for going on social media to out him, even though he'd never admit it.

"You never did tell me why you broke up with her in the first place," Tanner said. "What actually happened between you guys?"

"I told you," Cody said as he brushed the horse down. "I went to college and she stayed here. I wasn't going to screw with her head and pretend what we had was going to last, not when I knew I was never coming back."

"Maybe you should have told her that instead of leaving her here waiting for you to come back," Tanner quipped back.

"I wrote to her, actually." Cody cleared his throat, surprised with what he'd just admitted. "I was too gutless to say it to her face, so I got in my car hours earlier than I was supposed to leave just so I didn't have to see her before I left. And then I sent her a letter."

"A letter?" Tanner asked. "An honest to god letter on paper?"

"Yeah, a letter. It was something we did in school— she was always writing me little letters, so I finally wrote her one back."

Tanner whacked him around the back of the head as he jogged past. "Idiot. You should have just told her to her face." He watched as Tanner opened up his arms and enveloped Lauren around the waist, kissing her and then swinging her around in a circle. He'd like to tease his brother for being so sappy with Lauren, but he didn't dare. He knew what happiness looked like, and he doubted Tanner would even care what he thought, anyway.

"Hey, Harry," he said to the boy as he came closer. "You like horses?"

He went to jump toward the horse Cody had been grooming, but Tanner stuck his hand out and grabbed his shoulder.

"Whoa," he said, keeping hold of him. "You go fast at him like that, he'll be scared of you. Horses are flighty animals, which means they get scared really easily and the first thing they want to do is run away from whatever's scared them."

Harry looked up at him and nodded. "Can I touch him? He's huge."

"Yeah, you can touch him, but just hold your hand out when you're approaching, let him sniff you."

Harry did as he was told, and within seconds he was stroking the horse's nose and then his cheek. Cody was surprised Harry wasn't a little more nervous around one large animal since he'd clearly never been around one.

"You want to see something more your size?" Cody asked. "This guy here is my dad's horse, and I was just giving him a quick groom before he gets his rugs put on and turned out in the field for the rest of the day. We always cover them with warm rugs in this kind of weather, just like you and I need to put our jackets on."

Harry nodded and fell in to step beside him. "Why is a horse my size?"

"Well, we have an old pony still, it was Mia's pony

actually, and we loaned her out to some friends so their kids could learn to ride. But they've all grown too big for her now, so she's come back here just in time for Mia's daughter to ride."

"Can I ride her?"

Cody looked down at the eager face turned up to his, eyes wide and trusting, the kid so excited about seeing a damn pony. "Yeah, sure thing kid. You think your mom would mind?"

Harry squished his face up as he thought about it. "My mom was pretty mad at you. I kept hearing her say bad words a lot when she was saying your name."

"Yeah? Like what?" he cringed, imagining Lexi stomping around the kitchen cursing him.

"Whad'ya do to make her so mad? Mom never gets mad like that."

"Hey, you want to ride that pony or what?" Cody asked, quickly changing the subject and hoping Harry was too young to notice. The boy's face lit up and Cody chased after him, about to call out a reminder not to run toward horses but not wanting to curb the kid's excitement. Cleo was almost bombproof she was so quiet, and he knew that within seconds of meeting, she'd be nuzzling Harry and he'd be head over heels in love with her.

He hated the feud between him and Lexi, and he sure as hell hadn't meant to hurt her. But right now, he couldn't see a way out of it, or at least not one that made them both happy.

"What do you say we go for a little ride?" Cody asked.

Harry spun around, launching at him and tackling him around the legs with a big hug. He ruffled his hair, not sure what else to do, and he caught Tanner's eye when he looked up. Actually, Tanner *and* Lauren, who were standing together, both looking surprised to see him with Harry.

"What?" he asked, eyebrows tugging down as he scowled at them.

"Nothing," Tanner replied. "Nothing at all."

"Just because I don't want my own kids doesn't mean I don't like them," he muttered. "Come on, Harry. Let's find a little saddle for her and get you up there."

"Or you could ride my old mechanical bull and let Cody do some work!" Tanner called out, laughing when the kid suddenly let go of Cody and ran in his direction instead.

Cody shrugged and headed for the barn. There was something about the boy that he liked, and if he was going to freeze his ass off out with the horses, he was happy to be teaching Harry how to ride. Once upon a time, he'd loved being on the ranch. None of his siblings remembered it; hell, Tanner and Mia were too young and Angelina had never come outside to see him. They all laughed about him not having horses in his blood like Tanner, that ranch life wasn't for him, but they were all wrong. He used to be first out to catch and feed the horses in the morning, he'd been the first to learn how to ride on Cleo, and for a while he'd imagined growing up and spending his days on horseback and running their ranches.

But in the end, it had hurt too bad to stay.

"I have one question for you," Rosie asked, as she blew on her fingers to warm them up. "Are you sure we want to make an enemy of Cody Ford? I've been reading up about him, and he seems like the kind of man we'd be stupid to cross."

The last thing Lexi wanted was to open up to Rosie

about her history with Cody. "What more can he do? If we do nothing, he'll kick our moms out and tear the place down."

Rosie nodded, shifting from foot to foot now. Lexi did the same, feeling colder just from watching the other woman move around so much. The cold was biting, even through her woolly hat, gloves, scarf, and big jacket. Her face felt chapped from the chilly wind as it echoed through her entire body.

"You're right. I'm just new to all this. Have you ever joined a protest before?"

Lexi laughed. "No! But there's a first time for everything." *Not to mention my own personal vendetta.* "Look, there're more people coming. See? We're going to be just fine."

She was good at saying the right thing, but she was so nervous she could hardly breathe. Cody was going to be furious with her, but he'd left her with no other option, and it wouldn't have mattered if it was him or another developer, she'd have fought with everything she had to try to change what was happening.

"Hi!" she called out, trying to sound confident. "Thank you so much for coming! I know it's cold, but let's make as much noise as we can."

A few more cars pulled up and Lexi breathed a sigh of relief as some of the nurses, still in uniform, started coming out from the building, wearing smiles as big as Texas as they walked over to join them. This wasn't about her and Cody, this was about her standing up for the rights of her mom and all the other elderly people in there. This was their home, and it wasn't right that a developer could just buy the place and decide to rip it down.

"Let's go!" she called out, picking up her placard and clearing her throat.

The others gathered, at least fifteen of them now, grinned at her, and held up their signs too, and together they stood outside Bright Lights chanting as cars drove by, many tooting their horns in support as they passed. She slowly started to thaw out, her anxiety easing with every few minutes that passed, realizing that she was actually doing something good for their community. This was so much more than her feuding with Cody, and she only hoped that both he and his family understood why she was doing what she was doing. He'd left her with no other choice.

"Bright Lights, here to stay! Bright Lights, you can't take it away!"

But her quiet confidence hit the sidewalk with a *thud* when a local news station pulled up beside them, with a cameraman and news anchor she recognized from television suddenly bustling toward her.

Oh hell. She took a deep breath, forcing a big, bright smile as the brunette clattering toward her in heels waved out to them.

"Well, look at this!" the reporter exclaimed. "You all must feel very passionate about what you're fighting for to be standing out here in the freezing cold all day!"

The camera was suddenly pointed at her, and Lexi bravely held her sign even higher, feeling the power of the other men and women behind her as they chanted at her flank.

"Can you tell us why you're here today?" the reporter asked. "What's brought you all out to protest?"

Lexi opened her mouth to speak just as a Range Rover screeched to a stop in the lot, right beside the news van. Her nerves stammered, her voice faltered in her throat, but she held her head high and refused to be silenced.

Cody leapt from his vehicle, dressed just like she'd seen him that first day when he'd arrived. Part of her hoped he was dressed in suit pants and a big black overcoat because he was on his way back to New York, but she doubted she'd be so lucky.

"Ma'am?" the reporter asked.

She slowly lowered her placard and squared her shoulders as she faced the camera. A weird sense of calm slowly washed over her. "We're here because Bright Lights retirement, right behind me here, has been sold to a greedy, obnoxious developer who intends to tear it down in less than a month."

The reporter nodded, her eyes widening as if she hadn't realized what a juicy story she was on to.

"And how does this personally affect you?"

"My mother lives here. This is the only place she can be that's close enough for me to visit her, with the facilities she needs for her Alzheimer's, and it's the same for the people here with me today." A cheer went up from behind her, and Lexi realized a small crowd had gathered on the sidewalk now, listening to what she was saying. Only Cody stood alone, a tall, dark pillar among the regular folk, his face impassive as he stared at her. But he wasn't going to intimidate her, not today.

Tears pricked in Lexi's eyes when she started to talk again, the weight of what was happening was a weight on her shoulders she could barely stand any longer.

"This has been allowed to happen right under our noses, in our community, to the people who are most vulnerable among us," she said, clearing her throat when her voice wavered. "There are wealthy businessmen and developers who are allowed to do things that simply should not be permitted. We have to ask ourselves if too many envelopes are being passed under tables at local government offices!"

The people standing with her erupted into clapping and yelling, and even the crowd listening clapped their hands.

"And by envelopes?" the reporter asked, her dark curls bouncing as she nodded, eyes intent, waiting for something she could no doubt turn into an even bigger story.

Lexi took a step closer to the camera and stared down the lens. "I mean the type filled with a big wad of cash, to make sure the right papers are signed off on."

"That's enough!" Cody's voice cut through the frigid air, and Lexi fought the urge to scurry backward as he stormed toward her. "I will not have you insinuating that my decision or ability to develop this land had anything to do with corruption!"

Her heart was beating so hard she was sure Cody would be able to hear the thudding from where he was standing, but she wasn't going to back down. This was her chance, and she'd stayed quiet far too long—when Cody had left her, when her husband had acted like a jerk, and when she'd first found out about the development. It wasn't going to happen again.

"I'm not insinuating anything, Mr. Ford," she said, eyeballing him straight back. "There is a way that deals get done. I think we're all aware of this, but instead of thinking about our community, you're only seeing the dollar signs at the end."

She'd never seen his face turn red before, never imagined for a second he could even be embarrassed because he was always so cool, calm, and collected, but this? This had him rattled.

"I'm sure the community will more than appreciate beautiful housing being erected on this land," he said, his voice rising as his temper flared. "This was a business decision that any astute developer would have been crazy not to have entertained."

"What's next for you and all the people here?" the reporter asked. "Will the elderly be forced from here, Mr. Ford?"

Lexi jumped in before Cody could answer, raising her voice so he couldn't interrupt her. "The people behind me, the workers who've so diligently looked after our loved ones, will be out of jobs. A few weeks after Christmas they'll be searching for work." She paused, nodding and gesturing back toward the building behind her. "And our loved ones?" Tears pricked her eyes and she couldn't help the drop in her voice, the desperation that she knew was echoed in her words. "They have nowhere to go. The care many of them need will force their families to move them at least an hour's drive away, which means they'll lose the support they need. How many of us can drive an hour or more daily to visit our mothers or fathers, our aunts or uncles? And if we don't move them, then we're forced to care for them ourselves."

The reporter was nodding, her frown showing how sympathetic she was. "Mr. Ford, do you have a response?"

He folded his arms, defensive, before clearly realizing his mistake and dropping them to his sides, smiling as if he could win everyone over with his charm. "If the four-week notice isn't enough, I'm more than happy to extend it to ensure these people have the time they need to move. If only Ms. Murphy here had thought to come to me first, I'm sure we could have easily worked something out."

The bastard! He even had the reporter smiling at him now.

"But I—"

"Thanks for your time," the reporter said, waving at her cameraman that it was time to leave.

Which left her face-to-face with Cody, standing there, shoulders heaving as she tried to breathe, as she tried to see how he'd ended up with the upper hand.

"You're brave, I'll give you that," he said, his arms moving up to cross again in front of his body.

Lexi jutted her chin and stared up at him. "Brave? I'm not trying to be brave, Cody. I'm trying to fight for something I believe in, for something that's affecting me personally."

His frown made her laugh.

"Oh my god, you actually think this is about you, don't you? You think that I'm doing this as some pathetic way to get back at you?"

He grunted. "The thought had crossed my mind."

She stepped closer, staring up at him, eyes not wavering from his even as they watered from the cold. "You can put an end to this, Cody. You can be the good guy and put a pin on this entire deal."

"You really think it's as simple as that? That some other developer wouldn't jump straight in and buy it the second I pulled out?" He shook his head. "Don't be naïve, Lexi. This is a huge deal, and believe it or not, I'm not trying to be an asshole. The residents need longer, then you have my word, they can have another four weeks to find alternative arrangements, but you're better dealing with me than anyone else."

She folded her own arms and stared back at him. "Better the devil you know, huh?"

"Yeah, something like that," Cody said, before turning on his heel and storming back to the car.

"Honey, it's so cold out here, I think I'll go back in." Lexi turned and saw one of the nurses calling out to her, the rest of the workers gathering with her, and she crossed over to give the woman a big hug.

"Thanks for coming out to support us."

"You're fighting for your mom, we're fighting for our jobs. We're in this together, right?"

Lexi said goodbye and looked around at the small group slowly going their own ways, everyone cold and tired of being out in the open. Her shoulders slumped as she gathered her sign and her bag, the cold suddenly biting at her skin and making her want to scurry back indoors too. She walked around the back of the building and dumped her placard in the trash, staring at it before turning around and heading back to the front entrance.

She'd tried, but who the hell had she been kidding thinking she could shame or bully Cody into changing his mind? Stupid, that's what she'd been, and nothing she did was ever going to make a difference. Not a television interview, not a petition, nothing.

Lexi walked in the door, smiled at the receptionist and then trudged her way over to the elevator. She stopped and waited, staring up at the ceiling and biting down hard on her lower lip to stop the emotions threatening to spill over. The elevator *dinged* and the door opened, and Lexi stepped in, waiting for the doors to close and swallow her in solitude. As the doors slowly closed and shut her away from everyone else, Lexi let out a gasp, her body shuddering with a sob as she sunk to the floor. She dropped her bag, clamped her hand over her mouth as a noise so deep and guttural escaped from her it sounded more animal than human. Tears flooded her cheeks as her lungs fought for air.

Ding.

She scrambled to her feet, frantically wiping her eyes and clearing her throat just as the doors sprung open and a male nurse in scrubs stepped in.

"You okay?" he asked, eyebrows drawn in concern as he held the elevator door for her.

Lexi nodded and hurried out, not wanting pity or concern or anything even vaguely resembling sadness from anyone else. And just like she'd done all her life, she held her head high, refusing to let anyone see the cracks, refusing to give in for even a second to the bricks tumbling all around her trying to break down her carefully constructed wall.

She stopped outside the door to her mom's room, knocking before letting herself in. She waited a beat and then turned the handle, the familiar smell of her mom's perfume filling her nostrils. She glanced at the bed and saw her there, the television on low as she watched something mindless to fill the time, but at least it smelled good, better than the hospital smell of the rest of the place. She always made sure, no matter how tight money was, that her mom had her perfume to spray around the room and on herself.

"Hi, Mom," she said, spraying a touch of the fragrance to her own skin as she passed, before sinking down into the chair, reaching for her mom's hand. She wanted to lie with her, to have her hair stroked as if she were still a little girl, words of comfort whispered that always seemed to make everything better.

"Connie, why did you take so long to come see me?"

Lexi's tears made a fast return. "It's me, Mom. It's Lexi." Her mom often thought she was her sister, not realizing that she'd died many years earlier.

Her mother's face twisted into confusion and Lexi shuffled forward to cradle her, holding her mom and kissing the top of her head. All she craved was someone to look after her, but she was the mom now, and nothing was ever going to be the same, ever again.

"Oh, Lexi!" she smiled and hugged her, her eyes bright as if her old mom had suddenly appeared again.

"Hey, Mom." Sometimes she was normal, other times she was so forgetful and away with the faeries.

"How's your day been, darling?"

She loved moments like this, when she could forget the reality of her mom's disease.

"Interesting," she replied. "It's been interesting. Cody Ford is back. Do you remember him?

Usually her mom was great with things far in the past; it was the more present things she struggled with.

"The one who broke your heart," her mom said. "I should have given you the letter, shouldn't I?"

Lexi stared back at her. "What letter, Mom? Did Cody send me a letter?"

She must be confused. Maybe it was a letter from someone else.

"You were so upset I didn't think I should give it to you."

Lexi's hands started to shake, but she knew she couldn't push her mom too hard. "Do you still have it?"

Her mom smiled. "Of course. I have it with all those photos, in that box in my bedroom. I'll go get them for you, dear."

"No," she said quickly, knowing her mom was about

to get upset when she remembered all over again that her house was gone. "It's fine. I don't need to see it. Let's just sit and watch television together for a bit."

Her mom settled then, but Lexi didn't. Because all she could think about was this letter, and whether it was imaginary or real.

Chapter 12

"SHE kind of has a point," Mia said, her elbows on the counter as she leaned forward.

Cody opened the fridge and took out two beers, holding them out. Mia shook her head, so he put them both back in and returned with two Coca-Colas instead. She smiled and held out her hand.

"It's way too early in the day to be drinking."

Cody was going to sit down beside his sister, but instead he paced over to the window and stared out at the view, taking in the sprawling land that stretched farther than the eye could see. It was beautiful in a way that scared him, that made him wonder what it would be like to stare at it each and every day. But it also made him want to scurry straight back to the safety of his apartment and his office, where there were no distractions, no memories, and, more importantly, no emotions.

"If you'd had the day I just had, you'd be wanting to drink too," he said, turning around and watching Mia.

"Only I still wouldn't because I have to run around after little people and get up way too early in the morning."

He nodded. "Fair point."

"Talking about points, you completely ignored what I said before." Mia smiled, and he knew he'd never get away without answering her questions. *Or interrogations more like it.* "Lexi isn't the enemy here, she's just fighting for what she believes in."

"Yeah, well, so am I."

"You're like a dog with his hackles up," she snapped. "What is it about successful men acting like women shouldn't have a voice? She has *every* right to be as damn vocal as she wants to be."

Cody walked slowly over to her, put down his drink, and held up his hands. "Mom didn't bring just *you* up to be a feminist, Mia. She raised us all the same way, and this has nothing to do with Lexi being a woman."

Mia blew out a breath that raised the stray hair on her forehead. "You're sure?"

"Well, it has something to do with her being a woman," he muttered, picking at the label on his bottle. "She's beautiful and smart and sexy as hell, and until this all blew up, I . . ." His voice trailed off. "Nothing."

"It's not nothing. Spit it out," she said, her frown turning into a subtle smile. "You like her, don't you? Hell, you *really* like her! I can see it clear as day now."

Cody wasn't going to answer. If he gave Mia even so much as a hint of how he was feeling, she'd be like a dog with a bone. He'd already said too much.

"Cody?" Mia asked. "Come on, what's wrong with guys sometimes? What's wrong with just saying how you—"

"Fine," he interrupted. "I like her. Hell, I wouldn't have slept with her if I didn't like her. And what are you doing back here visiting already? Don't you have your own ranch to look after?"

"You *slept* with her?" Mia slapped the counter and burst out laughing, totally ignoring everything else he'd said. "You've only been home, what, three days? How the hell have you had time to sleep with her in between arriving, falling out with her . . ." Mia's eyes grew wide. "Ahh, when you had dinner together. I thought you'd have dropped her at the door afterward."

"Tanner and Lauren took Harry to their place," Cody said simply. "We had a great night, old feelings flared up and, well, I don't need to tell you the rest, do I?"

"I thought you guys had had a big blowup at dinner," she said. "I thought no one in this family could keep a secret, but it seems Lauren can."

Cody grunted. "Yeah, we can trust the ones who marry in, just not our own blood."

"Whose blood?"

He looked up as Angelina walked in, looking like she was about to head into the office or go out for an expensive dinner. It was only late afternoon, and she was dressed in polished cotton slacks and a silk shirt with her hair perfectly falling over one shoulder. Cody suppressed a laugh—*they thought he was the one dressed inappropriately for ranch life*. The only giveaway she wasn't going anywhere were her bare feet.

"Wow, and just like that you make me feel like a worn-out mom," Mia said with a sigh.

"You could make more of an effort," Ange said, walking around to her sister and stroking her hair back, before twisting it up and making a bun with it. "See, doesn't she look beautiful now?"

Cody just shook his head. "No way am I wading into this discussion, but yeah, Mia, you always look beautiful. Even without someone doing your hair."

"Thank you," Mia mouthed, giving him a wink, at

the same time as Angelina scowled and gave him a death stare.

"I'm surprised to see you so relaxed," she said. "Given your name is being dragged through the mud. I thought you would have jumped on a plane back to New York by now."

"Don't tempt me," he muttered, putting down his soda and deciding it was definitely beer o'clock. Where was his brother when he needed him? Tanner would always be up for a beer.

There was a bang at the side door, and Cody looked up to see Lauren entering, a bottle of wine in hand and a warm smile on her face. "Hey!" she said as she walked in, dusting the snow from her shoulders.

Cody stepped around to reach for her coat, smiling down at her as she shrugged out of it. He draped it over the back of a chair and went back to the fridge.

"Tanner joining us soon?" he asked.

"No." She sighed. "Something about a colicky horse?"

Dammit. He took two beers from the fridge, deciding he'd go find Tanner and see if he could help. Why the hell hadn't he called up to tell him instead of dealing with it on his own? But he knew the answer to that. He was probably the last person he'd think to call for help on the ranch.

"I might head down to see him, in case I can help," Cody said, as all three women looked up at him. Mia and Angelina were sitting, Lauren was standing, but they all had the same expression on their faces. He suddenly had the feeling he was trapped, and nothing scared him more than three women giving him their full attention.

"I was just telling Cody that I can understand where Lexi's coming from," Mia said, her voice soft as if she was talking to her children and trying to convince them of something.

"You can?" Ange asked, sounding incredulous. "Well, I can't. I'm firmly on team Cody. Business is business, and we haven't got to where we are by listening to every sob story."

"Ange!" Mia scolded. "You sound like a heartless bitch."

Ange shrugged. "When it comes to work, I am." She looked at Cody. "We have to be, right?"

Cody's eyebrows shot up but he didn't answer, more terrified of the sweet, caring women in the room than his sharp-as-a-tack businesswoman sister.

"I agree with Mia," Lauren said. "I know I'm not family, and you don't have to listen to me, but you have history with Lexi, and she's important to this family."

"You *are* family, Lauren," Cody said. "Don't you ever feel like you're not part of this family, because you are."

He saw tears swim in Lauren's eyes then, and he was surprised when she came closer to him and gave him a hug. He hugged her back, awkwardly to the side with one arm, and when she looked up at him he could see exactly why Tanner had fallen so hard. She was one of the sweetest women he'd ever met.

"Tanner and I had a lot of history before we found our way back to each other," she whispered.

"I think we're way past the point of no return," he replied. "But thanks."

He and Lexi were nothing like Tanner and Lauren. Were they?

"Cody, if this was our mom? If she were still here? You'd fight tooth and nail to protect her. I know you would."

He let go of Lauren as she slid away, and his eyes found Mia's. "No," he ground out. "You do not bring our mom into this."

"Why not? How is our mom any different than Lexi's? She's just trying to look after her, only she doesn't have the money for a private nurse and jets at her disposal to fly her around the country to see every available specialist!"

"Enough, Mia," Angelina interrupted.

"Yeah, enough," Cody said, turning to head for the door. "You don't bring Mom into this, okay? That was different and you know it."

"So it's not okay for Lexi to fight for her mom in her hometown?" Mia called after him. "This was your home too, Cody."

"Mia!" Angelina scolded, her high-pitched tone cutting through the air.

Cody spun around, but Mia was standing now, not about to be stopped. He'd never seen her so angry, so vivid about anything.

"You act like you're not even from here anymore, but you can't just forget what's in your blood, Cody. You're as much a part of River Ranch as I am. You just don't like to admit it sometimes."

Cody didn't know what to say. He stared, his mouth opening as he saw the pain in his little sister's face, the anguish as she finally, after all these years, spoke the truth. Why had she never said anything before? Why had they always just pretended everything was fine when it wasn't?

"I know that," he finally said, rooted to the spot even though he knew he should go to her. "I know that." Softer this time, as he took a big breath and stared back at her. "It's just, well, it's complicated. I'm sorry."

"It's a bit late for sorry," Mia said, shaking her head and turning away from him.

"Funny, that's exactly what I said."

Cody turned to see Lexi standing in the doorway, her hands wrapped around her body as she stared at him.

He fought the urge to groan and instead squared his shoulders and faced her straight on. "How long have you been standing there?" he asked.

The women behind him were silent, and even though he could feel them there, the way Lexi was staring at him made it feel like they were the only two people in the room.

She shook her head, her gaze sad as she looked into his eyes then turned away. "Long enough."

Lexi stared at Cody, wondering how he could be the same person she'd gone head-to-head with only hours earlier. Gone were the expensive threads, replaced with worn jeans and a plaid shirt that looked like it had been a favorite of his for years. She could almost recall the way it would smell, the way it would *feel*, just by looking at it.

"About before," he started, and she waited, thinking he was going to apologize but realizing he was just uncomfortable and didn't know what to say.

"When you belittled me on live television?" she asked, glancing behind him and seeing that both his sisters and Lauren were all watching her. Did they think the same of her? That she shouldn't be standing up for what she believed in? She wished she'd heard more of the conversation, wished she knew where she stood with the family.

But no one said a thing, so she didn't find out.

"Are you here for the rest of the afternoon?" Cody finally asked.

"Yes," she said, clearing her throat. "Unless you'd prefer me to leave?"

Cody opened his mouth, but it was Mia who leapt toward her, sheltering her in a big hug and speaking before anyone else could.

"Don't you ever say that," Mia said, holding her tight. "You have been the brightest of lights when none of us knew what to do or how to even go about dealing with Dad. Some members of this family run away when the going gets tough, so we need you more than ever, Lexi. You will always be welcome in this house, no matter what."

Lexi hugged her back, trying to disconnect from Mia's words so she didn't start crying. She wasn't allowed to crack, her moment earlier today was the only break in her resolve that she was giving herself.

"Thanks," she managed to mumble against Mia. Lexi didn't look at the others to see their responses; Mia's words were enough to tell her to keep going. Besides, she doubted Walter would let her go anyway, but she was still dreading what he was going to say about her having a temporary nurse assist him while she was gone that morning.

"Go after her," she heard Mia order.

Lexi shook her head as she walked. Cody had to be told by his little sister to go after a woman he was hurting. The irony wasn't lost on her—if only Mia had been older when she'd been dating Cody.

She was about to touch the handle on Walter's door when a hand settled over her shoulder instead. A heavy, big, masculine hand. A touch she'd have recognized anywhere. But instead of leaning into it, sighing into the warmth of another human connecting with her, she shrugged it away as she turned.

"Lexi, we need to talk."

She laughed. She couldn't help it, the laughter just bubbled out of her, and if she hadn't laughed she probably would have just burst out crying—and she sure as hell wasn't going to let that happen.

"Now you want to talk?" She folded her arms tightly across her chest. "Because Mia told you to come after me?"

Cody's face changed. The strong, confident mask slipped away, replaced with a look she hadn't seen for a long time. "No, because I care about you and I don't like the way this has played out between us."

"I don't want to go back into the past, Cody. I've held on to all that for so many years, and it was stupid and immature." She leaned back against the wall, wishing she had more space so she could move farther away from him. "We've already said all that though. It's over as far as I'm concerned."

"The way we both behaved today, like enemies, it—"

"We *are* enemies, Cody. We're on opposite sides of a very big void with very different opinions, so if that doesn't make us enemies, or adversaries at least, then I'm not sure what would."

"I never meant to hurt you, Lexi. Not back then and certainly not now."

"Well, you did, both times." She paused. "Cody, if you'd known this was going to affect me, or anyone else you knew personally, would you still have done it?"

He didn't say anything for a moment, but then he let out an audible breath and nodded, his mouth turned down.

"I'm not going to lie to you, Lexi. The answer is yes; I still would have done it. Because I only look at figures and returns, at whether something is a good deal or not. It's never personal and it's how I've grown my wealth and accelerated the growth of my company."

"Yeah, it's just business. You've told me that already."

She went to turn again, wanting to get away from him, needing to put some space between them before she flew off the handle and started screaming at him or launched at him like a wild cat wanting to claw at his skin. She'd never hated anyone in her life as much as she hated him right now.

"This is my mom, Cody. My *mom*," she finally said, grinding out the words. "You may not have fought for *your* mom, but I refuse to turn my back on mine."

"What did you say?" Cody's body language changed, his relaxed demeanor replaced by something more visceral as his eyes widened.

"You heard me. You ran away from yours, but I'll never turn my back on mine."

"Don't you dare," he said, his hand viciously running through his hair. "You don't, just don't talk about my mother."

"I always thought you were running from me, even though I couldn't figure out why. I just couldn't work out what the hell I'd done after that summer we'd had together, but then when I was listening to Mia, and something Angelina said the other night, it all clicked into place." Cody's hands were fisted now, his anger palpable, but she wasn't about to stop. Now that she'd started, the emotion was literally pulsing from her. "I won't turn my back, Cody."

"You don't get to talk about my mom," he said. "You know nothing about what I went through, what it was like for me seeing her wither away, knowing she was going to die and not wanting that to be my memory of her." Cody's jaw tightened; she could see the tick of him grinding it before he spoke again. "So yeah, I left, because it was the only way I could deal with that, and I've had to live the rest of my life knowing that when the going got tough, I disappeared. I turned my back on everyone I loved, and that includes you. Don't think it didn't hurt me, because it did. It damn well hurt but I was trying to save myself even worse heartache down the line."

She stared at him, almost pitying him now that he was finally being honest with her. But it hurt too, because he'd gone from the strongest man she'd ever known to one who'd been too scared to stay for fear of being hurt.

"I was there, you know," Lexi said, keeping her voice low, not wanting Walter to hear. "You left me like I meant nothing to you, but I was still there. I would have done anything for you, you could have talked to me, we could have figured it out together."

"You were where? Here?" he asked, looking confused.

"I was *there*," she ground out. "At the service for your mom when she passed."

"You were at the service?" he asked, not hiding the surprise in his voice.

"Your mom was kind to me, she always made me feel welcome, and whenever I saw her, after you left, I half expected her to cross the road or turn away so she didn't have to speak to me. But she never did." Lexi sucked back a breath. "She cared about me, she cared about what I was doing, and the last time I saw her alive, she gave me a hug and apologized for the way you'd just dismissed me, as if I was nothing more than a toy that you'd become sick of playing with. I think maybe I saw more of her in that last year of her life than you did."

She watched as Cody grit his teeth together, as he wrestled with what she told him. She may as well have stuck a knife into his side, she knew how painful the words were, but she wasn't about to stop, not now. If he wanted the truth, well, he was going to get it— every dirty, raw, unforgettable inch of it.

"I sat at the back of the church and grieved for her, Cody. I sat there and watched you walk past, carrying her coffin, and I felt your pain."

He blinked, nodding slowly. "I didn't know."

They stared at each other, before Lexi took a deep breath. "I have to go." And with that she opened the door and disappeared into Walter's study, not about to waste another breath on Cody goddamn Ford.

What the hell?

Lexi stared for half a second, paralyzed as she stared at the body on the floor. And then her training took over and she didn't hesitate.

"Cody!" she yelled. "Help!"

Chapter 13

LEXI's panicked call cut through the air like a hot knife through butter. One second Cody was walking down the hall, pissed as hell and about to storm back into the kitchen and give his sister a piece of his mind, and the next he was sprinting back down the hall as fast as his legs had ever carried him before.

Cody shoulder slammed the door at the same time as he turned the handle, about to ask why she was yelling like someone had been murdered when he saw his father on the ground and Lexi bent over him.

"Oxygen!" she ordered, and he didn't ask why or what, he just did as he was told.

Lexi put the mask over Walter's face, and breathed a guttural sigh of relief as she saw condensation forming on the mask and then a movement.

"What the hell happened?" Cody muttered.

She glanced up at him, her eyes filled with concern. "I don't know. I just found him like this."

"Has it happened before?"

She nodded and went back to checking him over. "Yeah, it has. I do my best to get him to rest, but the medication—not to mention his cancer—means that he needs to sleep more."

"And the old bastard won't stop working, am I right?"

Before she answered, his dad made a groaning sound and Cody reached out to touch Lexi, his hand on her arm as her big, beautiful brown eyes met his.

"Is it safe to lift him?" he asked.

She looked at his hand before answering, and just like that he felt something change between them. Everything else faded away as he felt her warm skin beneath his hand, her other hand on his father. If Lexi hadn't been there, hadn't found his dad and known what to do, it could have ended up being the worst Christmas any of them had ever had.

"Yes, let's get him to the sofa," she said quietly. "We need to work out if he fainted, had a medical event, or . . ."

Walter raised a shaking hand, his eyes open now as he attempted to take the mask off his face. Cody quickly helped him, lifting it below his dad's chin so he could speak.

"Fall," he croaked. "I was trying to hear what you two were arguing about and I slipped and fell."

Cody silently put the mask back over his father's face and then bent to lift him, surprised at how light he was. It wouldn't have been a year ago that it would have taken effort to lift Walter's big frame—but now it was easy.

"Cody, could you check in with Tanner and make sure Harry's okay?" Lexi asked. "I don't want to leave your dad, so I might need Tanner to keep minding him a little bit more. I'm so sorry."

"It's fine, you stay here," he said. "Are you even supposed to work nights?"

She smiled, her hand on Walter's shoulder as she looked down at him. "I'll sleep the night on the floor to make sure my favorite patient's okay, whether I'm supposed to be or not."

Cody watched her, amazed at her kindness. He knew his dad was paying her well, but he could see it ran deeper than that. Lexi was something special, and he would have volunteered to look after Harry all day if it meant she could look after his father.

"I'll go down and check on the little guy myself," he said. "But I can tell you that earlier today he fell in love with a pony, and I'll bet he hasn't let her out of his sight."

"Really? He spent the day with a pony?" Her smile put a small crack in his hardened heart.

"Yeah, he did."

"Thanks, Cody. And please thank Tanner too. This will go down as one of his favorite days, I just know it."

Cody pulled his phone from his pocket to call Tanner, quietly leaving the room so Lexi could get to work. There was no signal. He went to the front door and opened it, surprised to see a heavy blanket of snow had started to cover the ground again. He shut the door and jogged into the kitchen, surprising Mia, Lauren, and Angelina.

"Dad had a fall," he said. "Lexi's looking after him and he's fine but—"

Mia and Angelina were gone before he could even finish his sentence. He looked up at Lauren, who had a glass of wine half raised to her lips.

"I see it wasn't too early for drinking after all," he muttered.

"What should I do?" Lauren asked.

He felt for her, no doubt feeling like she was on the

fringe of the family in a crisis. "Try to get hold of Tanner for me. I can't get a connection, but if he's got the two-way radio on you should be able to get him."

"Where are you going?" she asked.

"Down to find him. I'll take a radio so you can call me if you need to." He grabbed the coat he'd left over the back of a chair along with his scarf and put it on. "Lexi needs to focus on Dad, and Tanner still has Harry. If she realizes the snow is closing in, she'll start worrying about him, and I want her focused on the old man."

Lauren nodded, touching his arm as she passed. "It'll be fine, Cody. She's a great nurse and your dad's a strong old bastard."

He gave her a kiss on the cheek, squeezing her arm in return, before disappearing out into the cold to find his brother. He knew he had the easy job—he got to leave the house and keep busy doing something else—but what else could he do for his father than what he'd already done?

Lexi's heart was finally slowing to its normal speed as she watched Walter take a sip of water. Even though his hand was shaking, she could see the normal color coming back into his cheeks. She knew it could have ended badly, that if she hadn't been close, if she hadn't walked into the room at that exact moment, that she could be looking into the eyes of two very heartbroken women right now. Lexi took a deep breath.

"Something stronger would help," he said, avoiding eye contact with her as he looked at his daughters.

"Absolutely not," Mia said, shuffling closer to him on the sofa. A cry echoed out from upstairs, the noises from the house filtering through the open door, and she saw Mia torn between staying with her dad and going to her children.

"I can go to them if you want to stay?" Lexi asked, knowing how it felt to be pulled between a child and something else that demanded attention.

"No, it's fine, you're the one I'd rather have with him," Mia said as she rose. "They've both had a long afternoon nap, they'll want cuddles with Mama when they wake up, and I need to get going soon anyway. Sam will be wondering where I am."

Lexi was starting to panic about her own child. Harry had been gone for hours now, and although she trusted Tanner with him, a quick glance outside at the darkening sky showed the snow starting to fall heavily.

"You'll stay with him?" Mia asked. "Is that too much to ask or—"

"Of course I'll stay," Lexi said without missing a beat. "You can count on me, Mia. I promise."

Mia nodded and gave her a warm hug, holding on tight before she left the room. Lexi turned all her attention to her patient then, deciding to act as normal rather than talk about what had happened. His own daughters had already scolded him enough.

"It looks like we're going to have a white Christmas after all," she said, smiling at Walter as she took his temperature again, pleased to see it wasn't too bad. She decided to do his blood pressure as well, not wanting to miss anything in case they had to get him to a hospital. Although she knew it'd be almost impossible to convince him about that being a good idea.

Angelina gestured with her head, and Lexi knew the cue. She'd been nursing long enough to pick up signals from worried family members. She completed the blood pressure test and then rose, walking with her to the other side of the room.

"Should we call his oncologist?" Angelina asked.

"I've been thinking the same thing, and I'm happy to, but all his vitals are fine and I honestly think he did just fall and bang his head," she murmured back. "If I was concerned at all, I'd be insisting we take him to hospital, but I believe his version of events."

Angelina nodded, her brows drawn tightly together. "I might get the helicopter on standby just in case. We can't be too careful, right?"

"I've got cancer, I'm not deaf," Walter boomed, surprising Lexi with his outburst. "I'm sick and tired of being cooped up like a sick animal in this room, and it's Christmas. Has everyone forgotten that with all the worrying and arguing going on in this house?"

Lexi didn't say a word, but she noticed Angelina bow her head. "How much did you hear, exactly?"

Lexi felt like Walter's eyes were on her, and when she glanced up, she saw she wasn't wrong. He'd heard too much, and he was right, the house certainly didn't seem to hold any of the joys of Christmas.

"Enough to know that your mother would be furious to hear her children arguing like that. I want to see gifts piled under the tree and laughter and happiness," he said, pausing as he fought to catch his breath. "I want to see my family enjoying Christmas instead of bickering with each other and worrying about me."

Angelina muttered how sorry she was and sat down beside him, but when Lexi looked up again she realized Walter was still staring at her. She shifted her gaze and was about to turn to give his daughter some privacy with him, when he spoke again. To her directly this time.

"That includes you," he said.

Lexi cleared her throat, uncomfortable. "I'm not sure what you mean," she managed.

"You're part of this family, Lexi, and I want this argument between you and my son to be over with." He looked annoyed more than angry, and she waited for him to continue, not knowing how much he was aware of. "I saw the coverage on television today, I know what's going on between the two of you." Thank goodness that's all he knew. She couldn't stand the thought of him knowing anything else about their relationship. "And I damn well know that there's a lot *more* going on between you two."

Well, goddamn. The old man did know more, a whole lot more, than she expected.

"I'm sorry you had to see that, I usually try to keep a very clear line between my professional and personal life." She swallowed. "Cody and I, well, let's just say there have been some old feelings there that we've had to work through."

Walter waved a hand dismissively in the air. "I see you for hours every day, I like knowing about your life, I just don't want to feel this division in my home at Christmas."

"Would you rather I left?" she asked, the words almost killing her just saying them. "Because if you no longer feel comfortable with me here, I completely understand." *Please don't fire me, please don't fire me.* Her heart started to pound again.

"No, I want to tell my son to pull his head out of his ass, that's what I want."

Lexi stifled her surprise, chewing on the inside of her mouth as her heart almost instantly slowed, but Angelina's burst right out of her.

"Dad!"

"With all due respect, Walter, I think I've told him that already in pretty much those exact words."

"Well, tell him again. Maybe he needs to hear it a few times before it sticks."

They all had a chuckle, Angelina included, before Lexi excused herself to go and make him something to eat. He was right, though, it was Christmas, and whatever was going on between her and Cody, or Mia and Cody for that matter, it might be Walter's last, and he deserved to have a harmonious family.

"Dad, if I didn't know you better, I'd think you were enjoying all this," Angelina teased, and Lexi watched as she dropped her head to her father's shoulder.

"Shouldn't someone be getting on to Christmas dinner?" he asked, an eyebrow raised as he looked at his daughter. "Is *anyone* in charge of the turkey?"

"I have *no* idea why you're looking at me," Angelina said with a laugh. "I don't even cook my own dinner, let alone cater for everyone at Christmas!"

Lexi left them to banter, imagining what it would be like to have siblings, and a father to laugh with and confide in. It had been just her and her mom for so long, until Harry came along, and it wasn't until she'd had a son of her own that she'd started to imagine how life could have been.

"Lexi?" Walter called out.

He wasn't wearing his oxygen mask now, and his cheeks were pink again, his eyes bright as he spoke to her.

"Yes?"

"Take the night off. You're only a short walk away if I need you, and I want you to enjoy that gorgeous boy of yours. Do you hear me?"

She nodded. "Thank you, Walter, but—"

"No buts," he said, and suddenly she didn't see a sick old man but glimpsed the strong, commanding Ford patriarch. "You soak up as much time with your boy as you can, and then you make sure you join us for Christmas dinner. Angelina can stay with me."

Lexi smiled; she couldn't help it. "Thank you," she said. "I'd love that, but I promised Mia that I'd stay with you."

He shook his head. "I don't want you here, Lexi, and I'm the one giving orders. It's enough that you're close by, and Cody can check in on me."

She watched his face, saw that it was his final decision, and smiled again. "Thanks, Walter." Lexi didn't want to let Mia down, but Walter was her boss, and she needed to accept whatever his decision might be on any given day.

Lexi did her final check and tucked Walter in with a blanket, resisting the urge to kiss the top of his head. He was almost a father figure to her now. She might hate what Cody was doing to her, to their community, but it wasn't going to stop her from enjoying Christmas in the company of a family who'd embraced her over the past few months as if she were one of their own.

"What are you still doing down here?" Cody shook off the snow from his jacket when he found his brother in the barn. "And where's Harry?"

"Here!" The little boy's excited call came from a pile of horse rugs on the ground, and he chuckled as a sandy brown head emerged.

"At least you've kept him warm," he said to his brother, grinning to Harry on the way past as he moved toward Tanner and the horse he was standing with.

"Good of you to come help me," Tanner replied.

"Hey, there's a worried mama up there at the house who hasn't seen her boy all day," Cody said. "Please tell me you've fed him."

"Do chips and soda count?"

Cody turned to find Harry standing beside him. His hair was sticking up, there was horsehair all over him, and he was filthy. The kid looked as happy as could be.

"Your mom's gonna kill us," Cody said, reaching out and unsuccessfully trying to smooth his hair down. "You look like you've been pulled through a haystack."

The boy giggled. "I kinda have."

"So what's going on here? Lauren said colic?" Cody asked.

"Maybe. I don't know," Tanner answered. "Could easily be a stomach ulcer, but colic seems most likely."

"You called a vet?"

He nodded. "Hope King's on her way over. Horses aren't her specialty, but she'll be able to give a diagnosis and she has meds to help if we need it."

The horse looked strained around the eyes, veins bulging where usually they wouldn't be noticeable, his coat streaked with sweat despite the cold.

"I don't think it's anything to worry about, but Dad took a fall before. Lexi had to give him oxygen but he seems alright."

Tanner stared back at him, his mouth falling open. "He's okay? I mean, I could leave . . ." His brother stared at the horse and then toward the direction of the house.

"Tanner, he's fine. If he wasn't I'd be sending you straight up there." Cody touched his shoulder. "Trust me."

"Okay, but tell Lauren that if anything changes, if he's not well, hell, *anything*, she's to come and get me."

Cody nodded. "I will. I'm going to take Harry back up to the house, then I'll come and stay with you."

"You don't need to come back, I'm used to going it alone."

His words packed a punch but one glance at Tanner's face, tense as he studied the horse, proved that he'd said it without thinking instead of trying to insult him.

"You know, I'd actually like to come back."

That got Tanner's attention. He looked up. "Yeah?"

"Yeah," Cody replied, surprised with how he was feeling. It was the first time he'd actually wanted to roll his sleeves up and get dirty. Usually he was battling hourly feelings of wanting to leave, but despite everything, this time he almost wanted to stay.

"I'll get Harry back and see you soon. Come on, kid," he said.

"Good work today, Harry. See you tomorrow," Tanner called out.

"Thanks, Tanner!" Harry called back.

Harry was grinning from ear to ear, and Cody slung an arm over his shoulders as they headed for the barn door.

"You had a good day today?" he asked.

"Yeah, it's been the best."

"Good." He peeled off his heavy coat and scarf, and wrapped the scarf tight around Harry's neck and then slid the coat on him, laughing at how enormous it looked.

"What are you going to wear?" Harry asked, giggling as he held his arms out and his hands were invisible beneath all the fabric.

"All I care about is keeping you warm and dry," he said. "I've upset your mom a lot lately, but not looking after her kid is not going to be one of the things she hates me for."

"My mom doesn't hate you," Harry said, his eyes so big and brown that he felt like he was looking straight into Lexi's.

"Why do you say that?"

"My mom told me that you were the best part of high school," he said, chatting away with no idea what secrets he was giving away. "She said she was only angry when she told me you were a jerk the other day."

"Well, that's good to hear," Cody said softly, watching Harry's face, wondering when Lexi had told him that. "I was pretty sure I was on the bad list."

"I'd know if she hated you, Cody. My mom doesn't hate anyone."

Cody scooped him up so he didn't slip, carrying him to the quad bike and putting him on the front. *Yeah, buddy, she does hate someone, and that someone is me.* And he damn well deserved to be that someone.

He got on behind Harry, the cold stinging his skin and making his back feel like it was going to ice over, wrapped his arms around the boy, and carefully made their way back through the snow to the house.

When they got back, he saw a silhouette in the window, the light from the house seeping out into the dark, and he raised one hand in a wave to Lexi. Cody leaned forward and spoke into Harry's ear so he could hear him.

"Give your mom a wave," he said, and the kid looked up and waved like crazy at his mom.

When they got to the house, Cody parked the quad under shelter and lifted Harry down, carrying him so he didn't trip over the enormous jacket and only stripping him out of it once the door was open so he could bundle him inside.

"Cody, you're soaked through!" Lexi exclaimed, going from hugging her son to fluttering her hands over his back.

"He's fine and so am I," Cody said, giving Harry a squeeze on the shoulder before he stripped off his shirt and kicked off his boots. "Nothing that a hot shower won't fix, isn't that right, little man?"

She was right, every part of him was sopping wet, but he didn't care. All that mattered was the little kid smiling up at him, unfazed by the weather and happy about the day he'd had.

Cody watched Lexi as he walked past, seeing the questions in her gaze, feeling the pain he'd caused her, that he was still causing her. He was just happy he'd brought Harry back to her so she didn't have to worry. He found his phone in the kitchen where he'd left it and headed upstairs, seeing that he had one bar of coverage now that he was higher. The hot shower was going to have to wait. He needed to use the phone while he could, in case he lost the signal again.

He closed his door and dialed, sitting down at the desk in his room and staring out at the falling snow, the outdoor lights illuminating the flakes.

"Cody Ford?" the voice on the other end boomed. "Aren't you supposed to be on vacation?"

He stifled a growl at the laughter that came with that question. Everyone in his life seemed to find it a joke that he was taking time off work.

"Look," Cody said, not about to make small talk. "I know it's Christmas, but we need to talk."

"Sure. What's the problem?"

"The Bright Lights deal."

A sense of calm came over him as he leaned back in his chair.

My mom doesn't hate anyone. He kept hearing the little boy say those words; they'd echoed in his head the entire ride back.

Well, he might be a lot of things, but being the only person that Lexi hated wasn't going to be one of them.

Chapter 14

LEXI wrapped a blanket around Harry and snuggled up beside him on the sofa. They'd had dinner together and he'd barely paused to draw a breath, and now as they watched television and sipped hot chocolate, she wondered if he'd ever stop.

"You know we're not going to live here forever, right?" she asked, hating to be a downer but wanting to make sure he didn't think this was their permanent abode.

"I know. Just while you look after Mr. Ford." Harry sounded so dejected all of a sudden that she wished she'd just kept her mouth shut.

"We've got months more here though, so there's plenty more fun to be had," she said, trying to sound upbeat. "So tell me all about the pony again. Did you *really* get to brush her and then ride her?"

"Yes!" Harry's excited little squeak of a voice made her laugh, and she sat with him, stroking his hair and kissing his forehead, his body tucked up beside hers, until his words started to slow and his breath became louder. She stared down at him, wishing he'd stay like that forever—little and warm and snuggly. And that they could stay tucked away from the world drinking hot chocolate while snow fell outside forever too. Except that hot chocolate made her think about Cody, and the way he'd been talking and laughing with her son that first night he'd returned home. She forced the thoughts away, refusing to let her mind wander.

When she was certain Harry wouldn't wake up, Lexi stretched her legs out and bent to pick him up, wondering just how long she'd still be able to lift him. She carried him up the stairs and placed him in his bed, tucking the covers up to his chin and bending to drop one final kiss to his head.

"Goodnight, little man," she murmured. "Sweet dreams."

She went downstairs and flicked through channels until she found *The Bachelor*, tidying up the living room and then the kitchen as she listened to it. She was just wiping down the bench when her phone rang. She looked at the number on her screen, sensing it was familiar but not sure who it was. She thought about not answering then changed her mind.

"Hello?"

"Lex! It's Jessica, Jessica Chapman from school."

Lexi laughed and smiled into the phone. "Jessie Chapman. It's been so long you thought you had to say your last name?"

They both laughed then and Lexi opened the fridge and took out a bottle of wine, pouring herself a half glass and curling up into the sofa, knees tucked up as she balanced the phone between her shoulder and ear. She muted the TV.

"It's been a long time. When did we last talk?" she asked.

"Two years at least," Jessica said. "I'm so sorry, I haven't been home in forever but when I saw you on television today, well, my mom did actually, I knew I needed to get in touch. I'm so sorry to hear about your mom."

"Thanks, Jess. It's really nice to hear your voice again," Lexi admitted. "It's lonely here now that everyone has moved away."

"Well, I might be back sooner than I thought," Jessica said. "I'm now a divorcée with two kids, and after splitting everything down the middle, well, let's just say I'm not left with a lot."

Lexi sighed. "I'm so sorry. When we all got married, I couldn't have imagined any of us not having our happy ever after."

Jessica's laugh was gravelly, filled with emotion. "Yeah, me too. Maybe we all jumped into marriage too soon."

"Or maybe the men we married were just assholes."

"God, I wish it wasn't snowing. I'd jump straight in the car and come see you. I think this conversation would be better over wine."

"I'm actually having wine!" Lexi laughed. "It's so good to hear from you."

"So I heard through the grapevine, which is actually my mother's gossip group, that you're working for the Fords? How's that going?"

She groaned. "You know what, it was going great before Cody showed up for Christmas."

"Yeah, well, that showdown outside the retirement home didn't exactly look pleasant."

"It wasn't. And the worst thing is there's nothing I can do about it other than try to fight him," she paused. "Ugh, I don't know. It's not even worth talking about."

"You still love him, don't you?" Jessica asked. "I mean, it's none of my business, but what you guys had back then, there's no way you just stop loving someone, even after all these years."

There was a knock at her door and she frowned. Who would be knocking? *Shit. Had something happened to Walter?* Why hadn't someone tried calling her?

"Hold on a sec," she said, interrupting Jess and leaping up. She swung the door open and found Cody standing there.

"Is everything okay?" she asked. "Does Walter need me?"

Cody shook his head. "No, the old man's fine."

He stared at her, his eyes intense, the desire in his gaze more than evident. A shiver ran through her, and she stepped back to let him in, not about to let him freeze out there in the snow. She shut the door.

"Jess," Lexi said, putting the phone back up to her ear. "Do you mind if I give you a call back tomorrow? It looks like I have to go over and check on Walter."

They said goodbye, and she took a long, slow breath before turning around, feeling bad for lying to her friend to get her off the phone. Cody was sitting on the sofa, in almost the exact place she'd been sitting. She'd have thought he'd look less intimidating sitting instead of standing, but the way he was tracking her with his gaze would have been terrifying however he was positioned.

"Is everything okay?" she asked.

"Yes."

When he didn't offer more she wondered if he was as nervous as she was. But then *he* was the one who'd turned up unannounced.

"Can I get you a wine?" she asked, already in the tiny kitchen and rummaging for a glass. She took one out, and when she turned back around he was standing just a few feet from her.

"Lexi, we need to talk."

She poured the wine even though he hadn't answered then slid it across the small counter so she didn't have to move too close to him. Then she moved back out to the sofa and collected her own glass. She sat on the chair rather than the sofa, not wanting him to sit down beside her.

"About earlier," he started.

"I know, seeing your dad like that—"

"I'm not talking about my dad." His voice was deep and raspy.

"Oh." She hadn't been expecting that.

Cody sat down, the wine glass in his hand looking completely out of place for a man who usually held a beer bottle or a tumbler of whiskey.

"I know you might not believe me," he said, leaning forward, elbows on thighs as he stared into her eyes. She wished he wouldn't, because he was impossible to look away from when he did that. "But I'm sorry. I'm sorry for what I've put you through with this whole land development deal."

She listened, wanting to hate him so badly but finding it impossible to. It didn't seem that many years ago that she'd loved the man more than anything else in the world, and however angry she was with him, she could never actually hate him.

"Did you truly write me a letter?" she asked, suddenly needing to know. "All those years ago?"

"Yes," he said. "Of course I did! Why are you even asking me?"

She sighed. "I just . . ." Lexi breathed deeply. "You know what, it doesn't matter."

He watched her so intently and she lifted her gaze, deciding she needed to be brave.

"Cody, would you have truly gone ahead with this deal, if you'd known how badly it would have affected me?" she asked. "If you'd known my mom was there?"

"The truth is, if you'd called me out of the blue and pleaded with me not to go ahead, I wouldn't have listened. I'd have tried to placate you, but just like I always end up doing, I'd have passed you off to an assistant." He took a sip of wine. "It's not pretty, but it's the truth."

She bristled at the thought he wouldn't have listened to her, but they'd parted a long time ago, and she could only imagine how many girlfriends he'd had since.

"And now?"

He shifted his weight again, leaning forward. "And now I'm in a goddamn pickle, that's what I'm in."

She laughed then, just a giggle to start with that erupted into something a whole lot louder, and Cody was laughing along with her, his eyes bright when they both finally fell silent again.

"What are you going to do about this *pickle* then?" she asked, feeling more relaxed than she had in a long while.

"I'm working on it," he replied, his voice lower this time, and she could tell he meant it. "I'm trying to come up with a solution, but I wasn't lying when I said someone else would have jumped on this deal if I hadn't. If I pull out, then I'll only be delaying the inevitable for you, and it's bad business to hold it like it is long term. I can't put my company in financial jeopardy just because I'm empathetic to a situation."

Her ears pricked at the word *empathetic*. At least he was starting to show that he had a heart.

"Can I ask one more question?"

He smiled. "Sure."

"Was I right when I suggested that envelopes full of cash were the reason for the change in the land zoning?" she asked, hesitantly, hoping she hadn't slandered him in front of a reporter. "Or was that completely out of left field?"

He paused long enough that she knew she wasn't entirely wrong, only she wasn't sure if it was relief or anger she was feeling more.

"Look, I'm not corrupt, if that's what you're asking," he said. "Did I make a generous donation entirely *aboveboard* to the local sports center? Yes, absolutely I did. And I made sure the mayor was aware of it. But I also do that publically, so the information is available to everyone. So to answer your question, the money is clean and there are no secret envelopes."

"It's just business, right?" she muttered.

"Yeah, it is. But just because I care about my bottom line doesn't mean I don't feel like an asshole for what I'm doing to you. For what I'm doing to all those people."

She wasn't sure she believed him.

"I promise you that I'll try to make this right. I just need you to trust me."

Lexi stifled a sigh. It shouldn't have been a hard request, but part of her just didn't trust him.

"Is there anything else you want to ask me?" Cody looked like he was about to get up, about to push up to his feet and walk straight back out the door if she didn't keep him talking, and for some reason she didn't want him to go yet.

"Your dad told me that we needed to stop fighting," she said. "Apparently we're ruining Christmas."

He chuckled. "Yeah, he told me the same thing."

"I need to know if you ever really loved me, Cody," she asked, lifting her glass and draining the rest of the wine from it. When she looked up, his eyes were locked on hers again. "I know it was a long time ago, but I just want to know if it was for real."

He dropped to his knees then, so close as he took the glass from her hand and held on to her palms, staring into her eyes with such intensity she could hardly stand to return his gaze.

"Yes," he whispered. "I loved you with all my goddamn heart, Lexi, but when I left here, it was like I just blocked everything out. It was like I put my old life on pause and just started a new one. It's almost like I can't remember that part of my past, like I just left and erased part of my history."

"Mia said before, when I overheard—"

"I left everyone, Lexi; she was right and I've had to live with that feeling for the past decade," he said. "It wasn't you, Lex, it was never you. I just felt so powerless, such a complete fuck-up that I couldn't deal with everything, and it was easier to run and just start over."

She pulled one of her hands from his and touched his face, running her fingertips down his smooth cheek and hovering when she reached his jaw. Hours ago she'd hated him with all her heart, and now she was thawing all over again, falling into the web that was Cody Ford. Shivering with anticipation, she recalled the sight of him stripping his shirt off at the door only a few days earlier, unbuttoning and discarding it, and giving her an eyeful of his golden-brown, smooth skin and muscled arms and chest. They might be feuding right now, but there had been nothing at odds when they'd spent the night together earlier in the week, and her body seemed to remember it. Every wicked, hard, delicious inch of it.

"I hate you, Cody," she whispered. "I hate that you left me, I hate what you're doing here, I hate everything about *this*." She just didn't hate his body. Or the way her own body trembled with anticipation at what was to come.

He leaned in closer, his mouth inches from hers as he lifted a hand and stroked down her hair, making her want to moan, making her remember just how good it had been with him the other night.

His mouth hovered, waiting for her, but she didn't close the gap.

"Promise me," she whispered. "Promise me you'll do something to help all those people."

His gaze dropped to her mouth. "I promise."

"Well, what are you waiting for then?"

The words had barely come out of her mouth before Cody's lips collided with hers, and somehow she was back in the web of her former lover turned enemy. And kissing had never, ever felt so good.

Cody hadn't come over to kiss Lexi. Or maybe he had. Ever since he'd seen that fire in her eyes today he'd wanted to kiss the snarl off her face and see that beautiful smile again and see her eyes light up, wanted to tell her what a damn jerk he'd been. And now here he was, in her living room, holding the woman he should never have let go.

And he must really like her, because he'd never, ever adjusted his profit line for anyone.

Her lips moved softly against his, pliable and warm, but tentatively as if she wasn't sure. He didn't push her, let her set the pace as he ran his hands over her shoulders and down her back, not putting any pressure on her as he stroked her.

It was Lexi who moved closer, who reached for him and deepened their kiss, her tongue exploring now like it was their first kiss. He was still on his knees, lower than her, which gave her the power, and he had a feeling she liked it. Her fingers found the back of his head and suddenly she was pushing him forward, her legs parted as she tugged him forward. Cody loved the feel of her strong thighs on either side of him, and the little moan in her throat when he plucked at her bottom lip, teeth grazing her sensitive skin, made it almost impossible to control himself. He wanted to rip the buttons off her shirt until she was left wearing nothing, strip her down to her underwear and take her on the sofa.

"We can't," she murmured as he attempted to get rid of her shirt.

Cody ignored her, mouth slipping to her collarbone, tracing kisses across her skin.

"Cody, stop," she whispered.

He raised his head. "Give me one good reason why," he whispered, kissing her ear lobe before moving back to her lips.

She kissed him back, slowly, groaning when she finally pulled away. "Harry," she said, and with that one word, he backed off and slipped her shirt back up over her shoulder.

Harry. How had he managed to forget she had a little boy who could walk in on them at any moment?

"Upstairs?" he asked, hopeful.

Lexi just gave him a look that managed to convey *not a chance.* He groaned and reached for her, drawing her in and indulging in one last slow, lingering kiss.

"You promise I can trust you, to figure out a solution to this whole thing?" she whispered, her eyes so wide as she looked at him.

"Yeah, I promise," he said. "And it's not just because of the bad PR."

She smiled and tipped her face a little, staring down at him. "I never thought we'd be in this position again," she said. "Not like this. Never like this."

He grunted. "Me neither."

"Mommy?"

Cody leapt back, connecting with the coffee table in his haste before landing with a thump on the sofa. He ran a hand through his hair and adjusted the front of his jeans.

"Hey, little man," Lexi cooed, shrugging her top back on her shoulder and giving him a raised-brow look as she rose.

"Cody?" Harry mumbled.

"Hey, buddy," he said, clearing his throat and giving him a half wave.

"Were you kissing Mommy?"

"Kissing? Ahhh . . ." He looked to Lexi for support but she was just biting down on her lip, clearly trying not to laugh.

Honesty was the best policy, right? "Yeah, I was. Is that okay?"

Lexi did crack up laughing then, or more like she made a strange choking noise that made Harry look back at her.

"I told you she didn't hate you."

"Hate who?" Lexi asked.

"Cody. He thought you hated him, but you don't kiss people you hate, do you?"

Now it was Lexi looking uncomfortable.

"Come on, back up to bed with you," she said, giving Harry a little push and turning him around. "I'll be up in a minute."

Harry did as he was told, shuffling up the stairs, a soft toy trailing from his fingers and bumping on each step as he walked.

"You were talking to Harry about me?" she whispered.

"Hey, we had a lot of time to kill today," he replied.

"Goodnight, Cody," she said, shaking her head before stepping in and grabbing a fistful of his shirt. She tugged him forward and kissed him, hard, biting his lip as she finished with a satisfied smirk.

"What was that for?"

"For talking to my boy about us without checking with me first."

Now it was him taking what he wanted, stepping into Lexi's space and wrapping his arms around her. He gave her a little push forward, his palm flat to her lower back as he nudged her body against his, his other hand cupping the back of her head, thumb against her jaw as he held her in place. Cody kissed her softly, over and over again, his lips plucking against hers until she sighed against his mouth.

"Merry Christmas, Lexi," he murmured. "It's been a long time since I've been happy to be home for the holidays."

She didn't say anything, but as he stepped back he watched as her hand rose to her mouth, colliding with her lips, touching where his mouth had been. He took his jacket, shrugged into it and blew her one last kiss before heading out into the freezing cold.

Something had changed. Not just between him and Lexi, but inside of him. Earlier that day he'd been so mad he'd almost left, had been so close to having the jet fuelled up and the pilot ready. But then he'd had a pull back to home, to the ranch, to trying to fix what he'd done instead of doing what he was best at doing—burying his head in the sand and doing a great impression of an ostrich.

He braced himself, head down as he jogged carefully through the snow back to the main house. When he got there, he looked back at the lights on in Lexi's apartment.

He'd always loved his life, thought nothing could be any better than what he already had. But after glimpsing what he'd missed out on by leaving Lexi behind, he wasn't so sure about that now.

"Son, is that you?"

He heard his father call out and went in to see him.

"I thought you'd be sound asleep by now," he said, finding his dad sitting at his desk, the lamps in the study putting out a warm glow and bathing the room in light.

"I want to talk to you about Lexi."

"You do realize that you've never asked to talk to me about a woman before, right?" He chuckled to himself as he crossed to pour two glasses of whiskey. He knew his father wasn't supposed to be drinking, but he also knew that without some indulgences, life would be pretty boring.

"She's special," Walter said, smiling gratefully as he took the drink before taking a long, slow sip. "Damn that's good."

"Couldn't agree with you more."

He sprawled on the leather club sofa and spread one arm across the back, thrumming his fingers along the smooth finish.

"Am I standing on your toes, Dad?" he asked, loving

the wide-eyed look his father gave him in response. Damn, it was a night for firsts. He'd never managed to rattle his dad before. "You want her for yourself? Is that it?"

"Oh for God's sake, Cody, I could be her father, heck, maybe even her grandfather!"

"I think *grandfather* is pushing it a little."

Walter sighed and swallowed the rest of the amber liquid in his glass. "If I wasn't on my deathbed, I'd give you a damn good run for your money, son. A girl like that doesn't come along often."

"Ahhh, so you *do* like her."

"I more than goddamn like her," he growled, and Cody raised a hand, accepting that their little banter was over. His dad was serious and he obviously had something to say.

"I want her looked after, if anything happens to me," Walter said. "There's no need to change my will. I trust you son, even if you are at odds with her."

"What exactly are we talking about here?" Cody asked, leaning forward, his attention more than piqued.

"I want her salary to continue for another six months after I pass away so she doesn't have to take just any job that comes along, and I want whatever care her mother needs paid for, starting as soon as possible."

Cody grimaced. "You're trying to buy my way out of my mess? You're the one who taught me that business is never personal."

"And it's not, because this has nothing to do with you." His father rose, glass in hand, and when Cody jumped up to help him all he received was a fast frown in response and he knew to let him be. He watched as his father poured himself another short whiskey.

"Lexi has given me dignity and allowed me to stay in my home," his father continued. "She's become a close friend to not only me, but to this entire family, and regardless of what you do, I want her mother taken care of. Am I understood?"

"Yes, you're understood," Cody replied, catching his father's eye when he turned. He could see a glint there, a steeliness he hadn't expected. "Dad, is this to do with Mom?" he asked, lowering his voice this time.

"Yes."

His dad sat down across from him, and Cody refused to look away even though he wanted to. He was a man now, not a boy, and he had to learn to confront his father's mortality head on instead of pretending it didn't exist.

"We had access to the best of everything for your Mom," Walter said in a low, shaky voice. "It didn't help her in the end, but money was never an object. I just want Lexi to see her mother well cared for, that's all."

Cody nodded. "And you want this generosity to start after Christmas?" he asked.

Walter sat silently for a moment, before nodding. "Yes. Start it in the New Year. The lawyer can draw it all up when he's back from vacation."

"Of course."

"I'm pleased you came home, son. Christmas wouldn't have been the same without you."

They sat in silence, until Cody finally rose, taking both glasses with him to the kitchen. When he returned, he bent and put a hand on his father's shoulder, standing there, the closest to a hug they'd shared in years. Walter grasped his wrist, holding him back, and

Cody felt the unfamiliar prickle of tears in his eyes as he imagined what life would be like without this incredible, strong, inspirational man in it.

It might even be Cody's last ever Christmas on the ranch, because without Walter here, maybe he'd never come home.

Chapter 15

"I can't believe it's Christmas Eve," Lexi said, one arm around her son as they stared at the little tree in the corner of the room.

"Can we have a real tree next year?" Harry asked.

She frowned, staring down at him. "Harry, what's wrong with this tree?"

He giggled. "It looks like you stole a baby tree from a mama tree, it's so tiny!"

Lexi laughed with him, pulling him firmly against her waist. "I guess it does look more like a large branch than a real tree. I promise next year we'll have a bigger one."

Trouble was, she had no idea where they'd even be living this time next year. She kissed the top of his head and turned him around. "Okay, milk and cookies for Santa, then it's off to bed with you."

Harry groaned, but she just kept pushing him forward.

"If you don't go to sleep you won't get any presents. Now come on."

She had so much to do still. The living room and kitchen to tidy up, presents to wrap and put under the tree, and she was dying to watch at least one cheesy Christmas movie on Hallmark before bed.

She played along with Harry and put the things out for Santa, then ushered him up the stairs. He was predictably hard to get into bed, but once his teeth were brushed and a story read, she turned the lamp off and snuggled up beside him.

"Is it still going to be snowing in the morning?" he whispered.

"Yes," she whispered back, stroking his hair. "It's going to be one of the coldest Christmases we've had in a long time I think."

"Can we go and give Cleo apples for Christmas?"

Her sweet boy was obsessed with the pony Tanner and Cody had introduced him to. "Of course."

He snuggled even tighter up beside her and it wasn't long before his breathing was heavy and she was able to slide out. She tiptoed into her room and reached into the back of the wardrobe to retrieve his gifts, smiling down at the toy tractor and farm she'd bought him, as well as the latest Nerf gun with glow-in-the-dark bullets. She went downstairs, gave the kitchen a quick wipe down, and then settled in to watch television while she wrapped her presents. Lexi glanced at the empty spot beside her, feeling the familiar numbness of being alone. When Harry was awake, she never felt it, but when he was in bed and everything was silent, she was painfully aware of just how alone she was.

When her short-lived marriage had ended, it had almost been a relief. He'd been the wrong guy at the right time, and although she'd thought she'd loved Harry's dad, she could see now that it hadn't been the kind of love she deserved. And as soon as Harry came along to complicate things, he was gone, too immature to deal with the sleep deprivation and energy required to raise a tiny human. The only thing she wished was that he'd make his child support payments, because the extra money sure would have come in handy when her mom had gone into care.

She placed the presents under the tree and snuggled beneath a blanket, smiling as the beautiful blonde on the screen spun around with her skirt flaring out around her in the town square. It was just the type of movie she needed.

Lexi woke with a fright and looked around, wondering how long she'd been asleep. The TV was still going, but it was no longer the movie she'd been watching. She'd been so tired she must have crashed the second she snuggled down. She stood up and turned the television and the lamp off, before using her phone as a light to walk upstairs. She went to the toilet, then brushed her teeth, before creeping into Harry's room to make sure he was still tucked in warmly under the covers.

She froze. What the hell? She slowly pulled the covers back, expecting him to have wriggled down low, but he wasn't there. She flicked the bedside lamp on, and scanned the little room, but there was no sign of him.

"Harry?" she said, hurrying out and realizing that he must have padded into her room to climb into her bed. But there was no little body in her bed either. Panic started to rise within her, heart thudding, pain stabbing in her chest as she systematically turned all the lights on.

Lexi took a deep breath and dashed into the bathroom, but there was no sign of him. She ran down the stairs, still flicking lights on, wondering if he'd been trying to catch Santa in action. Surely that was it. He must be downstairs, maybe he'd crept down when she'd been in the bathroom brushing her teeth. He'd be hiding behind the sofa, ready to pounce when he saw the big guy dressed in red.

He wasn't there. The place was small, so there was nowhere he could be hiding, nowhere he could be, without her finding him.

"Harry!" she called out. "Harry!"

He wasn't the type of kid who hid. He wasn't the type of kid to play games like this. It had been the two of them for too long.

"Harry!" She screamed this time, before turning and seeing that his coat was gone. The coat that was always hanging right beside hers. It was gone. And so were his boots.

Her baby was gone!

Lexi kicked into action then, grabbing her coat as she stuffed her feet into her boots and yanked open the door. Tears pressed against her eyes as a shock of wind and snow blasted her. No. *No, no, no!* Her little boy could not be out in this weather, in the dark, on his own!

"Harry!" she screamed, but her voice was lost on the wind. "Harry!"

She ran through the snow as fast as she could to the main house, about to start banging on the door before realizing it was probably open. She ran inside, not taking her boots off as she bolted down the hall, past Walter's library and up the stairs.

"Cody!" she called, too frantic to care who she woke. "Cody!"

Lexi pushed open the door to his old room and ran toward the bed, grabbing hold of Cody's broad shoulders, his skin warm beneath her icy fingers.

"Cody, wake up!"

He turned, sitting bolt upright when he saw her.

"Geez, Lexi, what the hell is going on?"

"It's Harry. He's gone. He's—"

"Whoa, slow down." He rubbed at his eyes and pushed the covers back, swinging his legs over the edge of the bed. "Where's he gone? What's happened?"

"I went to check him, I went to tuck him in, and he was gone. His coat, his boots, he's out in this weather, in the dark somewhere."

She could hear her teeth chattering, knew she sounded half demented as she told Cody what had happened.

"Stay here," he ordered, rising and pulling on jeans and a shirt.

"No, I'm going to look for him. I can't even think about him out there."

He turned and stared at her; even in the half light she could see the intense stare he was giving her. Or maybe she could just imagine it.

"I'm going to go get Tanner. Then we're going to find your son, okay?"

She nodded, letting Cody take her hand and pull her close. He dropped a quick kiss into her hair, holding her hand tight, before marching out the door and running down the stairs so fast she could barely keep up.

"What's going on?" Walter called out from his library.

"It's Lexi's son," Cody called back as tears spilled frantically down Lexi's cheeks just hearing the reality of what was going on. "I'm taking the radio, you call me if he turns up, okay?"

"Thank you, Cody," she stuttered from behind him.

He disappeared into the kitchen and returned with a two-way radio hooked onto his belt. "Thank me when I find him," he said through gritted teeth, and then he was marching out into the snow with her trailing behind.

She called over and over again as Cody alerted Tanner and Lauren, and she knew that within minutes Tanner would be out searching, too. If anyone was going to find her son, it would be the Ford brothers. They knew the land, they'd been little boys here themselves, and she would trust both of them with her life.

"He say anything? Before he went to bed? Was he upset?" Cody shouted over the wind.

As snow fell on her face, Lexi shut her eyes and thought back. "Yes," she said, eyes popping open as his words came back to her. "He asked about the weather, and then he asked about taking apples to the pony in the morning."

"The pony? You mean Cleo?"

Tanner appeared, his face grim. "We need to find him fast."

"I'm going down to the horses," Cody called out. "I have a gut feeling he's gone down there."

"I'll search closer to home," Tanner said.

Lauren was there too, running through the snow, her eyes wide. "Any sign?" she asked.

Lexi shook her head, biting down hard on her lip. "No."

They held hands as Cody disappeared and Tanner

started to run through the snow, shouting out Harry's name.

"Honey, they'll find him. If anyone's going to find him . . ."

Lauren's words trailed off, but Lexi knew she was right. But it didn't stop her mind from racing off and wondering if she was ever going to see her boy again.

"Let's search the house, just in case he went in there," Lauren said.

Lexi nodded, numbly following her. At least it gave them something to do other than worry.

Cody trudged through the snow until he reached the quad. He'd considered going on foot, so he could call out to him, but he had more than a hunch that the boy was down with the horses. *If he'd made it that far.*

He turned the key and made his way slowly through the snow, the lights fighting a losing battle against the pitch-black night and heavily falling snow.

Where are you, Harry? He refused to think about what could have happened, not until he'd made his way down and checked the barn and small field where they'd turned the pony out.

Once he was there, he leapt off, leaving the lights on for the little help they gave and running into the barn. He fumbled and flicked the lights on, illuminating the entire barn and the exterior as well.

"Harry!" he called. "Harry!"

He cupped his hands around his mouth as he moved back outside.

"Harry!" he yelled.

Nothing.

He stared around him, wondering if he'd been wrong, if his instincts were off. He'd been so sure, but now that he was down here he was starting to feel less optimistic.

"Harry!" he yelled again as he let himself into the small field and scanned for the pony. Within seconds little Cleo was coming toward him, snorting and blowing her icy breath onto his gloved hand when he extended it.

He searched the field with the pony following close behind, and it wasn't until he turned around that he heard a noise. What the hell was that? He was sure he'd heard a banging sound.

He jogged back through the snow, into the barn again. Cody listened, waiting, but there was nothing.

"Harry!"

This time when he heard movement he bolted through the barn, and then he saw a lump of blue.

"Harry!" he yelled as he sprinted and dropped down beside him, the little boy in his blue Spider-Man pajamas huddled up beside the hay, arms wrapped around himself, coat unzipped as he huddled to keep warm. Cody scooped him up and held him tight, hearing his teeth chatter against the cold.

"Harry, buddy, you gave us one hell of a fright," he whispered, heart pounding as he cuddled him even tighter to try to warm him. He'd never been so damn pleased to see someone in his life. "You okay?"

"Cleo," he mumbled. "She's c-c-c-old. I wanted to give her a-a-a-apples and . . ."

His head fell against Cody's chest, arms looping around his neck, and Cody took him back into the hay.

"You need me to bring her in for the night?" he asked. "You want to know that she's warm?"

The little boy nodded as he shook. "Y-Y-Yes," he chattered.

Cody grabbed a horse blanket down from where it was hanging on the wall, tucking it around Harry. "I'll bring her in. Then I'm getting you home."

He bolted outside, not even bothering to get a head collar and grabbing hold of Cleo by her cover and tugging her along beside him. If the boy needed to see the pony warm and dry, then he'd do it. And tomorrow he'd tell him just how well horses dealt with all kinds of weather, especially if they had rugs on to keep the wind chill off them.

"Your lucky night," he muttered, leading her through the barn and into one of the stalls. Cody quickly filled the hay up and ran to cart a bucket of water, conscious of the cold little boy waiting for him. Then he ran back and scooped him up again, horse blanket and all.

"Come on, let's go."

Harry shook his head and Cody stopped, knowing instinctively that the boy needed to see the pony. She leaned over and snuffled, and Cody moved closer so Harry could feel Cleo's breath against his face, remembering the desperation to be close to a horse, how much he used to love it too. Tears pricked his eyes as he held Harry and watched the smile, despite the cold, as her whiskers tickled his face. The poor kid had been so worried about the pony being cold, he'd made it all this way on his own.

"Come on, your mom's so worried about you," he said softly, hefting him up a little higher and reaching for the radio, realizing he hadn't alerted anyone that he'd found him. "Let's get you home."

He stopped at the door, about to turn the lights off, but felt Harry shake his head against him.

"You want her to have the lights on, huh?" he asked, trying not to laugh. He flicked the main lights off and left one on in the entrance. No wonder so many of his friends declared that parenting was one of the hardest jobs they'd ever had. The kid was as stubborn as a mule. "She won't want them all blaring, but she can have a night light."

He turned the radio on before they stepped out into the cold.

"Anyone there?" he asked.

"Here, son," his father answered, the line crackling but clear enough to hear his words.

"I have Harry. On my way home now, over."

There was a delay before it crackled to life again.

"Take it slow. Over and out."

Cody clipped the radio back on his belt and carried Harry to the bike, putting him up front and tucking the horse blanket around him before scooping himself in tight behind him and slowly driving him back to the house.

Thank God for small miracles. If the boy had been out any longer on his own, if he hadn't been in the barn . . . he clenched his jaw and pushed the thoughts away. Harry could have died in the dark, out in the snow, he knew it and Lexi would know it, but he was alive, and that's all that mattered.

Between him and Tanner, they would have searched all night if they'd had to—his brother was as determined as he was.

"You okay?" he asked, speaking into Harry's ear so he could be heard above the motor.

The boy wiggled even closer back into him, and he sped up a little, wanting to get him back in his mama's arms and tucked up in bed. It was going to be a Christmas Eve the kid would never forget, and one Cody'd never damn well forget either.

Chapter 16

"HOW am I ever going to thank you enough?" Lexi whispered as they sat in front of the blazing fire. Harry was nestled in her arms asleep, far too big for her to hold, let alone carry, but Lexi hadn't let him go.

"You don't have to thank me," Cody said. "But you can let me carry him upstairs to bed."

She glanced at him, her eyes bright even in the dim light. They had lamps going and the fire was bright, the logs licked with flames as they burned, casting a light across to where they were sitting. A wave of longing came over him, wanting to hold her against him, to whisper to her that her son was okay, that he'd never, ever let anything happen to them.

"I should take him back. It's Christmas Eve and he'll expect to wake up in his own bed."

Cody frowned. "You want to take him out into that snow? Not a chance I'm letting you do that."

Lexi looked like she was torn between what decision to make. "I—"

"Let me carry him upstairs. You can stay with him and I'll go back to your place and get his presents."

She smiled, the first smile he'd seen that night, and the color was slowly coming back into her cheeks, too. "Could you also get the note he wrote Santa, and the milk and cookies?"

Cody chuckled. "Glad to. But you know we do have all that stuff here."

"I know," she said, her eyes back on her sleeping boy. "But he chose the plate and glass, and I want everything to be perfect for him. He'll notice if it's different."

Cody nodded. "Of course." He stood up and stretched before bending to scoop Harry from Lexi's arms. His fingers brushed her skin and he looked down at her, that familiar feeling of longing surging through him again. He had a sudden desire to protect her, to look after her. And he sure as hell had a desire to love her too.

Harry was light and he carried him up the stairs and into a guest bedroom. The entire house was warm, but Lexi tucked him in tight, the covers snuggled up to his chin as if he were still out in the snow. Cody stood at the door for a moment, watching the way she touched him, the way she *looked* at him. He was a special little boy with a damn special mother, and for the first time in his life, he felt the pang of loss. For what he'd never have. He was never going to hurt again, and that meant never letting himself love. And as far as he could tell, parenting was as much about worry and pain as it was about love.

He left them and jogged silently down the stairs, slipping out the door with his jacket and heading for her place. He let himself in and located the gifts under the most half-assed tree he'd ever seen. Cody looked around, going into the kitchen in search of a bag. There was a wineglass with a lipstick stain on it sitting on the counter, a letter from the boy's school discarded nearby, and beneath it, peeking out, was the letter he'd found the last time he'd been alone in Lexi's kitchen. He nudged the school letter aside and stared down at the other one, at the reality of what he'd done to so many people, his sweeping decision to close the retirement complex and the message that had been sent out at Christmas time. The same letter that had ruined what had been an otherwise perfect night with Lexi. Was he so cold-hearted? Or had he become used to having so much money at his fingertips that he'd forgotten the stress the holidays put on so many people? And all he'd done was add to it.

He found a bag and carefully put the gifts inside. He was going to make this right. What he'd done was wrong, he'd reacted wrong, he'd seen Lexi's decision to protest as a personal vendetta, when in fact all she'd been doing was giving a voice to everyone he was hurting by trying to make the biggest profit he could. How the hell hadn't he been able to see that?

Lexi deserved better. He stared around the little apartment again, wishing he could be the one to give it to her, wishing he could be the man she thought he'd been, the man she needed. But he couldn't give her that. Now then, not now. *Not ever.*

He finished collecting the things for Santa and bundled everything inside his jacket, flicking the lights off and heading back to the main house. He could make Christmas special for Harry, he would give as much of himself as he could to Lexi while he could—and then he was going home. To New York. To the place where he could hide everything that made him feel, and go back to being hard-as-steel Cody Ford; *Fortune*-magazine-list Ford; the-guy-who-jumped-higher-than-anyone-else-to-get-a-deal-done Ford.

There was something to be said about staying in control, and being back home made him feel very, very *out* of control.

The Ford's Christmas tree looked like something from a display at Barneys. It towered to the high ceiling, twinkling as if a million lights covered the greenery and filled with enough decorations to be worthy of an advertisement. And now the presents she'd wrapped only hours earlier for her son had been added to the piles of gifts lying beneath it.

"Thank y—"

"Don't say it again."

Lexi smiled. "Sorry, I just seem to have so much to thank you for."

Cody had just returned from the kitchen, two glasses in hand, filled with an amber liquid that she guessed was whiskey.

"Have this," he said, standing close as he passed it to her. "It'll help you sleep."

She took it from him, one little sip filling her throat and sending fire through her entire body as she swallowed.

"Lexi," Cody said, stepping closer, his gaze dropping to her mouth before slowly raising to meet her eyes.

She swallowed, wishing she'd had more of her whiskey. The way he was looking at her, the way her body was tingling, pulsing just from staring back at him, this man she'd loved for so long, this man who'd found her son for her. Lexi bravely raised her chin.

"Lexi, I'm not going to be here long," he said, his tone low, voice gruff. "But I know that I want you."

She wanted him too. She lifted her glass and took a long, slow sip, before closing the distance between her and Cody. Harry was safe upstairs asleep, there was no chance he would wake after such an eventful night, and right now, in this moment, she wanted to take something for herself. And that something was Cody Ford.

"Close the doors," she said, so close to Cody now she could feel the warmth of his breath on her face, could smell the intoxicating blend of aftershave and whiskey on his skin.

Cody was holding his glass in one hand, the other at his side, but he didn't reach to touch her. Instead he shuffled the space between them, their bodies brushing now, as his lips came down to meet hers, teasing at first, so soft she could barely feel his touch, but then he deepened the kiss, mouth moving hungrily against hers.

He grinned when he finally stepped back, downing the rest of his drink in one gulp and sweeping the big doors shut. She was pleased to see he could lock them, clicking them and then turning to face her, his eyes hungry, his expression like a wolf finally closing in on his prey.

"I want you too," she whispered.

"You're sure you want to do this?" he asked, stalking back toward her.

She downed her drink too, the fire in her throat almost making her cough. But she held it down and nodded. They were alone. The big living room was at the far end of the house downstairs; no one could hear them, no one was awake. Harry was safe.

She'd wanted something just for her, and now she had it.

"This is just for tonight," Cody said as he reached for her, fingers sliding down the back of her head and then curling around her neck, his touch so light.

She moaned as he pulled her closer, as he bent and

kissed where his fingers had been, his other hand sliding around her lower back, drawing her closer to him. His body was hard, his mouth soft, his touch just . . . *right*. Everything about being with Cody now felt so right.

"I remember how good I felt with you," she whispered. "I've never forgotten."

His chuckle was low. "Honey, I was just a boy then."

She moaned as he pushed her harder against him, feeling just how much he wanted her. Lexi tipped her head back, Cody's kisses like wildfire across her skin. "And now?" she whispered, not reminding him that he'd been anything but a boy the other night when they'd reconnected.

"Now I'm a man," he murmured as he dropped kisses, plucking at her skin ever so softly. "And I'm gonna make damn sure you're satisfied."

Lexi knew she should feel guilty, that she should never have let Cody lock the doors, but this was just one final night. One night for her to feel good and block everything else out.

He stroked her shoulders and edged her top down, kissing her exposed shoulder before glancing up at her.

"Tell me what you want," he said.

"I want you," she said simply. And she did. She reached up and cupped his face, one hand slipping to cup his skull as she lifted her face and kissed him, sighing into his mouth as he took charge. Cody kissed her gently, he kissed her hard; he paused, stroking her face, before kissing her all over again, tongue teasing her, sending shivers of desire through her body as she soaked up every second of being in his arms.

Cody's fingers expertly worked the buttons on her shirt, leaving her in the tank top she had underneath, and then he slid the straps down, his mouth following everywhere his fingers traced. But when he went to take off her jeans, she stopped him, reaching for his belt buckle and taking it off him. He grinned down at her and she loved the look on his face, the desperation she could see that was the perfect mirror of how she felt inside. She slipped her hands beneath his T-shirt, pleased that he'd already discarded his heavy shirt earlier. Her palms slid against his bare skin, against firm muscle, his stomach sucking in as she explored.

And when she gripped the hem and tugged it up, Cody complied, lifting his arms and letting her pull it the whole way off. He didn't wait for her to fumble with his jeans, stripping them off himself until he was wearing only his briefs and then setting his sights on her.

"Your turn," he murmured, reaching out for her and skimming his fingers down her top until he reached her jeans again. Back to where he'd been before, ready to unbutton her until she was standing as naked as he was.

She wanted him to do it, standing as he pulled her jeans down, lifting her feet for him to take them off her completely. And then she let him pull her top all the way down her body too, until she was standing, shivering despite the heat from the fire. *And the heat from Cody's gaze.*

Cody swallowed hard as he stared at her body, bathed in the flickering light from the roaring fire behind her. She was almost bare now, standing in her panties and bra, her long hair tumbling down her back, skimming past her bra, and all he could think about was how she'd look without her underwear, whether her hair would fall over her breasts far enough to cover her nipples. She was so beautiful standing there, and he reached for her, taking her hand and tugging her gently forward.

Her body moved against his, not as warm as he was as she pressed into his chest and looked up, mouth parted, just waiting to be kissed again. He leaned in to claim her mouth at the same time as he reached for her bra and unclasped it. She moved back slightly and it fell between them, so this time when she pressed to him, her bare breasts crushed against his chest.

Longing swelled inside him and he skimmed his hands down her back, wanting her full breasts in his hands, needing to feel every inch of her to satiate himself.

But Lexi wasn't as demure as he'd expected her to be this time.

"You're sure the door's locked?" she whispered.

"Positive," he murmured back, kissing her before she could ask any more questions.

Hell. Her hand slid down his thigh as her mouth moved to his chest, sucking as she touched him, nails scraping ever so slightly against him, moving down to the front and . . . *fuck.* Her fingers slid inside his briefs and closed around him, just the lightest of touches that had him groaning as she took charge.

Cody battled the primitive need to turn her around, to pin her against the wall and take her from behind, to take charge, but it was obvious Lexi was enjoying the control and he didn't want to take that away from her. If she wanted to take the lead, then he was damn well going to enjoy the ride.

There was something different about her tonight, more confident, determined maybe. Or maybe it was just that they both knew it was only this one last night and they had to make the most of it.

She traced her fingers back up his leg then, up his side, reaching for his face, cupping his cheeks, and leaning in to kiss him. He'd expected fast and rough, but she took her time, kissing him so carefully, so softly, as if they'd changed gears to slow down. Cody took her into his arms, held her close as he kissed her back. Their lips were brushing, so tender, her tongue touching his, exploring, tasting him like it was the first time they'd been together. The spark between them hadn't dulled, the electricity like a current that just continued to burn despite the years.

"I've been dreaming of a repeat," she told him, one hand still to his face, her legs tangling around him as he started to walk her backward.

"I know the feeling," he whispered back, lips on hers again before she could say anything else, carrying her until they hit the sofa and slowly putting her down on it.

He covered her body with his, pulling her panties down and then discarding his briefs, but he didn't push her. Their kisses were endless, unhurried. Cody had no idea whether minutes had passed or an hour, but for once his impatience didn't get the better of him when it came to Lexi. He reached behind her, took his weight off her completely so she could arch her back and let him unclip her bra. It was lacy, like all her underwear seemed to be, and he slowly took it off her, savoring her body like a Christmas present he got to slowly unwrap and discover. The best damn Christmas gift he'd ever had.

Cody reluctantly stopped kissing her, moved away from her lips and down her body, trailing kisses across her breasts instead. He cupped one, loved that it fit perfectly in his hand. He licked and sucked her nipple, smiling to himself when her toes clenched against his leg, her moans only spurring him on more. Lexi's fingers were in his hair, tugging, trying to encourage him back up, but he was on his way down her body and he wasn't planning on stopping.

"Cody," she murmured, fingers loosening their hold as he ran his mouth over her belly. Her skin was so soft, her flat stomach taut as he rained kisses over it, wanting to feel and taste every inch of her.

"Slow," he muttered, "tonight we're gonna take it slow."

If tonight was all they had, he wasn't going to make any mistakes. He wanted to pleasure her and make love to her, to enjoy every moment, because the memory was going to have to last him a lifetime.

"Cody . . ." This time she hissed out his name on her breath as her knees lifted, her body quivering beneath his touch as he ran his fingers up her thigh, stopping when he reached the top of her leg and trailing the rest of the way with his tongue instead. He touched her so delicately he doubted she'd even feel it, but her body bucked, jumping away from him before resting down again, sensitive as hell.

Cody smiled and tasted her again, carefully, slowly, wanting her to enjoy every sensation. Lexi's moan only made him more determined to take his time, to push her to the brink and guide her to climax. He wanted to please her, wanted her to know that he was as interested in her pleasure as he was his own.

"Cody, stop," she begged quietly.

He ignored her completely, her groans of pleasure telling him that she didn't really want him to stop, legs locking around his head like stopping was the last thing she wanted him to do.

Cody reached up and cupped Lexi's breasts, loving the hard pebble of her nipple, trying not to laugh as she almost choked him when her legs tightened around his head.

And then her body arched and he cupped her backside, caressed her with his tongue until she climaxed, her legs stiff around him one moment, then soft and supple the next.

He kissed her thigh and then her belly, trailing his way back up her body and then staying poised above her, holding his weight with his elbows to either side of her, knees in between hers.

"You're wicked, Cody Ford." Her eyes were still shut, lips moving and tempting him to kiss her.

His willpower was in tatters and he did exactly that, covering her mouth with his and pressing down into her, showing her just how much he wanted her. He was still hard and he was ready to pleasure her all over again in an entirely different way.

Cody nudged at her entrance, groaned at how slick she was, but he cursed as he realized what he was missing. He dropped a quick kiss to her lips but she pulled him down before he could move.

"Do you have protection?" she asked.

He groaned. "I was going to check my wallet but it might be so old it's disintegrated."

"Anything I should be worried about?" she sucked on his earlobe and made it impossible not to slide back down on her again.

"No."

"I'm on the pill," she whispered with a smile. "Stop making me wait."

Cody growled as he playfully bit on her lower lip, before dropping more of his weight onto her; then suddenly her eyes were locked on his when he slowly slid all the way inside of her.

Lexi's nails dug into his back as she pushed her body up, meeting his thrusts with her own. She was making it hard for him to take it slow, but he did, determined to enjoy every single minute without rushing any part of making love to her.

"Why the hurry?" he whispered in her ear, kissing her neck as he kept sliding back and forth into her.

"Faster, Cody," she begged, "*please.*"

He ignored her wishes, wanting it to last, but eventually she wriggled so hard that he did start to move faster, slowing only when she forced him to.

"Stop," she said, voice firm.

Cody stopped immediately, looking down at her with concern. Only he was met with a smug grin as she moved from underneath him and pushed at his shoulders, palms flat as she forced him to his back. She climbed on top, eyes twinkling as she stared down at him and positioned herself, head arched as her hair tumbled down her back.

"Don't move," she murmured, sitting astride him and leaning forward, her hair covering his face now until she shook it away and kissed him on the mouth.

He groaned as she lowered herself over him and started to rock back and forth. Her head was tipped back again, long hair touching his thighs as she moved, brushing against him, teasing him. Lexi moved slowly at first, and he raised his hands to cup her breasts, loving the fullness of them above him, holding them as she rode him. Lexi's eyes were shut, but he didn't shut his for a second, wanting to watch every move she made, keep his eyes locked on the breasts that drove him crazy.

Then she started to ride him faster, her body locked

to his, and he cupped her backside instead, held on to her hips, and rocked hard inside her. Just when he started to lose control, knew there was no way in hell that he could hold back, Lexi slowed, her body more gentle, the intensity of her actions gone at the same time as he gave in to his own climax. Cody kept hold of her, not letting go of her butt until her body relaxed, then scooping his arms around her so she could collapse on top of him.

He kissed her neck, held her tight, their bodies still fused together as they lay in silence.

"You're so beautiful," he whispered. "As beautiful now as the day we met."

She nestled into him and he stroked her shoulders and down her back, not wanting to let her go or stop touching her.

"I needed that," she whispered back with a giggle. "Best Christmas present I could have asked for."

"Hey," he teased, leaning in for one more kiss. "I aim to please."

Cody stared at her, at her lashes against her cheeks as she shut her eyes, at the soft way she breathed, at the beautiful naked body stretched out on the sofa beside him. If he wasn't so scared of getting close to someone, he'd have scooped her up in a heartbeat and never ever let her go.

Lexi could have laid there forever in Cody's arms. They were warm, the fire still roaring nearby, and the only noise was the embers crackling and falling. He had one arm loose around her, the other was still stroking, thumb brushing back and forth against her skin. She sighed and nestled tighter against him.

"We should go upstairs," he said, kissing her head as

she gazed up at him. They were stretched out side by side, still naked, still enjoying the peaceful aftermath of sex. But he was right, she wanted to get up to Harry. And it was only a matter of hours before he'd be up and excited about Christmas, anyway.

He took her hand and pressed a kiss to it, before helping her up as he rose. She was about to pull away to retrieve her clothes when Cody tugged her back, not letting go of her hand until she was standing against him. His eyes were shining, it could have been the light from the fire, but she saw something there, something she hadn't seen before, only she didn't know if it was happiness or sadness or a combination of both.

Cody's hands rose and cupped her face on each side, his kiss warm and gentle. They stood like that, connected, lips moving slowly in time with each other, until he finally dropped his hands.

It felt like a last kiss. It was bittersweet, painful almost, knowing he was going soon and, just like last time, she was never going to see him again.

"Cody, what did the letter say?" she whispered.

"You don't know?" he asked, sounding confused.

"I never got it, Cody. And my mom can't remember what she did with it. All I know is that I never saw it."

"I can't believe it," he muttered, tucking her tight to him, his chin resting on the top of her head. "It said that it was easier to just go instead of saying goodbye, because I knew I might never leave if I had to look you in the eye and say it." He paused and she tried not to cry. "And it said that I loved you, and that even though I had to go, it had been the best summer of my life with you. Or something along those lines."

Cody didn't say anything after that and neither did she, and she'd never felt so close to someone yet so far away at the same time. She would never know why her mom had kept the letter all those years, or whether she'd ever find it, but it changed everything. Because all this time, she'd believed she just didn't deserve to be loved, that somehow it was her fault, but now she knew that Cody hadn't just turned his back on her so easily.

When she was dressed, and Cody had slipped on his shirt and jeans, he took her hand and unlocked the door, leading her out of the room and down the hall. Their feet made quiet padding sounds as they crossed the timber barefoot and then made their way up the thickly carpeted stairs.

She stood outside the room where Harry was, the low light from the hall providing just enough illumination to see his face on the pillow. He was a tiny lump in a very large bed.

"I should go snuggle up with him," she whispered.

"Come with me, just for a little bit," Cody replied, still holding her hand. "Please."

She nodded and followed him down two more rooms, smiling to herself as she stepped inside. Earlier when she'd come looking for him, she'd gone straight to his old room just presuming he'd be in there, and it hadn't surprised her when he was. But now she could look at it properly, and it took her straight back down memory lane.

"We had some fun times in here," she whispered.

"Not as fun as the times we had outside, but yeah, the memories aren't bad."

She swatted at him and he laughed, catching her wrist, his gaze burning a hole straight through her it was so intense.

"Take a shower if you want; I'll be out here."

Lexi was so tired, and she hadn't realized just how

tired until she'd come upstairs and looked at the beds. She was ready to collapse into one, but he was right, a shower would feel good.

"I'll just take a quick one."

She left the cardigan she was carrying on the bed and smiled at Cody as she passed. His abs were on show from his open shirt, and she resisted the urge to reach out and glide her fingernails across his stomach as she passed. How the hell had he gotten even better with age?

Lexi entered the bathroom and looked around. She'd been working in the Ford house for months now, and she'd never gotten used to the opulence. The number of bathrooms, the floor-to-ceiling tiles and exquisite taps and thick, embossed towels—it was all just so indulgent.

She touched the towel hanging on the heated rail and wondered if Cody had already used it. She had no problem being wrapped in something that smelled of him. Even after everything—their years of no contact and their spat over his development—she still wanted him. He was the only man who'd ever made her feel so alive, and her body seemed to defy her even when she was point-blank furious with him.

She turned the faucet on and started to strip down, leaving her clothes in a puddle on the ground to come back to later. She reached out a hand and felt the warm water, and stepped in, face straight under the steady stream, water teaming over her forehead and down her body, before reaching for the soap and lathering up her body.

But then something else touched her body. Something big and silent, moving in behind her, hands stroking across her slick wet body. His mouth closed over her neck, puckering a kiss there, the body behind her as rock solid as the kisses were feather-light.

Lexi let him stroke her, closed her eyes and gave in to the feelings pooling inside her, the heat she felt for him flaring all over again. And then she turned, slowly, arms looping around his neck as he scooped his hands beneath her buttocks and lifted her up, her legs locking around him.

She stared through the steam and water at him as he rocked slowly inside of her, kissed him as water streamed between them. It was like everything they both wanted to say was pulsing between them, their actions the only words they needed, and when they were done Cody held her and kissed her, before slowly lowering her to her feet again.

He reached for the soap and gently lathered her again, washing her down and waiting for her to rinse herself, before quickly washing himself. And then he was stepping out, passing her a towel and wrapping her up in it.

She dried herself, silently, watching him as he wrapped a towel around his waist and bent to collect her things. He opened the door and they walked back out into his bedroom.

"Here, wear this," he said, passing her a soft shirt from his wardrobe.

She took it, lifting it and inhaling, loving the scent of him stamped into it. "Thank you."

Lexi put her underwear back on and then buttoned up the shirt, and she watched as Cody pulled on fresh briefs and a T-shirt before pulling the covers back and lying down.

"Come here."

She looked at the warm spot beside him, wanting nothing more than to snuggle up to him and fall asleep in his arms, just this once. But she couldn't.

"I don't want Harry waking up in a strange bed alone," she whispered.

"Just for a few minutes. I promise I won't let you sleep here."

Lexi glanced at the door, knowing she should go. "Okay, but just for a minute."

She climbed in beside him, scooting over close to him as his arm came around her, mouth against her hair. He felt so good; so big, so warm. *So right.*

And when he started thrumming his fingers against her skin, she knew she should never have taken up his offer because now she didn't ever want to leave his bed.

Cody stared down at Lexi, wishing he could find the right words to say to her when she was awake.

"You were the one," he whispered as he stroked her cheek. "You were the one and I was too damn scared to stay and find out."

He would never have been happy staying in Texas, or maybe he could have been but he just didn't want to admit it. He lived for his work, loved the city and everything about it, but he was lonely. He'd known it for months, maybe even years, but he'd refused to acknowledge it. But now, here with Lexi, he could see as clear as day just how lonely he'd been.

Just how lonely he'd *be* when he returned.

Why had he never been brave enough to ask her back then if she wanted to go with him?

He waited one more minute before carefully extracting himself and standing, bending to scoop her up in his arms and carry her the short distance to the guest room, just as he'd carried her son earlier. Cody lowered her beside Harry, watching as she instinctively nestled into her son on the bed.

Tomorrow it would be Christmas, and the day after that, he'd be gone. Seeing what he could have had, looking at mother and son tucked up, it made him realize what he'd been missing all these years.

Chapter 17

LEXI woke up to hands pressed to her cheeks and a nose smooshed against hers.

"Mommy, it's Christmas!"

She groaned and shut her eyes for another few seconds, before Harry started to yank at her, tugging on her arm.

"Mommy, come on! We have to see if Santa came!"

Lexi laughed and sat up. No matter how little sleep she'd had, Harry's excitement was contagious. She'd always loved Christmas—her mom had made it special for her no matter what—and she'd tried to ensure that Harry always had an amazing one too, no matter how low her bank account was or what was going on around them. This year was going to be no different.

"Okay, let's go. Just let me put my jeans on."

She touched the shirt she was wearing, not ready to take it off just yet. It was so soft and it smelled so nice, and when she shut her eyes it brought back memories of the night before that she hoped she'd never forget.

"Come on!"

"Alright, alright!" She tried not to laugh at Harry

when he grabbed her hand, dragging her behind him.
She glanced at the bed and felt bad for not making it
straightaway, but it was Christmas morning and her son
wasn't going to wait.

"We need to get back to our place. Why did we stay
here?" he asked.

"Um, because someone decided it was a good idea
to run away in the snow last night and we ended up
here," she said, ruffling his hair and wondering how
he was so unaffected by what had happened. "Talking
about that, you owe Cody and Tanner a big thank-you.
They were so worried about you that they went straight
out looking to find you."

She was pleased to see he ducked his head and looked
at least a little guilty.

"And *then*, when you were asleep, Cody went over to
our place and brought the letter for Santa and the milk
and cookies you'd left out and left them here."

Harry stopped, one foot on the stairs. "Did he write
a letter to Santa, to tell him to come here? What if he
thought we didn't leave anything out for him?"

Lexi bent down and kissed his cheek. "Of course he
did. Cody knows what he's doing."

She had no idea what the time was, but from the light
filtering through the windows she was guessing they'd
slept in a little. And when they got downstairs, she realized they'd definitely slept later than usual.

Cody was in the kitchen already, barefoot and wearing jeans and a shirt that was undone and rolled up at
the sleeves. She gulped seeing him standing there, so
muscled, so strong, and so damn sexy as he held up his
coffee cup.

"Merry Christmas, you two," he said with a wink.
"Coffee?"

"Yes, please." How did the man look so fresh and handsome after so little sleep?

"Cody, has Santa been?" Harry asked.

"Huh, you know what, I don't know. But there was an empty glass over there by the tree."

Harry's squeal cut through the air, and Lexi gave Cody a grateful smile and mouthed "thank you." It was one thing putting everything out, but she'd forgotten completely about actually drinking the milk or eating the cookies.

He walked a coffee over to her and she took it gratefully, inhaling the strong aroma. "Thanks. Just what I needed."

Cody looked like he was going to embrace her, but then something passed over his face like he wasn't sure how to react. She stepped in to him, not waiting for him to initiate contact, palm to his warm chest as she stood on tiptoes to brush a kiss to his cheek.

"Thank you for last night," she said quietly. "For everything."

Cody softened again then, his easy smile replacing the faint frown he'd been wearing as his arm slipped around her. He bent then and placed a gentle, sweet kiss to her lips.

"Honestly," he said, "it was the best night I've had in a long time."

Lexi let go of him when Harry excitedly started asking which presents were his, giggling with excitement as he ripped through paper and triumphantly showed his gifts off. She sat down with her coffee, watching Harry, her heart filled to overflowing as her son zoomed around the room with his new farm toys. But what choked her up was seeing the way he was so eager to show his things to Cody, and the easy way Cody spoke to him and laughed.

For a man determined to keep a wall up, a man who was apparently so happy focusing on work and nothing else, he did a damn good impression of a guy who would make a really, really good dad.

Later that day, Cody looked around at the table, happy that Lexi had decided to join them. She was sitting beside his father, and Harry was happily sitting between him and Tanner, talking a mile a minute and making him remember just how exciting Christmas had been for him as a kid. It was so easy to forget. He swallowed away a lump of emotion as he realized that Lexi was sitting in his mom's seat. It hadn't been hers for more than twelve years now, but still, she would have been sitting there if she'd still been alive.

When he was at work, he lived and breathed it, refusing to think about the past or pain or memories, which was why coming home was always such a shock to him. Everyone else thought it was that he didn't like ranching life, but after being back this time, he knew it was a façade he couldn't keep up forever. Ranching was in his blood, and he damn well loved the place. He just didn't like the way it made him feel sometimes.

Mia called out to him across the table and he grinned as he saw the way her husband, Sam, had his arm slung casually across his sister's shoulders, even at the table. It was clear they were just as in love now as they'd always been. But it still didn't make him crave the same life or love; all he saw was the potential for so much heartache, and he preferred situations he could control.

"Can you pass the cranberry sauce?" Mia asked.

Beside her, her Sophia squished turkey in her hands and then stuffed it in her mouth, grinning the entire time.

"Really nice manners, Sophia," Cody teased.

"That's my girl," Mia said, laughing as her daughter ate like she'd never seen food before.

Everyone chatted and filled their plates a second time, their family so rarely all together that they were largely on their best behavior. Even Angelina, who usually looked so out of place when she was home on the ranch, seemed relaxed. Although he'd put money on it they'd be fighting over who got to use the jet first to get home as soon as the day was over.

The sound of a spoon being tapped against glass pulled Cody from his thoughts, and he looked up to see his father standing, one hand on Lexi's shoulder as he steadied himself. He looked well today, his cheeks full of color and his eyes shining bright, and Cody tried to soak it in, wanting to remember him like that forever.

"I should have said something before we ate," Walter said, looking around the table and smiling when he met Cody's eyes. "But I'm an old, sick man so I suppose I can make my own rules."

They all chuckled, and Walter lifted his glass of wine and gestured at them all before continuing.

"It's so good to have you all home. I thought the best moment of my life was when Tanner gave up riding those damn bulls, but I think I've changed my mind. It's this, having you all home at Christmas this year."

Tears shone in his father's eyes and Cody stamped his jaw shut tight as he fought his own surge of emotion. It was what he hadn't said that hit him hard. This could be their last Christmas together, and they all knew it. Walter's doctor hadn't given him a timeframe specifically, but he had said to make the most of every month, and they all knew the cancer was a ticking time bomb.

"This year, we're lucky enough to have Lexi with us, and I think it goes without saying how much I like this little lady." They all laughed then, even Cody, and he met Lexi's gaze. Her cheeks were flushed a deep pink at being singled out, and he loved the way she glanced sideways, shy and uncomfortable in a way, but his family loved her and he hoped she knew it. "It's been a privilege to have her and young Harry living on the ranch, and mark my words, she's the reason I'm not moping around the place feeling sorry for myself. I think she'd give me a good kick up the backside if I started moaning, so we've been good for each other."

Cody stared at her, finding it impossible not to, and wondering if she would have been sitting at this table for another reason entirely if his mom had still been here, if he hadn't left like the devil was chasing him out of his home state.

"Anyway, enough of hearing this old man speak. It's just damn good to have my house and table full again."

They all raised their glasses and sipped wine, the noise level rising again as everyone enjoyed the festivities. Cody talked ranching with his brother for a bit, before moving to sit with Angelina. He'd barely had time to talk to her when she'd arrived, and he wanted to know more about her work—she was usually desperate to talk shop, but when he'd brought it up earlier she'd been quiet about her new ventures and he wanted to know more.

"You looking for an exit already?" he asked.

Angelina shrugged. "Maybe, maybe not." Then she laughed. "You know me too well. Of course I am."

They sat quietly for a moment before his sister laughed again.

"Don't you think it's weird, how those two got the ranching gene and we got the, what? I don't even know what to call it?" she said.

"The get-the-hell-out-of-dodge-and-make-a-name-for-yourself-in-the-business-world gene," he said dryly. "That what you were trying to say?"

"Well . . ." She shrugged before grinning back at him.

Cody nudged her with his shoulder and laughed. "Something like that, right?"

She leaned in, voice lower this time. "Or maybe we're just the screwed-up ones who can't deal with relationships or emotions."

He gave her a sideways look, but she just smiled.

"Takes one to know one. More wine?"

Cody nodded and watched as she filled his glass. He hadn't realized that Angelina wasn't interested in, or struggled with, relationships either, he'd just presumed she didn't want a husband or family because she was so focused on her career.

As Angelina started to talk to Lauren, Cody glanced down the table and saw Lexi watching him. He needed to go down there. In less than eighteen hours, he'd be gone, only she didn't know that yet. He'd decided to leave early, wanting to figure out the Bright Lights deal before there was any more negative publicity after the holiday period, and he had a stack of work on his desk to return to. He'd been back at the ranch too long, and if he stayed any longer, he had a feeling that it might suddenly become too hard to leave.

"Hey," he said as he walked down to the head of the table and sat in his father's seat for a moment. Walter was off inspecting toys with the kids, who'd long since left the table to play.

"Hey yourself," she said.

Cody went to touch her shoulder, then thought better of it. "I'm pleased you're here. It's been a great day, and you're so important to Dad."

She smiled and he inwardly cringed. She was damn important to him, too, only he seemed incapable of saying that.

"Thanks. We've been good for each other."

Suddenly Harry was giggling behind him, and when he turned he saw that he was holding a sprig of greenery, high in the air as he stood on tiptoes and tried to hold it higher than their heads. He dangled it and then jumped up and down, so excited he managed to whack his mom on the head with it.

"Harry," Lexi spluttered, looking mortified as the table went quiet and everyone looked at them. "Stop!"

"Walter said it's mistletoe!" he announced gleefully. "Kiss, kiss, KISS!"

Cody looked at Lexi, loved the dark stain on her cheeks as she stared back at him. If this was going to be the last time he kissed her, he wasn't going to miss it. One last kiss to say goodbye, one last moment before he slowly put up the walls he usually kept so carefully constructed around him all over again. Because once he left, once he was on the plane heading back to New York, he wouldn't let himself think about this again. He didn't do regrets, and that meant he blocked out the past even to this day.

He leaned in, cupping her face with one hand, gently against her jaw, his lips pressing ever so softly to hers. She kissed him back, mouth moving against his, so soft, a whisper of goodbye that lasted barely a few seconds until it was over. He slowly pulled back, staring into her eyes one last time too, feeling the swirl inside of him as she somehow seemed to look right through him.

Harry ran off giggling and Sophia stole it from him and ran to her parents, who happily obliged in a big smooch for all to see when she dangled it above their heads, but all Cody could see was Lexi sitting before him. Beautiful Lexi, whom he'd never meant to hurt but had, and from the looks of it, he'd managed to do it all over again. He should never have let her close again.

"I'm sorry," he whispered, reaching for her hand.

She nodded, holding him back. "I know."

Somehow she understood, knew that he was too screwed up emotionally to offer her any more, but her expression told him that it still hurt her. Dammit, it hurt him too! He held her hand for a second longer, before going back to his seat. He passed his dad on the way and gave him a hug, holding him tight.

It had been a Christmas he'd never forget, but he was ready to leave. This wasn't home anymore. New York was, and no amount of walking down memory lane was going to change that.

Lexi grinned as she watched Harry play, her heart full to bursting with love for her child, and for the day they'd been invited to be a part of. Being invited into the Ford family fold, it had been incredible, and she knew it was a day that neither she nor Harry would ever forget. Before her mom had moved into Bright Lights, they'd had small but memorable festive occasions, always full of love and laughter, but it was something else to be part of a large family get-together. There seemed to be a revolving amount of laughter versus arguing, accusations versus teasing, and it was something she hadn't been witness to for a long time. Even when she and Cody had been dating, she'd never been invited to get-togethers like this because they'd been so young and she would have always been with her own family.

Lauren was suddenly sitting beside her and she let her top her glass up with more wine, smiling as they both settled into their seats.

"I've never gotten used to this many people around one table," Lauren said, "or all this noise."

Lexi smiled. "It's a lot to get used to."

"You know, Tanner would love Cody to come home. I think he's spent years hoping his brother would want to come back to Texas eventually."

"Tell him he could be waiting a long time," Lexi said, watching Cody, drinking in the sight of him while she could. "I don't think he's the settling-down type, so if he's waiting for him to start a family and move back to the ranch . . ."

Lauren nodded. "That must hurt." Her voice was low as she sipped her wine and gave her a quick look. "I've had my heart broken by a Ford before, so I know how much it hurts."

Lexi closed her eyes for a beat. "Yeah, but at least Tanner came to his senses eventually. You two were made for each other."

Lauren snorted and made Lexi laugh. "Trust me, it didn't feel that way at the time. It took us a long time to find our way back to each other."

"We found our way back, it just wasn't meant to be," Lexi replied sadly. Maybe if things had been different, if her mom was still healthy, if Cody hadn't been the developer she was at war with, if he hadn't still been so damn afraid of the past. There were so many reasons why they just weren't meant to be, but nothing could change what had happened, so she just had to make peace with it.

They sat side by side, the table growing louder around them as everyone continued to drink and eat. Cody caught her eye and smiled, and she smiled back, but he was gone. She could see the way he was pulling away already, the relaxed line of his mouth and shoulders replaced by something slightly more reserved. It wasn't just her he was pulling away from, it was everyone.

She'd already lost him, and even though she'd known it was coming this time, it still hurt.

Chapter 18

THE next day, Cody had wanted to sneak away without having to see Lexi, but when she walked out of her house, looking between him and the car he was walking toward, he knew he wasn't going to get away so easily. He smiled but he could see she wasn't going to smile back. He changed course and moved toward her as she kept walking to him.

"You're leaving?" Lexi asked.

He lifted his hand and touched her shoulder, smile sad and wishing he could kiss her one last time for something to remember. "I'm going back to New York today."

He saw the tremor inside of her, the way her face changed, the invisible wall between them rising.

"You were just going to leave, without . . ." Her voice trailed off. "Never mind."

He should have said that he was going to call her, but that was a lie because he'd thought about it and decided he had no idea what to say. Besides, they'd agreed it was a one-night thing between them—he hadn't promised her anything. And anyway, he thought they'd said their version of goodbye yesterday.

"I'll never forget that you brought Harry home to me that night," she said quietly. "Thank you, Cody."

"I did what anyone would have done," he said. "And I want you to know you have my word on the development."

"You're not just going to leave and then forget about it?"

"I promised you I'd make this right, Lexi. I just haven't worked out the logistics yet, so you need to trust me."

She nodded, but he could imagine what she was thinking. She'd trusted him once already and he'd let her down, so what was any different this time?

"We could have been great, Cody. I just want you to know that," she said, her eyes brimming as she stared at him.

He watched as she quickly wiped at her cheeks.

"I wish you weren't so afraid of being home."

Cody stared back at her. "Me too."

I wish things could be different. He stared back at her, grinding his jaw as he fought for the right things to say. *I think I love you.* That's what he wanted to say now, that's why he was scared as hell and running before he got in too deep. But he was never going to say it, because no matter what he felt, no matter how much he wanted to let his guard down, he couldn't. It wasn't worth the pain.

"I'm sorry, Lexi." And he was. He was so, so sorry. For everything.

She shut her eyes then opened them and looked away. "Yeah, I'm sorry too."

He dropped his hand and turned, because what the hell was he going to say? He'd told her he'd sort the development issue out, and he would, but it was time to go back to work. The ranch life wasn't for him—it never had been—and what had happened between him and Lexi? He pushed the image of her in his mind away, not looking back, not about to start wondering *what if*. She was a great girl, but he wasn't looking for a great anyone. He had his work. He had his life in New York. He *loved* his life.

He didn't need anymore.

He didn't *want* anymore. Love and broken hearts were for other people; he was single for a reason.

"Cody!"

A little body hurled against him, slamming into his legs and holding on tight, and Cody was forced to stop walking.

"Hey, kid," he said, ruffling Harry's head and trying to pry his fingers off his jeans.

"You're leaving? Why didn't you say goodbye?" His face was so warm, so full of innocence as he looked up at him, and it hit Cody like a nail into his heart. He'd already left Lexi like that once before, and now he'd almost made the same mistake with the kid.

He decided to deflect the question.

"You gonna keep up your riding? Tanner's keen to teach you."

"Yeah, and when you come home I can show you how good I am."

Cody bent down to his level and looked him in the eye, holding his hands. "Don't forget to give your mom lots of cuddles and tell her you love her, especially tonight," he said. "Be a good boy for her, and no more running away, you hear me?"

Harry nodded and Cody opened his arms to give him a hug, surprised when the boy launched at him, arms around his neck as he held him around the waist. His little body was warm and tight to him, the hug so fierce and full of so much emotion, Cody didn't know what to do. He cleared his throat, standing the second Harry released him.

"I'll see you around, kid."

Cody patted his shoulder as he passed, only turning when he got to the car. Tanner was waiting behind the wheel for him, his bag already in the back, and Cody held up his hand in a final wave to Harry. The boy was still standing where he'd left him, eyes wide, hand held high as he waved back, and then past him was Lexi. She was walking toward her son but her eyes were focused on him and Cody wished to hell he hadn't looked back at all.

"Drive," he said when he got in the car and slammed the door shut.

Tanner didn't say a word, he just started the engine and turned the vehicle around, slowly driving down the long drive and turning out onto the road. Cody kept his eyes trained straight ahead. He didn't want to look at anything, didn't want to remember anything. Dammit, he didn't want to *feel* anything!

He'd spent the past decade trying to make sure he didn't have to deal with any emotions or feelings, so he sure as hell wasn't going to let one Christmas vacation at home change everything for him.

"You want to talk about it?" Tanner asked.

"Talk about what?"

Tanner was silent for a beat before shifting his weight and glancing at him. "You're all bent out of shape, I just thought you might like to talk."

"Well, you're wrong. I'm fine." Cody leaned against the window before slamming his palm into his leg. *Fuck!* "I'm sorry. I didn't mean to bite your head off."

Tanner glanced at him again. "It's fine."

"Leaving wasn't as easy this time," Cody admitted. "I usually pack up, can't wait to leave, and I get the hell out as fast as I can. I'm wheels up before I've even had time to miss anything."

"And this time?" Tanner asked.

Cody thought about his question. He didn't even really understand himself how he felt. "This time," he said slowly, "this time, I'd almost trade what I have in New York to stay."

Tanner was silent for a long time, and Cody stared out the window, the snow-covered fields blurring past his vision. He couldn't believe he'd even said those words out loud.

"You could have stayed for a bit longer," he finally said. "And it's not too late to change your mind."

"No," Cody said, shaking his head as if he needed to convince himself. "Nope, I couldn't do that."

"And why the hell not? Would it be so bad to see more of your family for a while?"

Cody balled his fists, squeezing them in and out.

"You're scared, aren't you?" Tanner said, putting words to something they'd never talked about before. "You're scared of losing Dad, of it being like when we lost Mom. You're scared of getting too close to us again, and you're sure as hell scared of letting Lexi close."

"Screw you," Cody swore.

"Yeah? Well, you can insult me all you like, but I'm just telling it like it is and you know it."

Cody angled himself away from Tanner, not wanting to engage with him. He was getting pissed with his brother because he needed someone to get angry at, and it wasn't fair.

"They say you're better to have loved and lost, than not to have loved at all," Tanner said in a low voice. "And now that I'm with Lauren, I can see that. I'd do anything for that woman, *anything*, and even if I lost her tomorrow I wouldn't trade anything in the world for the time we've had together. It would all be worth it."

Cody grunted. "Yeah? Well, anyone who says that hasn't known loss. It's bullshit."

Tanner's voice was louder this time, more aggressive. "I haven't known loss? Is that right? Because I lost Mom too, in case you forgot, and I stuck around for her. And I lost Lauren and made my way back to her, too."

If Tanner hadn't been driving, Cody would have slammed his fist into his face.

"Fuck you," he swore. "*Fuck you*, Tanner! Don't even start."

"You can swear at me all you like, but it's true. And now you're going to let the same girl go twice." Tanner turned and Cody realized they were getting close to the airfield. "You're the one making mistakes, brother, not me."

"She wasn't mine to lose this time," he muttered.

"You really think that?"

He nodded. "Yup."

"Then you're an even bigger idiot than I thought."

They didn't speak the rest of the way, and when they finally got there, Cody jumped out of the car as quickly as he could. Tanner didn't get out of the driver's seat as Cody retrieved his bag from the back. He held up a hand in a wave, not wanting to talk, not wanting to look back.

"Let me know when you come to your senses!" Tanner called out through the open window.

Cody shook his head. "See you at Thanksgiving."

The sleek black jet was waiting on the tarmac—he could see it as he walked toward the terminal building—ready to take him home.

New York was his home now, and he wasn't coming back to Texas until he had to.

Lexi refused to think about Cody. She refused to be sad, she refused to imagine *what if*, and she absolutely refused to wonder if he'd change his mind and come back. Because she'd been right here before, waiting for him, believing that he'd come back for her and realize what he'd left behind, only it had never happened. And what would bring him back now? A single mom all these years later wasn't as interesting as an eighteen-year-old in her first year of college, so why would things be any different this time around? If he loved her, if he'd ever loved her, he couldn't have left her the way he did . . . twice.

She stopped for a second, halfway through making sandwiches for her and Walter, and dropped her head to the cool granite counter. She just needed a moment to pull her thoughts together, to refocus.

"Honey, are you okay?"

Lexi stood bolt upright, wiping her eyes to find Mia standing in the doorway, watching her, her eyes filled with sympathy. The other woman walked toward her, arms outstretched, and that little moment of kindness set her off. As Mia held her close, arms so warm and tight around her, a sob erupted from deep within Lexi that she couldn't stop. And then she cried and cried, holding Mia, crying for so many things that she'd been holding in for too long. Her mom. Her son. Cody. *Everything.*

"He's gone, hasn't he?" Mia said, rubbing her back with her palm.

Lexi nodded as Mia kept holding her.

"He's a damn fool for leaving you behind," Mia whispered, before releasing her and standing back, gently wiping Lexi's face with her fingertips to brush away the tears.

Lexi didn't trust her own voice, but she braved a smile at Mia.

"He left us all those years ago too, Lexi," Mia said. "I've tried to get him to talk about it, but he's put up so many walls, pushed everyone away so he doesn't have to feel."

"I wish I didn't love him so much, but even after all these years . . ."

Mia took her hand and held it, palm to palm, her smile and her touch so warm that it made Lexi hurt even more.

"We can't help who we love," Mia said. "Or for how long."

"Want a sandwich?" Lexi asked through blurry eyes, smiling at Mia.

"Hell yes," she replied, moving to stand beside her and taking more bread out. "And after we eat, you're taking the afternoon off."

"I'm fine, honestly, I just needed a minute."

Mia shook her head. "No way. You need to take a few hours off, enjoy playing with Harry. I got this."

"You're sure?" Lexi asked.

"Sam has the kids for the afternoon and I want to spend some time with Dad," she said. "Not everyone in this family runs away from their emotions."

Lexi grinned at Mia. If only Cody was more like his sister, her heart wouldn't feel like it had been sliced in two. Twice.

"You're going to get through this," Mia said, nudging her with her shoulder.

"Yeah, I know." And she would. She'd survived a broken heart before—she'd survived *Cody* before—and she'd learned how strong she was when her mother was diagnosed. Life had thrown her more than one curveball, and she'd refused to let it ruin her life. But she couldn't help wondering, *hoping*, that she'd catch a break. That she'd find happiness and love, and that someone would step into her life and make things a little easier for her. Look after her. *Love her.*

She blinked away fresh tears as she sliced a tomato.

Was that really so much to ask?

Chapter 19

Three weeks later

LEXI held the letter in her hand, the paper heavier than
normal and embossed with the Ford Corporation em-
blem. She wondered if everyone affected had received
the same letter, or whether she'd just been singled out,
but then she doubted Cody had written it himself despite
the fact it bore his name and was signed in black ink
at the bottom. She'd been looking for the old letter he
claimed to have sent and her mother claimed to have
hidden, but still hadn't found any trace of it. And then
this letter had arrived.

*Please be advised that your loved one will be able
to continue her care at Bright Lights until the new
state-of-the-art facility has been fully completed. Your
existing contract will be honored and transferred, and
all current Bright Lights residents will have the opportunity to visit the new establishment prior to moving day.*

*The proposed development will still take place as
publicized, but we will not be proceeding until every
resident has been moved, giving sufficient time for the*

adjustment. The new facility will be within a fifteen-minute drive of the current assisted-living complex, and we trust your loved ones will enjoy the peaceful setting and state-of-the-art facilities.

She'd done it. She'd actually taken on a Ford and won. So why didn't it feel better? *Because she hadn't won.* Cody had left; her heart was shattered again; and even though she'd known what had happened between them was a holiday fling and nothing more, still, it hurt. It didn't feel like a win at all.

She folded the letter and placed it back in the envelope as relief coursed through her. Her mom was safe, the only thing she had to worry about was money now, and what she was going to do for a job. Because one thing was certain: she couldn't stay living at River Ranch and working for the Ford family, no matter how many times Walter asked her to reconsider.

She finished what was left of her coffee and put her cup in the sink, before heading to the main house. This was something she'd been dreading for weeks, but it had to happen. Other than the letter she'd just received, she hadn't heard from Cody since he'd left almost three weeks ago—and she had no idea what she was waiting for anyway.

He was never going to ride in on a white horse and rescue her; hell, he hadn't come back for her when they'd been joined-at-the-hip inseparable, so he sure as hell wasn't going to come riding back for her now. Cody's life was in New York. She needed to keep telling herself that.

She let herself into the main house and listened. No one was there. Mia had gone back to her own ranch, so there were no little squeals or the pitter-patter of children. Angelina was long gone, Lauren was back at work, and Tanner was no doubt out on the ranch or gone for the day. Which meant it was just Walter.

Lexi padded down the hall, expecting to knock but finding the door to the library open.

"Morning, Walter," she called out before stepping in.

He was sitting at his desk, but his back was turned, and he was looking out the window. The sun was just starting to break through the clouds, and she wondered if it was the weather he was looking at.

"Morning," he said, without turning.

She busied herself by going over to make his bed, now that he'd decided to move into the library more openly instead of trying to hide it, and plumped the big soft cushions on the leather sofa.

"Can I make you a cup of coffee?" she asked.

When she turned, she saw he was standing, and he looked so much older when he was up, his frailty more obvious.

"You were walking with your shoulders down and a face like your dog had just died," he said.

Lexi swallowed. So he hadn't been watching the weather. "Lucky I don't have a dog then," she teased, but Walter was no fool and he wasn't falling for her joke.

"Let me have it. What's wrong?"

She decided to make him a coffee anyway, and herself another one too, using the fancy coffee machine that had seemed so foreign to her when she'd first tried to use it.

"You know I've loved my time here with you, Walter, but I don't think I can stay anymore," she said, not turning around until she had his coffee made. Her hands were shaking as she took it to him, setting it down on his desk.

"This because of my boy?"

She forced herself to look up. "I knew when I took this job that I might find it difficult, but I haven't. I've actually loved every minute of it, and I'm so grateful that you allowed us to stay on site, too."

"Then stay," he boomed, taking her by surprise. "Cody won't be back until Thanksgiving and who knows if I'll even still be here by then?" He started to cough and she went to stand with him, rubbing his back and helping him lower into the chair.

"Walter," she said softly. "I'm not going to leave until I've found you a wonderful replacement, but it's time for me to move on. I'm so sorry."

"Is there anything I can do to change your mind?" he asked.

Lexi blinked away tears and turned, going back to retrieve her coffee. She refused to show emotion at work, and she quickly cleared her throat and smiled when she turned back around.

"You and your family have been nothing but kind to me, Walter, so no, there's nothing you can do. It's just time I moved on."

He nodded and sipped his coffee, looking out the window again. She would have sworn she could see tears in his eyes, but he never wiped them and she never said a word.

"You've brightened up this old man's life, that's for sure," he finally said.

Lexi didn't reply, she just went and stood beside him, hand on his shoulder, and stared out the window with him. There was so much she could have said, but nothing seemed right, and so she just stood in silence, watching the clouds drift and the wind slowly whisper through the enormous trees flanking the driveway into the property.

It was the most beautiful property she'd ever stepped foot onto, and it was going to be so sad to leave it all behind. Once, she'd dreamed she might live there with Cody, but that dream had died long ago. She was just a fool who let herself imagine it all over again.

Cody sat in his office and stared out at the city twinkling beneath him. He'd watched as darkness had blanketed every building in his line of sight, replaced by the brightest of lights that illuminated New York. He never tired of the view, never wished to be anywhere else, but tonight all he could think of was the ranch. Of the way it had felt wearing his boots and feeling the grass beneath him; the smell of horse and the way the bulls had moved around him when he'd walked among them with his brother.

And a certain someone he'd left behind on it.

His phone rang and he glanced at the call screen before answering. What the hell was wrong with him, daydreaming about the ranch?

"Hey, Simon," he said, stretching out and standing, making his way over to the screen as if by going closer he could convince himself it was where he was supposed to be.

"I'm here. Are we heading out or am I coming up to you?"

Cody looked around and decided he needed to get out of the office instead of staying in it another minute. "Heading out. I'll be down in a sec."

He pressed a mahogany timber wall and it opened, displaying suit jackets, shirts, an overcoat, and a selection of scarves. He virtually lived in the place and he kept half his clothes in the office—it beat going home to his empty, modern chrome apartment after the warmth of staying back on the ranch. He yanked off his tie and shrugged into a suit jacket, throwing his overcoat over his shoulder to stave off the cold once they were outside. He made a quick trip into his adjoining bathroom, staring at his face and barely recognizing the dark circles under his eyes and his pale skin. Something had to change, and it had to change fast.

He flicked off the lights, leaving the lamps going for when he came back to work later. Working through the night was the only thing keeping him sane right now.

Simon was waiting for him in the lobby, and he held out his hand to shake it, pulling him in close and slapping him on the back at the same time.

"Good to see you."

"You too," Simon said. "I thought you'd be away somewhere exotic at this time of year instead of suffering through this cold."

"Not a chance, you know me," Cody joked. "Workaholic to the extreme. What's your excuse?"

"Patients to see," Simon replied. "We take turns every year to go away over New Year's, but someone has to stay behind in case we have any emergencies. This year it was my turn."

They started to walk, out into the brisk cold and down the road. They made small talk and headed into a nondescript bar, and Cody waved out to the bartender and directed Simon to a table tucked away from everyone else. He settled into the booth-style seat and planted his hands on the table.

"So, you about to tell me why we had to meet tonight, and why Sophie wasn't allowed to come?" Simon asked. "I'm going to get those puppy-dog sad eyes from her tonight when I get home, and you know I have to tell her the truth and blame you."

"I need help," Cody admitted, clearing his throat and knowing how uncomfortable he must look. "*Professional* help. But if you tell your beautiful wife that, I'll kill you."

Simon laughed, and then his smile died to a frown as Cody watched on.

"Tell me you're fucking with me, Cody," he said. "You know I can't help you professionally. You're my friend, so there's a big conflict here. If you need help you can make an appointment with my partner or—"

Cody shook his head. "No. I'm not making a goddamn appointment with a stranger. And I don't care if there's a conflict. I need help, and you're one of the most highly regarded shrinks in the city."

Simon stared at him like he was speaking an undecipherable language. "Cody, seriously—"

"Have you ever, *ever*, in the entire time we've known each other, ever heard me ask anyone for help?" he ground out. "Come on, do I have to beg?"

Simon let out a low groan before slamming his palms to the table. "Fine, but this is just an informal talk, this is not a proper session. And you're buying the damn drinks."

Cody rose and ordered two top-shelf whiskeys. He let out a long, shuddering breath as he thought about what he was about to do. All these years he'd kept it bottled inside, refusing to talk to anyone even when Mia had

begged him to see a professional the year after their
mom had died. And now here he was, about to spill
his guts to one of his friends who had no idea he didn't
have his shit together.

He sat back down, drinks in hand, and slid one over
to Simon.

"So what is it you want to talk about?" Simon asked.

Cody gulped down half the whiskey before looking up. "The past," he said. "All these years I've been
running away from what I left behind, and I need to
know why. I need to know if there's something wrong
with me, if I, hell, I don't know. It just doesn't seem
right, or even normal, anymore."

Simon frowned. "Why do *you* think you ran away?"

"Because my mom was dying and I couldn't handle
it," he said. "I left for college, and I've only been back
for holidays and her funeral since. Until recently, it's
been like pulling goddamn teeth every time I have to
go back there, but this time it's different."

Simon took a sip of his drink. "So you know why,
then. What do you want from me?"

"I want to know if it's possible I . . ." Cody knocked
back the rest of his drink. Talking about his past, or his
feelings, was as pleasurable for him as poking needles
into his eyes. "Look, I had a beautiful girlfriend who I
loved, but I also had a mom I loved, and she was withering away in front of me, dying before my eyes, and I
just fled. I couldn't handle it; hell, I didn't want to remember her being that way, and so I just left and never
went back."

Simon waited. Cody signaled to the bartender for another and leaned forward.

"I remember we had a great time, my girlfriend and I,

but it was just so painful and I think I kind of just blocked out the way I left her. I didn't forget, I mean it was there somewhere in my head, but I just didn't let myself think about her or anything about home once I left. I wrote her a letter goodbye before I left, but that was it. All these years and I've never thought about her. Hell, I've barely thought about my mom either. I go home for Thanksgiving and Christmas, and if the memories start or it gets too much, I just get on a plane and fly back to work." He didn't tell Simon that he could barely look at a photo of his mom without it making him want to bolt in the opposite direction. But it was true. He was a coward when it came to pain, when it came to feeling anything other than the thrill of a deal.

Simon nodded and sat back, looking more relaxed. "This girlfriend, did you see her recently? I'm guessing your crossed paths when you were home and all these feelings, these old memories, flared up for the first time in a long time. Maybe even years?"

Cody grunted. "Yeah."

"And suddenly everything started coming back?"

"At first, I didn't even recognize her, and then it came back like someone had opened the floodgates. I just, I know I left her, I know that because it's a fact, but the physical act of leaving or how I felt—it's like I blocked it all out and the memories are patchy at best. But when I think about what we had together, when I think about being with her? I remember all of that and wonder why the hell I blocked it out because it was so damn good."

Simon seemed to be considering his words, staring at him hard before finally opening his mouth. "Look, we'd need more sessions to really work through all this, but if it's an answer you're wanting, I'd say the memory loss and haziness is likely PTSD. And then going home, seeing this ex-girlfriend again, has triggered some memories. But you'd need more help to work through it all, to remember everything."

"I don't want to remember any more," Cody said quietly, grinding his teeth together, not wanting to revisit anything painful. "I just needed to know why."

"PTSD is the most likely cause," Simon said. "You were what, eighteen? And your world was falling apart at the same time you had an opportunity to leave home and put it all behind you. Hell, I'd be surprised if you *didn't* have a form of PTSD."

Cody wasn't sure whether to feel relieved or pissed, but just to have a name put to it, to make sense of the jumbled memories and guilt he'd started feeling over how he'd treated Lexi, made him feel better. Not to mention how he'd treated his mom, the person in his life he'd loved more than anyone, when she'd needed him so bad.

"Thanks, Si," he said, clearing his throat when he heard how gruff he sounded. "I needed to hear that."

"You need to see someone, Cody," Simon replied. "I'd prefer it wasn't me, but I just want to know that you're going to talk about all this. It might be painful, but you need to open up and let it all go."

Their next round of drinks arrived and he lifted his to clink to Simon's. "To getting help."

Simon laughed. "Thought I'd never see the day." He clinked his glass back. "*To getting help.*"

They both sat back and Cody relaxed into the chair. This didn't give him an excuse, but it did help him to understand what he'd done. And maybe, just maybe, it'd help him to make amends.

"So this is completely off the record, but this girl, what happened when you saw her again?"

Cody laughed. "I wondered how the hell I'd ever walked away from her, and I honest to God couldn't remember."

"And what about her? What did she have to say about it?"

"Trust me, that's an entire story in itself," Cody said. "In a nutshell, she hated my guts and had never forgiven me for leaving her behind. Something along the lines of me being too good for country girls and too big for my boots."

"Ouch."

"Yeah, ouch." Cody sipped his drink. "But it was kinda nice, too. I'm used to everyone telling me what I want to hear, and she didn't hold back, not for a second."

Simon nodded. "So when are you going back?"

"Going back where?"

"To Texas, you idiot! To get the girl?"

Cody stared at Simon, downing the rest of his drink as Simon's words sunk in. "Now." He leapt up and pulled out his wallet, dropping a handful of bills on the table and grabbing his coat.

"Go get her," Simon called out, but Cody was too far away to call back.

He fumbled for his phone and made a call. "I need the jet fueled up and ready to go at sunrise. Destination, Texas."

Cody hung up and ran the few blocks to his office, letting himself in and grabbing his laptop and some files. When he left the office this time and flagged down a taxi, it was to head downtown for some late-night shopping and then to his apartment to pack his overnight bag. He was going home, and for the first time in as long as he could remember, he wasn't going under duress.

And this time he wasn't coming back until he got what he wanted.

Chapter 20

"SWEETHEART, we can't take the pony with us," Lexi said, her heart breaking as she watched her son's face crumple. This was the real deal, his pain almost tangible, and completely unlike the usual fake tears that came with a tantrum.

"But I love Cleo, Mom," he whispered, his voice catching as he started to cry again. "Why can't you talk to Mr. Ford?"

She wished Harry knew how hard it was for her too. She wanted to collapse and cry, and admit to her son that she was leaving behind something, *someone*, she loved too, but that wasn't going to help her.

"We don't have anywhere to keep a pony, and besides, Mia's kids are going to want to learn to ride on her. We can always come back to see him whenever you want."

"I hate you!" Harry screamed, eyes frantic as he threw his soft toy at her and ran out of the room. "Why do we have to leave, anyway?"

She didn't bother going after him or yelling back that that wasn't the way they spoke to each other, because she knew what he was going through. They'd had so much change to deal with over the past couple of years, and being here had been a welcome reprieve. For a while, she'd felt like she belonged too, but staying just didn't feel right any longer. She'd found a replacement before formally handing in her notice, despite Walter insisting that he wasn't allowing her to leave, but it was just too painful anymore. Maybe it had been a bad idea right from the start, but it had seemed like the perfect job—with the exception of Cody. For the first few months, before he'd come back, she'd almost been able to pretend that caring for Walter would have nothing to do with Cody.

When Cody had been at the ranch, it had seemed impossible; and now that he was gone, it was somehow even more impossible. She was a muddle of thoughts and worries, her heart yearning for something her mind knew wasn't even possible.

A knock at the door took her by surprise, and she looked around, wishing the place wasn't such a mess. She'd already started boxing up some of her belongings, so there were things stacked everywhere.

"Just a minute!" she called out, running her palms down her jeans and smoothing her hair down.

She swung open the door and was surprised to see a man in a suit standing there, briefcase in hand.

"Hi," she said. "Should I have been expecting you?"

He shook his head and held out his hand. "Bryan Gordon. I'm the Ford family attorney and I've just been up at the house to see Walter."

She nodded. "Okay. Is there something I've done wrong or . . ." Her voice trailed off. Was she going to have to sign something? "I've already signed a confidentiality agreement, as part of my employment, if that's what you're concerned about." She hadn't realized it would be so involved to leave her job with the Fords. "You're not going to have any issues with me post-employment, if that's what you're worried about."

"No, nothing of the sort. May I come in?"

She stood back and waited for him to pass, before following him to her small kitchen table. He sat down and pulled out a wad of papers. Lexi wasn't sure whether to offer coffee or to just sit, so she went with sitting.

"I'm sure you're aware that Walter is very fond of you and is extremely upset about your departure," the attorney said, pushing some papers toward her. "However, he put this in place some weeks ago and insists that it remain in place despite your imminent departure." He chuckled. "However, he did offer me a very generous bonus if I managed to convince you to stay."

Lexi coughed, or maybe she choked, her hand flying to her mouth as she glanced over the papers. She didn't need to be a lawyer to understand what he'd done. Her eyes ran back over the words again, and then again, more slowly the last time as she digested what it all meant.

"I . . ." She didn't even know where to start. Walter had made a name for himself as the toughest business-man in Texas, and yet here he was wanting to give her so much.

"I understand it's a lot to comprehend, and I need to explain that, although Walter would prefer you stay in his employ, he understands and respects your decision. This is something he'd like to do as a gesture of friend-ship from the Ford family."

Lexi started to shake her head. "This is so very generous, but I can't accept it. There's no way I could accept it."

He looked amused, but seemed to ignore her state-ment. "Your mother's care will be paid for as soon as the documents are signed, and that includes all future care regardless of the facility required. The financial responsibility will be taken over entirely by the Ford family trust, and I don't think Walter will take no for an answer."

"No," Lexi said as disbelief flooded her. "N-No, he can't do that. H-He can't pay, it's too much." She realized she was stuttering, that she was trying to speak too fast and not getting her words out properly. "I simply can't accept it."

"Walter *can* do this, and he wants to," the attorney said. "He told me you might be reluctant at first to accept help, but he also told me that he wants your mother to have the best care money can buy." He lowered his voice. "Just like his wife had while she was alive, and what he's had since his diagnosis."

Lexi gulped. It would be so easy to say no, because she didn't want to be indebted to Cody in any way, but what Walter was offering her? It was enormous. Life changing, even. It would mean that she could make decisions that didn't revolve around the monthly bill she had to pay for her mother's care, or worry about having to take her in and give up her job to care for her.

"What do you need me to do?" she finally asked.

"Sign the papers," he said. "We can either do it now or I can leave them for you to consider or send to your own attorney."

Her hands were trembling and she fisted them, forcing herself to meet the attorney's gaze. "Thank you for delivering the papers, but I'm going to have to seriously consider this for a few days before signing."

He closed the folder and left it there on the table, and Lexi rose to let him out at the same time as a loud thumping echoed on the door. No one ever came to her door, and suddenly she had two visitors within half an hour.

"Thanks for coming over. I'll go and speak with Walter later today, if that's okay?"

The knock sounded again and she walked fast to the door.

The attorney chuckled. "It's more than okay. From what he told me he's missing you already and he's hoping you'll, in his words, *feel sorry for the old bastard* and stay a bit longer."

The door suddenly burst open and big, deep dark brown eyes met hers.

"Cody?"

"Ahh, sorry," he muttered when he saw she was with someone. "Should I go and wait outside until you're finished here?"

"I'm just leaving, so don't mind me," the attorney said, holding out a hand to Cody as he passed. "Good to see you again."

"You too, sorry, I wasn't expecting . . ." Cody's voice trailed off and suddenly his attention was directed at her.

"What are you doing here?" she asked, taking in the suit, the shiny black boots, his coat, and the immaculate leather bag dropped at his feet. "And why the hell did you just burst through the door like that?"

Cody strode across the room and then marched straight back to her, his eyes wide as he dropped to his knee. He reached for her hand and she numbly let him take it as she watched him. *What the hell was he doing?*

"Cody—" she started before he abruptly cut her off.

"Please, Lexi, I've been up all night and I . . ." He squeezed her hand. "Lexi, I have so much to say sorry for, but the thing is, I came back here for Christmas and saw you, and everything I've done since then has been one big fuck-up." He let out a breath and brought his lips to her hand. "Well, almost everything."

"Cody, get up. You don't need to be—"

It seemed he wasn't worried about what she thought, he had a look in his eyes she didn't recognize, a desperation that seemed so unlike him. Cody always looked like he had it together. He was dressed perfectly, he looked perfect, he spoke beautifully, he seemed impossible to rattle. Until right now, when he looked genuinely unhinged and . . . a sense of calm settled over her. He looked vulnerable. That's what it was, he was vulnerable, and it was a side she hadn't seen before—at least not in a very long time.

"Lexi, I love you," Cody said, his voice raspy as he stared up at her. "I think I always have, only I pushed everything away when I left here, including you."

Tears pooled in her eyes. "I don't want to go over the past again, Cody. We've already talked it to death."

She saw tears sparkling in his eyes too, and it was her squeezing his hand now.

"Lexi, I think I've always loved you," he repeated. "No, I *know* I've always loved you, but somewhere along the way I lost myself and I managed to lose you too. I pushed away everyone I loved. My mom, my sisters, my old friends, *and you*."

Lexi dropped to her knees then too, wanting to hold him, wanting to comfort him, because this wasn't like the apologies he'd given her. This wasn't him telling her what she wanted to hear or what he thought he needed to say. This was raw Cody Ford like she'd never, ever seen him before. She didn't even remember him being this open as a teenager.

"We had something great, Cody, we did. I know we

were young and it was probably too soon for either of us, but I loved you, too."

He lifted his hand, hovering as if waiting for permission, giving her the chance to push him away, before carefully cupping her face so tenderly she couldn't help but lean in to his touch.

"Lexi, I need help. I need to go into the past and figure a lot of stuff out, but I promise you I'll get the help I need," he said. "I think, well, I know, that I suffered from a form of PTSD. When Mom became sick, I changed, and I don't remember how or why, but all I really knew was that I had to get away from here. And you became part of my collateral damage."

"Oh, Cody," she whispered, as tears started to plop slowly down her cheeks. She smiled when he gently caressed them away with his thumb, seeing the man she used to love and wanting to grab hold of him and never let go. "I know we were young and it was a long time ago, but—"

"Marry me," he said, staring at her so earnestly she couldn't break his stare. "I've been an ass and I never should have left you the first time, let alone the second time, but if you say yes, I promise I'll never leave you again."

Marry him? First Walter offered her money, and now Cody was asking her to marry him? What was it with the Ford men today?

"Cody, I—"

"You know what, don't say anything," he said, interrupting her. Her dropped her hand and reached into his jacket pocket, pulling out a little velvet box and slowly opening it. "This is for you, Lexi. I love you and I'm sorry it's taken so long for me to find my way back to you, but I know that I want to spend the rest of my life with you."

She felt tears welling again, her body shaking as she stared down at an enormous diamond set on a band of smaller diamonds, all twinkling up at her.

He snapped the box shut and passed it to her.

"When you're ready, if you decide to say yes, I'll be here waiting. Either way, this ring is for you. I want you to be my wife, Lexi. Being with you, being back here, it made me feel alive in a way I haven't felt in years."

"Did you know your dad wants to take over all costs for my mother's care?"

Cody's smile said it all. "Yes, I did. Only he expected you to keep working for him as long as he was able to stay at home."

"Did you ask him to do it? Was this actually—"

"No," he interrupted. "This was all the old man. He called me into his office over Christmas to tell me his plans, and to make sure I'd have the documents executed if anything were to happen to him. He really likes you, Lexi, and he knows what it's like trying to get the very best care for someone you love."

Emotion choked her, lodging in her throat as she realized that this was as much about Cody's mom as it was about hers. The Fords were a loving, generous family, and she could see why Walter was doing it now, and why she needed to let him.

Lexi held the soft box in her hand, thumb brushing across the velvety surface, struggling to breathe as his words played over and over in her mind. Cody leaned in then, his eyes on hers as he cupped her chin and covered her mouth with his, his kiss so soft she barely felt it. But she wanted more, she *wanted* to feel it, so she wrapped an arm around him and pulled him closer, lips firm to his, wanting him so badly. She wanted his body against hers, his mouth whispering against hers all night. Hell, she wanted Cody for a lifetime, she always had.

"Yes," she whispered when they finally broke for air.

"Yes?" he repeated, pulling back to study her face.

"Yes," she said again, laughing as his hands came up to frame each side of her face, grinning as he leaned in to kiss her again.

"Cody!" Harry's squeal of excitement had them scrambling apart, and Cody was on his feet before she was, running a hand through his hair before opening his arms to her son. As she watched, slowly finding her way up, Cody swung him into the air, so natural with him as her little boy's face lit up into one of the biggest smiles she'd ever seen.

Lexi looked down at the box in her hand then, opening it and studying the solitaire as it twinkled up at her, and Cody slowly took it out and slipped it onto her finger, his eyes catching hers for a moment as she smiled at him, before looking down again. It was the most beautiful piece of jewelry she'd ever seen, and once she'd finished admiring it, feeling the weight of it on her finger as she lifted it, she realized the room had gone quiet.

She lifted her gaze and found Cody and Harry staring at her, a slow smile spreading across Cody's lips as he watched her.

"What's that for, Mom?" Harry asked as he clambered from Cody's arms to his back, little hands looped around his neck like it was the most natural thing in the world to be climbing all over him.

"I asked your mom to marry me," Cody said for her. "And she said yes."

"Marry you? Like you're gonna be my dad?" Harry asked.

Lexi moved toward them, tucking into Cody's warm chest and reaching a hand up to touch her son.

"You've already got a dad, little man, but I'll be your second dad," Cody said. "If you're okay with that?"

Harry giggled and he made them all laugh. "I'm *so* okay with that," he said. "Mom, does it mean I get to keep the pony then?"

"Harry!" she scolded. "The pony wasn't yours in the first place!"

"Cleo?" Cody asked. "Of course! You can share him with Mia's kids. And when you're ready, I'll get you your own pony. Every boy has to have a horse, Mommy, you know that, right?"

Lexi play punched him, but he expertly caught her hand, slowly raising it and pressing a kiss to her ring finger. Lexi felt light-headed as they stood, the three of them, in the little apartment she'd loved for the months she and her boy had lived there. The place she'd been planning to leave and never come back to.

"Do we still have to move?" Harry asked, his voice sad as he leaned over Cody's shoulder.

"I'm not sure," she said, looking up at Cody. "Cody lives in New York and—"

"No one's going anywhere," Cody said firmly. "We're a family now, and that means we stay on this ranch. Unless there's somewhere else you'd rather be?"

Lexi shook her head. She was *exactly* where she wanted to be. "No, there's nowhere else I want to be, Cody."

"Well, good." He dropped a kiss to her lips that had Harry groaning. "Because I'm going to build you a house by our tree, and we're going to spend the rest of our lives living on this ranch together."

"What about New York? Your job? Your—"

"I'll have to commute, and there's this little thing called work-life balance that I might need to figure out."

She laughed as he caught her around the waist and kissed her again, but even with Harry begging them to stop, she let him kiss her, over and over again, his lips warm and sweet against hers and filled with so much promise it filled her heart.

"I love you, Lexi," he whispered.

She sighed against his mouth. "I love you, too."

Epilogue

"ARE you absolutely sure you want to build here?" Cody asked, as they stood on the hill overlooking their tree. It was picturesque, the river full of icy cold water as it ran through the valley, but the last thing he wanted was to push her into something she didn't want.

"Cody, stop asking me," she said, snuggled to his side, one arm wrapped around his waist as they stood together. "I can't imagine anywhere more beautiful to build our home. Besides, I thought I was the one in charge of the design? That means I get to decide where it's built."

"But if you'd rather have our own ranch, somewhere of our own—"

"Stop," she said, reaching up to tug him down, her hand slipping around his neck. She kissed him, and just like that all his worries disappeared. "I love it here. I love your family, I want to be close to your dad, and this is our place. I can stare at this tree all day and remember the way we stripped each other's clothes off and made love for the first time in the sun."

He grunted and ran a hand down her back, loving the

way she felt against him. "I don't need to stare at a tree to remember that."

Lexi laughed. "Come with me."

He let her tug him along, making their way around and down the incline, hand in hand toward the tree. When they got there, Lexi took both his hands and he let her take the lead, letting her walk him backward and push him against the trunk. She held his hands down and stood on tiptoes, kissing along his jawline and then finally finding her way to his mouth. He slipped his hands to her waist and she laughed, taking them off and putting them at his side again.

"Why can't I touch you?"

"Because I'm in charge, that's why."

He grumbled, planting his hands firmly back on her hips. "Maybe I don't like you being in charge."

She laughed and leaned in to him, her body firm to his as she tipped her head back and looked up at him.

"I'm the one studying to be an architect now," she teased. "And that means I'm in charge of everything to do with our house, including this tree."

"Did I mentioned how pleased I am that I found my way back to you," he murmured, leaning down and kissing her, slowly, gently, loving the warmth of her soft lips against his.

"Me too," she whispered back, her fingers running through his hair as she tugged him back down for another kiss. "What do you say we give this tree some new memories?"

He scooped his hands under her bottom and lifted her up, turning them around so it was Lexi's back against the tree. Her legs wrapped around him, hands slung over his shoulders as he kissed her, over and over again, never tiring of the feel of her in his arms or the way she seemed to melt against him.

"What do you say we give Harry a sibling?" he whispered in her ear, his heart pounding as he held the woman he loved in his arms.

"I say slow down, tiger," she whispered back, kissing his earlobe before gently nibbling it. "I want to enjoy every second of being back together again, and I'm not dropping out of college again."

"Yeah?"

"Yeah," she murmured. "Doesn't mean we can't practice though."

Cody didn't need to be told twice. He'd wasted a decade away from Lexi, and he was going to spend the rest of his life making up for lost time.

Coming soon. . .

Look for the next novel
in **Soraya Lane**'s
River Ranch series

My One True Cowboy

Available in April 2020
from St. Martin's Paperbacks

Don't miss the first two novels
in the River Ranch series

Cowboy Stole My Heart
All Night with the Cowboy

And look for **Soraya Lane**'s
Texas Kings novels

The Devil Wears Spurs
Cowboy Take Me Away
I Knew You Were Trouble

From St. Martin's Paperbacks